AFTER *the* STORM

CHRISTINA BERRY

Published by PVR Publishing

Edited by Christina Consolino

Cover design by KiWi Cover Design Co.

To Dad,
My first hero and the man who has always inspired me to expect goodness
from the men in my life.

NOTE FROM THE AUTHOR

Hello Readers!

I hope you enjoy the book. Some content within may be triggering or upsetting to some readers. This book contains details about Hurricane Katrina and Hurricane Rita, PTSD, suicidal ideation, alcoholism, substance abuse, and racism.

Christina

1

THURSDAY, DECEMBER 16, 2004

NEW ORLEANS, LOUISIANA

In a part of New Orleans that's fallen on hard times, the theater is a strange little diamond in the rough. It's close to the French Quarter but not quite there. A busy store stands on the corner of the block, but otherwise the area seems abandoned—though a few doorways have the faltering foot traffic associated with drugs or sex for sale.

And then there's Paradise, or rather, a theater called Paradise. The neon blade sign with its glowing letters, retro curves, and brilliant color is a beacon in the dark. It doesn't belong here, so conspicuously vibrant in an area so depressed, but then perhaps it's exactly what belongs here, exactly what this place needs.

Beneath the blade is a bright white marquee with black block letters that read, *It's a Wonderful Life*. What a great surprise. When I first saw the glow of the sign from afar, I assumed it was a porn house. That's been the fate of a lot of these old forgotten gems. But the place looks too loved for something so seedy.

It's a beautiful building, one of those classic old theaters from the heyday of Americana. The front alcove is brightly lit and freshly painted a cheery seafoam green. Beneath the marquee awning, there's a wash of white hexagonal tiles, scrubbed to a brilliant shine, with the word *Paradise* spelled out in black. The walls of the ticket window, too, shine with bright pink ceramic tile, a terrific match to the pair of pink doors with porthole windows that open into the theater.

The lights are on inside, but no one is in the ticket window. I check my watch; it's early evening still. Am I on time for the screening? A night of watching George Bailey tackle his problems seems like a good remedy for avoiding my own.

I lean close to the small voice box set into the plexiglass window, trying to see through to the other side, but the glare of the lights only reflects my own face back at me. I finger comb my hair where the breeze has tussled it, then run my hands over my dark suit and loosened tie before I move around the ticket window to one of the pink doors and step into the lobby.

To my right, a set of red-carpeted stairs leads up to the auditorium, I presume. At my left, the brass and glass expanse of a concession counter glints in the amber light of a pair of overhead spotlights, revealing bare shelves. Behind the counter, a retro popcorn popper sits idle.

I turn my attention to the rest of the foyer. It's so quiet here, too quiet. After a moment's hesitation, I raise my head and, in my loudest voice, call out, "Hello?"

Nothing but silence.

I walk toward the back hall with its doorways to bathrooms and an employee-only office. There is no movement, no response. Nothing in the balcony overhead, either, with its sole set of double doors leading into the theater. After a brief hesitation, I make my way up the stairs, drawn to the theater by some curious compulsion.

"Hello?" I holler again when I'm halfway up. Silence is the only reply.

The place is apparently deserted, so I continue to explore. Why I don't leave, I don't know. I could blame my curious nature, my tendency to wander, or my fascination with mid-century modern architecture. Regardless, it's stupid to wander through an empty, unlocked building in a forgotten corner of New Orleans, and yet my feet take me farther up the stairs.

At the landing, I make my way to the doors at the far end. As I draw near, though, my footsteps falter when I hear something. It's music. It's…Prince? The sign outside says *It's a Wonderful Life*, but are they actually screening *Purple Rain*?

I love that movie, and it's been too long since I've seen it. I grow excited, imagining I will steal into the back row to watch it. It's been years since I snuck into a movie; the last time that happened was during college, when my best friend Jake and I slipped into whatever movies were showing at the cinema in the mall where he worked.

I push the door open. There is no film playing, and rather than darkness, the theater is flooded with the blazing, bright light of giant overhead fluorescents. The most notable surprise, however, is the woman bouncing and spinning and singing her heart out to Prince's *Let's Go Crazy* a few feet in front of me.

The brightness of the room and the brightness of her fritz out my brain. I stand there, stupidly staring. I'm intruding, I know this, but I can't make myself leave.

She is petite and curvaceous with rich, dark skin well complemented by her bright purple top, her figure gorgeous in a pair of tight, paint-speckled jeans. Her hair is a short cap of curls, trimmed to draw attention to the striking lines and angles of her face, her lush lips, and big, dark eyes. Her energy, too, is stunning. I am entranced as she swings her hips to the beat and sings along, using a paint brush tipped with red as her microphone.

She bobs her head as she spins to the sounds of the guitar solo, giving her body over to the music in a beautiful rhythm. On her second revolution, she stops abruptly and screams.

I blink, confused by the sudden shift in her mood. Then I realize it's me she's screaming at.

"I'm so sorry." I try to be heard over her shouting and the music, but it's no use.

She points the red-tipped paint brush at me like it's a gun instead of a mic. I'd be inclined to laugh, except there is real terror in her wide eyes as she stares at the stranger who's wandered into her space.

Sticking up my hands, I try to seem less threatening as I say, "I didn't mean to frighten you. I won't hurt you. I promise."

It's the truth, of course, but why should she believe it? I'm a stranger. Plus, I'm taller than her and male, so by default, I'm perceived as a threat to a woman alone.

"What do you want?" she barks at me, a bite to her tone.

I keep my hands up. "I wanted to watch *It's a Wonderful Life*."

She frowns. "We're not open yet."

"Yes. I see that now." I nod sheepishly, my hands still over my head.

"How did you get in here?"

"The door was unlocked."

"*WHAT?*" Her fear seems to be replaced with anger when she says, "Fucking idiot!"

My ego sinks with the insult.

"Not you." She lowers her paint-brush gun, so I lower my hands. With a huff, she explains, "The kid who's supposed to be helping me. He keeps leaving that door unlocked. Now I have to search the toilets…again."

"The toilets?" I'm so confused.

Incredibly, she smiles a bit at me. "Last week, the kid left the door unlocked overnight. I came back in the morning to find a guy high on heroin sprawled across the floor of the ladies."

"Oh. That sucks."

"I don't have time for this," she grumbles. "Come on, I'll walk you out."

I comply, turning and leading the way out of the theater and down the stairs. The woman follows close behind. I glance back to see she's collected a baseball bat from somewhere in the theater. It rests on her shoulder, and she looks like she's ready to crack my skull if I try any funny business.

Something switches inside me at that moment. The image of her alone in this big empty building, in this forsaken corner of the city, her toilets regularly invaded by drug addicts, with that bat as her only defense—it fills me with a strange sense of protectiveness.

She wants me to leave, and while I don't want to harass her, I worry about what could happen if I leave her here alone. What if there is someone in the bathroom? Will a bat be enough to protect her?

What sort of Neanderthal nonsense is this? She wants me to leave; I should go. This is her space; I'm intruding. To her, I'm no better than the random trespassers in the toilet. Still…

"I can help," I offer as we reach the bottom of the stairs.

"What?"

I turn to face her as we near the door and try to look as nonthreatening as I can for a six-foot-tall man who towers over her petite stature. "I can search the bathrooms. Make sure they're empty."

Her hands tense tighter on the grip of the bat.

She doesn't say anything, so I continue, "When I came in—it was only a few moments ago—I didn't see anyone else around, but let me do the search, just in case."

"Just in case of what?"

"If someone's in there—"

"I can take care of myself."

"I don't doubt that. But I'd like to help regardless. Consider it my apology for wandering in here and ruining your…dance."

That gets a smile out of her, which she tries—and fails—to hide from me. "Who are you?"

I reach into my pocket, and she grips the bat defensively. I raise my hands again, explaining, "I was going to show you my ID."

She nods. Slowly, I reach for my wallet, produce my license, and hold it out for her.

She leans toward me, trying to read the small card while remaining out of reach. So I read it out to her: my full name, my full address, my Texas state driver's license number and expiration date, my date of birth…

She smiles again.

I keep going. "Height: six feet; sex: male; eye color: brown; restrictions: none; endorsements: none." I turn it over. "Organ donor."

She chuckles, and it's a warm, lilting sound. Something I'd like to hear again. "Why are you here?"

"Like I said, I wanted to see a movie—"

"I mean in New Orleans."

"Oh." Now I reach back into my wallet, producing one of my business cards. "I'm here for work."

She reads the card aloud. "Gregory Hendricks, Senior Structural Engineer and Director of Forensic Inspections at Crawford & Son Engineering Services." With a raised brow, she adds, "Sounds important."

I shrug. "So what do you say? Can I search your bathrooms?"

"And that would be one of the strangest things a man has ever said to me," she says with a shrug. "Go ahead. Knock yourself out."

Across the lobby, I check the men's room first and swing the door open. A motion sensor triggers, and the light flickers on, illuminating an empty room. Still, I give it a full inspection, pushing the stall door open to be sure no one is hiding. It's empty. I repeat the process in the ladies' room, and it, too, is empty.

Back out in the lobby, the woman's grip has loosened a little on the bat she wields. I indicate I've found nothing, then cant my head toward the door labeled Employee's Only. She gives me a quick nod, and I push into that room next. It's empty except for the computer and monitor on a metal desk in one corner and a kitchenette beside a fire exit.

"All clear," I announce as I return to the lobby. "I'm the only trespasser here."

The woman lowers the bat from her shoulder with a sigh of relief.

My spirits sink when she still directs me toward the exit. I don't want to go. I like this place with its rich colored walls and thick red carpet dotted with gold stars, the faint scent of popcorn buried beneath the strong odor of fresh paint. And I like her, too, this proprietress of Paradise. I don't even know her name, but I want to. Out of the blue, I announce. "I'm handy."

She looks confused by the non sequitur.

"I can help," I clarify.

"You want a job?"

"I already have a job. I just want to help."

"Why?"

"Why not?" My flippant answer is clearly unsatisfactory to her, so I add, "I like to work with my hands."

Seeming almost irritated with me, she asks, "Don't you have anything better to do?"

"Not really." That's not true. I have quite a lot to do. I need to review my site notes for tomorrow's meeting, and my assistant, Kate, had mentioned wanting to connect over dinner to look at the numbers. But after today's meetings, I went for a walk. That was almost two hours ago, but I can't force my feet to take me back to the hotel.

"There's a great drag show about a half mile from here. They would love the attention of a pretty little white boy like you."

Pretty little white boy? "I'm not that little."

The woman surprises me when she throws back her head and laughs. It's enchanting, and I stare rudely at the deep dimples that form in her cheeks and the twinkle of mirth that dances in the depths of her onyx eyes. As her laughter subsides, she considers my offer.

"You'll get paint on your suit."

I'd forgotten I was still wearing it, not that it matters to me. I step over to the concession counter and shrug out of the jacket, laying it neatly over the glass case. I tug off my tie, too, and roll my shirtsleeves up to my elbows.

The woman watches me, seeming amused, then with a shrug, she bolts the door shut with me still inside. I grin like an idiot when she gestures for me to lead the way upstairs.

Back in the theater, Nina Simone is singing about the spell she's cast over me. It's awkward, somehow, to be in this big room, alone with this beautiful woman, as the jazzy strains of a saxophone fill the air. To break the ice, I ask the burning question, "What's your name?"

She extends a hand toward me. "Violet Devollier. Pleasure to make your acquaintance."

"Violet Devollier," I repeat with awe. What a great name, and it suits her—dark, vivid, vibrant: Violet. I shake her soft hand, marveling at her firm grip. "That's a fantastic name. A Hollywood sort of name."

Violet chuckles softly and glances at our clasped hands, then takes a step back, severing our connection. I feel the loss acutely. Crossing her arms over her chest, she says, "So Mr. Hendricks—"

"Greg, please."

"Greg," she says so sweetly. "How do you feel about heights?"

"Love 'em."

"Well, then," she points to the corner where a ladder leans against the wall, "I could use some help cutting and rolling the top of the room."

I glance from the ladder to the plaster walls that stretch twenty-five feet overhead. The ladder, an extension sort, looks like it's seen better days. I nod. "It would be my pleasure, Ms. Devollier."

"Violet, please," she says.

I get to work with the wobbly ladder, making quite a clatter as I extend it to its greatest height and test its strength under my weight. It'll hold.

Back down on the ground, Violet pours me a pan of paint and sets it in my idle hands with a fresh brush and roller. Carefully, I climb to the top of the ladder and get to work outlining the black ceiling with a smooth stripe of red before I roll out the top portion of the wall.

I work quickly and efficiently, enjoying the mindless task of painting. Like mowing an unruly lawn or vacuuming a dirty carpet; it's shaping chaos into order. It's cathartic. It's good work if you can get it. I paint as far as my arm can reach, then come down to move the ladder and do it all again until the top of the room is a warm Tibetan red.

As I finish the last stripe, I catch Violet staring at me. She looks amused and maybe a little impressed. My chest puffs up with pride, but I try not to let it show as I return to the ground and collapse the ladder to set it aside, then join her down below, painting what remains of the lower section of the room.

I like being in Violet's company. It's easy. It's so rare that interacting with people is easy for me. Usually, it's a strain on my introverted mind—exhausting. My best friend, Jake, was the first person I ever knew who was this easy to befriend. The two of us fit together from the start, peas in a pod. My wife was the second. I knew from the moment I laid eyes on Ari, I was in love with her. And while the thought of that made me nervous, her presence never did. Like them, Violet seems to be someone I can share comfortable silence with.

"So, Austin, huh?" Violet asks.

"Yep. Austin." Now I'm the one watching her, the way she stretches her whole body when she rolls paint onto the wall.

"Do you like it?"

"Yeah, it's a good town."

"What do you think of New Orleans?"

"One of the greatest cities in the world."

"Wow. High praise." She does that long stretch again to reach a high spot, and I stare at the place where her shirt lifts, revealing the soft cleft at the base of her spine above the curve of her ass in those tight jeans. "And have you been to all the cities of the world?"

"I've been to a lot of them."

She catches me staring. I turn my attention back to work, hitting the high points for her.

"So what sort of work brings you to this great city, Mr. Gregory Hendricks?"

"Safety inspections."

"And what does that entail?"

With a sigh I didn't intend to be audible, I explain, "I'm sent in to assess the integrity of municipal structures and determine if there's need for repair or replacement."

"Honestly, that sounds boring."

It is. Once upon a time, I loved my job. I enjoyed working in the field, climbing into a safety harness, and scaling a structure to look for fissures or cracks, rusted bolts, metal fatigue, and the like. I was good at it, had a true eye for detail. I was so good at the job, in fact, they promoted me.

Now, I push paper. My on-site work is generally limited to one walk through at the start of the project. Then my team does all the fun stuff, and I run the numbers, write reports, and sit in meetings.

In response to Violet's observation, I shrug.

"So what are you in town to assess?"

I don't see the harm in telling her, vaguely. "A bridge."

"And does it have integrity?"

I chuckle at her phrasing but answer her in the only way I can. "That's confidential."

She glances at me curiously. "Well, that's less boring. Are you the Agent 007 of structural engineering?"

"I'm definitely not that interesting."

"I'll be the judge of that."

With that, Violet lets the inquisition end, and we paint again in silence. It's nice, the quiet, strangely intimate. Too intimate, perhaps. Suddenly nervous from the prolonged pause in our conversation, I blurt out, "Tell me about Paradise."

Violet glances at me, and the lights glint in her dark eyes. "What about it?"

"I assume you own this place."

"Yep," she says with a prideful grin.

"Alone?"

Her expression slips into an exasperated grimace.

I backpedal. "I didn't mean that the way it sounded. I'm just impressed."

She narrows her eyes at me, and I fidget nervously beneath her gaze. Finally, she says, "My dad died a little over a year ago."

I don't understand the relevance, but still I say, "I'm sorry."

"He left me with some money. It wasn't much, but it was enough for me to buy this place and give it a go." As we finish the last strokes of paint and the room is awash in a brilliant coat of red, Violet sets her roller in the tray and looks out across the theater, *her* theater. "Dad was a big movie fan. When I was a girl, he'd take me to the pictures every week, buy us both a popcorn and a Coke. We'd see anything, didn't hardly care what it was. Those are some of my best memories."

Her eyes glisten with unshed tears as she turns away from me and collects her paint supplies off the floor. I help her clean up, assuming the topic is closed, but she says more. "Sidney Poitier was his favorite actor—*In the Heat of the Night, Guess Who's Coming to Dinner*—he saw those movies right here."

"Here in Paradise?"

She nods. "He grew up in this neighborhood before it went downhill. He and his sister would come here a lot in the summers with their mama because there was air-conditioning in Paradise."

"I can't imagine a New Orleans summer without air-conditioning."

Violet chuckles. "Me neither."

"You bought your dad's favorite old theater as an homage to him? That's extraordinary."

Violet shrugs, then claps her hands excitedly. "Want to see the full effect?"

"Definitely."

With much fanfare, she leads me to a panel of switches on the far wall, and when she flips one, we're sunk into total darkness. For a split second, it's terrifying. But then she hits a switch. The room lights back up with the soft amber illumination of sconces mounted high on the walls and floor runner lights to mark the stairs on either side of the seats.

I gasp at the sight. It's breathtaking. I've been inside countless theaters, sure, but I've never noticed the nuances of every corner and curve. I've never considered the tender loving care that goes into a place like this. "It's incredible, Violet. You've achieved something truly amazing here." My gaze moves over the undulating wave of red velvet chairs and the soft folds of the velvet curtain that flanks the wide screen, and I stand there, mesmerized. "When is opening night?"

"Tomorrow. It's a soft opening. You should come." She elbows me in the side. "You've earned yourself a seat."

The invitation is nice, but my shoulders sag as I decline. "I fly home tomorrow evening."

"That's too bad." The way Violet pouts at the news is oddly validating. Almost like she'll miss me.

An uneasy silence falls between us, and not knowing what to say next, I ask, "How else can I help?"

Violet bursts into laughter. "Seriously? I'm calling it a night. With your help, I'm way ahead of schedule now. All I have to do is a bit of cleanup and sort out the concessions—all of which can wait until tomorrow."

"Okay." I try to mask my disappointment. Is this goodbye? I've enjoyed my evening with Violet. It's been a welcome reprieve not having to think about everything that's happening in my life right now. The prospect of going back to my hotel room to try to sleep, alone with my thoughts, weighs heavy.

In as casual a voice as I can muster, I ask, "Then could I interest you in a drink? I hear there's a great drag show about a half mile from here. Being that it's my last night in town, I thought I might check it out."

As we move through the crescent streets of the Crescent City, I take in the sights. It is truly one of the greatest cities in the world—that wasn't an exaggeration said simply to get a smile from Violet.

I've loved this city since my first visit, thirteen years ago, when the band Jake and I started in college went on our first tour of the South. It's a hell of a town to get drunk in, but with its many quirks and unique characteristics, it's mélange of cultures and histories, this city is so much more than that.

New Orleans is a fascinator, a colorful kaleidoscope of cultures, loosely woven and layered with sparkling beads. There is no other place in the world quite like it. Built like an old European port town but with Creole flair, a child of the American South and a cousin to the Caribbean, all right here at the bend of the Mississippi River.

I gawk and marvel at the Easter egg-colored Creole cottage homes with their ornately carved corbels and brightly colored shutters. I pause to admire the occasional Spanish colonial-style façade with its intricate ironwork on the galleries that hang out over the sidewalks. As we move from one neighborhood to another, the beautiful spectacle transfixes me.

Beaux Ballroom fascinates me too. It's in a building that looks hundreds of years old. Layers of plaster chip off the brick walls in a rainbow array of colors—coral, yellow, green, and a deep, dark purple. Inside, the high ceiling is draped with swags of holiday lights, and people dance beneath the twinkle and spark of a disco ball slowly spinning.

Along one wall, a small stage sits squat before a blue velvet curtain bejeweled by rhinestones, like the night sky spotted with stars. At the other end of the room, a wooden horseshoe bar is crowded with patrons.

Everyone knows Violet, who navigates a gauntlet of hugs and hellos, handing out tickets to tomorrow's show as she leads me toward a pair of stools at the bar. When we're seated, Violet leans across the bar to air-kiss the bartender, a middle-aged Dolly drag queen in a scarlet red pinup dress. "Good evening, Miss Jewel."

Miss Jewel smiles at Violet then turns her attention to me and fans herself, fluttering her feathered lashes when she asks, "Well goodness me, Sweet Vee, who's this tall drink of water? He's the spitting image of Montgomery Clift, before the car accident, of course."

Violet purses her lips, then she introduces us. "Miss Jezebel Jewel, allow me to introduce to you, Mr. Gregory Hendricks. He's come all the way from Austin, Texas, to meet you."

"A real Texan cowboy? Be still my heart," Miss Jewel says in a sugary southern accent as she gives me a long wink.

"You're making him blush." I'm fairly certain she's right—I can feel my face warm with embarrassment at the attention. As if to take some of the scrutiny off me, Violet makes a production of ordering our drinks, exchanging a couple of inside jokes with Miss Jewel, who makes quick work of pouring my whiskey and Violet's vodka.

Once we're served, Miss Jewel winks at me again, saying, "Stick around, Cowboy, next show starts in ten minutes," then sashays to the opposite corner of the bar to serve other patrons.

Violet gives me a devilish grin. "I figured you'd be popular here." With that, she clinks her glass against mine and we drink.

"Why?"

Violet guffaws. "Because you're a Texan cowboy who looks like Monty Clift before the car accident, silly."

"Oh." I lean in and talk loudly to be heard over the throb of the music. "I'm not actually a Texan cowboy. I grew up in Tennessee, real close to Dolly Parton's hometown. I even worked at Dollywood for a summer."

"Is that right? Doing what?"

"I was the guy who'd decide if you were tall enough to ride the Thunder Express."

"Oh yeah?" She hops off her seat. "Tell me, Mr. Hendricks, am I tall enough to ride?"

Are we flirting? This feels like flirting, but it's been a long time since I flirted, so I can't be sure.

Violet is about five feet tall, well above the height line. Still, I add a little twang to my accent. "If you stand on your tiptoes, I'll let you ride."

My answer earns me a wink, and she shimmies back onto her seat to take a sip of her cocktail before asking, "Is that what a Tennessee accent sounds like? It's cute."

She thinks my accent is cute?

Violet's onyx eyes are unreadable over the rim of her glass as she watches me, assessing. Then, she sets her drink aside and—with her skin still chilled from the ice in her glass—rests her hand on mine and touches the gold band on my ring finger. "What's the story with this, Mr. Hendricks? Is there a Mrs. Hendricks to go with the ring?"

I nearly choke on my drink but answer simply, "Yes."

"Wow, not even gonna lie about it."

"Lie about what?"

"Most of the tourists out here chasing townie tail slip the ring off. Let it jangle in their pocket with the rest of the loose change."

"Chasing townie tail?" The words sound so crass, but is that what I'm doing? Suddenly exhausted, I say, "I'm not a cheater. I've never cheated on my wife."

"Okay. Okay. I didn't mean to hurt your feelings, just wanted to point out the elephant in the room."

"You didn't hurt my feelings." *Maybe a little.* "It's just... complicated."

Violet raises a skeptical brow. I'm sure she's heard it before. Probably every cheating husband calls his situation "complicated" right before he tries to get in her pants. I hate that she sees me that way. I don't want to be anything like those men.

My mind starts to race with the same torrent of thoughts that have plagued me for days. Thoughts that have made it almost impossible to concentrate on my work during this trip and drove me to drink myself to sleep every night.

Violet seems to be waiting for me to explain my *complicated* marriage, and maybe I should. Maybe what I need to organize this chaos in my head is to talk about it. Talking is not something I normally seek solace in, but with Violet, for some reason, I feel an urge to share, so I do.

"Four days ago, the night before I flew to New Orleans, my wife told me she wants to open our marriage."

Violet slants her head, curious now. I half expect her to speak, but she waits for me to say more.

How to talk about this? I try to put the words together, but what words would be appropriate? My focus moves to my half-drunk glass of whiskey, where I smooth my finger along the rim, a perfect circle. One revolution, two, three…

"She says she wants to give us both space." *Space.* The word sounds foreign and wrong. Like it's a cypher, a code for something else. And of course, it is code for something else. With a bit too much bitterness in my tone, I spell it out. "She wants to have sex with other men, and she's asked my permission to do it." I shrug and add, "But hey, she's granted me permission to have sex with other women, so that's nice."

I drink what's left of my whiskey and, in a tone I try to keep somewhere north of pathetic, admit, "If I've come off as a creepy tourist to you, then I'm sorry. That wasn't my intention. I've enjoyed my evening with you, platonically speaking. Though, I'll admit, I've enjoyed the flirting, too, if that was flirting. I don't know. To be honest, I don't know what I'm doing. I can't remember a time when I wasn't in love with my wife. I don't know how to be anything other than…hers. So when she laid this on me it was… Well, it was exciting at first. But I think I was excited because she was excited about it, and I can't remember the last time she was excited about anything. But the more I consider it, the more the whole idea feels….messy. And then the day after our talk I flew here to this incredible city filled with beautiful women"—I gesture to Violet to make it clear who I mean—"and I have no idea what to do. At what point do I stop being a faithful husband? I mean, do I even want to date other people?"

Dizzy from the warmth of the whiskey, the intensity of the music, and the sparkling motion of the lights, I pause to take a breath. With a huff, I add, "I like to think I'm an open-minded guy, but the idea of having sex with other people then going home to love my wife confuses and exhausts me. If you're with someone you trust, monogamy is so easy. This seems…difficult. So then I think, I just need to give her the space she asked for, let her do what she needs to do and wait for her to get it out of her system and come back to me. But I picture it. I imagine her with God knows who, and I wonder if she likes him better than me. Is she auditioning for my replacement right now?"

"Oh, Honey Eyes, wow. I didn't know you had all those words inside you."

Honey Eyes? "It's the whiskey. It loosens my tongue."

"Well in that case, let's get you another drink."

I nod when the bartender comes back to refill our glasses. I shift closer to Violet, feeling an odd sense of comfort with her, despite everything I've shared or, perhaps, because of it. Right here, right now, she knows more about this mess in my head than any other person. Not even Jake knows what's going on with Ari and me.

On the other side of the room, a set of lights over the starry-night stage spark on. Everyone's attention turns to a toweringly tall Black drag queen. She steps onto the stage in a silver dress and matching silver hair, lips, and nails, performing a quasi-robot routine to Kylie Minogue's "Can't Get You Out of My Head."

Awe fills me as the performer dances and lip-syncs, the spotlight sparking off her dress like the disco ball over her head. At my side, Violet sways and sings along with the song. And when the performer steps off the stage, standing a full head and shoulders above most of the crowd, she struts straight toward us, winking at me. She takes the money I hold out for her and stuffs it into the neckline of her dress before she moves deeper into the cheering crowd.

Talking loudly over the music, Violet asks, "So why did you agree with this open thing if it doesn't sit well with you? Why not say no?"

I turn my attention to my glass, tracing the rim once again with my ring finger, my perfect circle glinting golden in the twinkling lights. "What kind of person would I be if I told her no?"

"You'd be a husband who loves his wife."

"I'd be a husband who *controls* his wife, and that's not me."

She seems to like my answer. "It's like that proverb about the butterfly."

"Huh?"

"You know, it's something like: If you love something, set it free. If it comes back to you, it was meant to be."

"Oh. That's about a butterfly?"

"Hell if I know. I remember seeing it written next to a picture of a jar with a butterfly inside. And I remember thinking you could poke air holes in the lid and feed the butterfly nectar to keep it alive."

"That's bleak." I laugh.

A new performer is working the crowd now, but I'm too engrossed in my conversation with Violet to pay much attention. There is something about her that is so disarming, so refreshing that I want to keep her talking. She could talk about anything, and I'd pull up a chair to listen.

The music thumps louder, so Violet leans a little closer, and I do the same. "It's not often that people surprise me, Greg, but you sure have."

"Why, because I'm not a Neanderthal who keeps my wife in a jar with air holes?" This conversation has veered into the strange.

"Well, yeah. Because you recognize that subjugation isn't love. Gotta say, it's kinda hot."

"Yeah, well, a lot of good it's done me. I don't want to control her, and I don't want to be a jealous asshole, but the thought of her with…" I pause and take a gulp of my drink.

"How long have you been together?"

"Twelve years."

"Wow. Y'all were babies when you started."

"I was twenty. She was seventeen. She was in high school when I met her. I was…" *Her first.* I don't finish the sentence, feeling like to do so would be a betrayal of Ari's trust. "Yeah, we were young. *She* was young. I think she's restless. She's curious about the world outside of…us. And I don't blame her—it is a beautiful world. I'm not going to stand in the way of her exploring it. I just wish…"

"That she wanted to explore the world *with you.*" Violet finishes my sentence for me. She watches me closely, too closely, her keen eyes piercing my armor to see the parts of me I normally keep hidden.

"Yeah." I frown, remembering the look on Ari's face as we discussed the terms and conditions of our new marital status. And, when it was all decided, there was the way she mounted and fucked me, rough and hard and no-holds-barred, and how strange it felt to be loved by her so completely, even as she was pulling away.

"But it's weird. I think I understand her need to explore, now more than ever. I travel a lot for work, but I've never really explored…until tonight." I smile at Violet. "Tonight, I wandered off the beaten path, I worked with my hands, I laughed and relaxed and got to meet a lovely person. Honestly, I wouldn't have done any of that if she hadn't changed the terms of our marriage. Maybe she's right. Maybe there are layers of life that are off-limits when you're married, and she wants to experience them… I'm talking a lot. Say something, please. Save me from myself."

Violet's smile is brighter than the disco ball behind her. "I like you, Greg."

That shuts me up.

"You're very thoughtful and honest. I like it."

Ready to talk about something other than me, I ask, "What's your tale of woe?"

"Honey Eyes, I've got no troubles of the heart. That's the main perk of celibacy."

I nearly spit out a mouthful of whiskey. "You're celibate?"

"Yep."

"Why?"

"Because I'm not into women, and men are a pain in the ass I don't need. No offense."

"None taken."

Violet grins at me over the rim of her glass before elaborating. "When my dad died, my boyfriend at the time tried to be understanding, but he lost patience pretty quickly. He became practically obsessed with the fact that I wasn't in the mood to have sex. He complained that I was 'sad all the time,' but he'd have been fine if I was sad all the time, as long as I was still giving him blow jobs on the regular."

"He sounds like an asshole."

She shrugs. "He was great in bed but ultimately not worth my time. So I dumped him, dumped all my money into that theater, and never looked back. I've got a fly swatter and fresh batteries in my vibrator. What more could I possibly need from a man?"

I stare at her for a good twenty seconds before I'm overtaken with laughter. "You and my wife would get along well."

"And that's, possibly, the strangest thing any man has ever said to me."

"That's the second time you've told me that."

"Well, you say strange things."

I open my mouth to say more, but my phone vibrates in my pocket. I pull the thing out, and Violet watches me read the caller ID display.

"Your wife has incredible timing."

I stare down at my assistant Kate's name. "It's not my wife. It's work."

Rubbing my palm over my face, I apologize to Violet. "I need to take this."

Violet nods, sipping her drink as I stick a finger in my ear to block out the noise and answer the phone.

"Kate." My tone is gruff, curt.

"Greg, where are you?" Her voice is strange, softer than usual.

"What's going on?"

"I thought we were going to have dinner and go over the measurements before the meeting tomorrow."

I check the time on my phone. It's almost ten, but I don't want to leave this place. I'm enjoying my time with Violet too much. But the job is the whole reason I'm in this city.

"Okay, where do you want to meet?"

"The hotel bar?"

Is she already there? She sounds like she's been drinking. "I'll be there in half an hour."

I hang up, and Violet seems sad when she says, "I guess that's your cue."

"I guess so." I frown. "I'm sorry about having to cut this short. Can I walk you home?"

Violet chuckles. "Such a gentleman. No, thank you. I live nearby, and I'm going to stick around here for the next show."

Neither of us are in a hurry to end our night, sitting together a moment more. Finally, it's Violet who speaks first. "Well, Greg, thank you for all your help tonight. I am sincerely grateful."

"It's been my pleasure." Bashfully, I add, "And thank you for listening. I really laid it all at your feet, didn't I? I'm sorry about that."

With a wide smile that settles deep in the dimples of her cheeks, Violet stands from her barstool, and I follow suit. She reaches for me and pulls me against her, wrapping her arms around my waist in a great hug. I hug her back, squeezing my arms around her shoulders as I rest my chin on the top of her head. I like the way she fits against me and the way her breath warms my neck. Her hair smells like flowers, night-blooming jasmine. She fills my senses, and I don't want to let go. Eventually, though, I do.

Pulling away, I'm entranced by the way the twinkle lights warm the apples of her cheeks and sparkle in her onyx eyes. My breath shudders out of me as our gazes lock, and I'm overwhelmed with a desire to kiss her.

I don't.

Seeming to sense my hesitation to leave, she squeezes my hands before letting them go. "It's time to flap those butterfly wings and fly back to your life, Honey Eyes. I set you free."

"You never know—maybe I'll come back."

"I wouldn't mind if you did. In fact," she pulls a movie ticket for tomorrow's debut of *It's a Wonderful Life* out of her pocket and hands it to me, "this ticket is good for a free hug and a show if you ever find your way back to Paradise. You're always welcome, Greg."

2

MONDAY, AUGUST 15, 2005

AUSTIN, TEXAS

Nine months later.

Alex keeps touching my wife. He's subtle: a gentle stroke to the small of her back, his rough hands carefully brushing aside her dark waves of hair to whisper something in her ear, something that makes her smile. But of course he touches her. Ari is his girlfriend.

That's right. My wife has a boyfriend. She lives with him. His name is Alex. He's bigger than me, beefier than me, and nicer than me too. I wish I could hate him as much as she loves him. Because she does love him, more than she loves me.

I know they don't mean to torment me, but it's torment all the same. I try not to watch but can't help myself. I'm sitting across the table from them, and after twelve years together, my eyes are trained to seek and find her. It's a habit I need to break. I look away, down at my beer, and guzzle half of it—another habit I need to break.

Alex takes a bite of au gratin potatoes and ends up with a bit of food stuck on his bottom lip. Ari carefully wipes it away. Their eyes meet, and he winks at her. It's a sweet moment. Their bodies lean closer together as they both eat more of the potluck food.

It's Family Dinner Night at Nicole's house. Or is it Nicole *and* Jake's house now? I don't know, I just know that Jake, my best friend of twenty years, is head over heels in love with his roller derby queen. Even now, he sits with Nicole on his lap as they cuddle and eat their food, surrounded by their found family. The fact that Ari is my wife and dating Alex, who happens to be Nicole's ex-boyfriend, doesn't seem to faze anyone but me.

It's silly to keep calling Ari my wife. Legally, it's accurate. Emotionally, Ari divorced herself from me a while ago. She's his now. He's hers.

And I'm alone, sitting here rubbing the sheen off my movie ticket. That little piece of cardstock has become something of a grounding stone for me lately. It reminds me of New Orleans, and I imagine vibrant, vivacious Violet Devollier in her theater, dancing and singing as the paint dried. It seems like a lifetime ago since I was there. And in a lot of ways, it *was* a lifetime ago. Those moments spent with Violet were some of the last moments of my simple life before everything got horribly complicated.

"You're serious? You're having a baby?" Sheryl, Ari's eccentric new best friend, squeals at the top of her lungs as she jumps up from her chair.

Wait. What? Who's having a baby?

My stomach plummets as I look over at Ari and Alex with dread. Are they pregnant? I've always wanted to be a father, but Ari was never ready to start a family. I'd resigned myself that we never would. But was it me? She didn't want to start a family *with me*?

My wife and her boyfriend do not act like expecting parents, though. They stare at Jake and Nicole, their jaws hanging open. I turn as the tiny tornado known as Sheryl barrels into Jake and Nicole with a bone-crushing hug. *Oh. Okay. Wait.* Jake and Nicole are pregnant?

Jake catches my eye over Sheryl's shoulders and gives me a smile wider than I've ever seen on him. It's like every emotion I've ever known washes over me, but mostly it's joy that swamps me. Whether he knew it or not, Jake was always a family man without a family, and now he has one.

I stand and hug my best friend. "Good for you, brother. I'm happy for you."

And I am happy for him; of course I am. But when Jake goes to hug the others around the table, a chill sinks through me, loneliness like frostbite nipping at my toes. It's so loud in here—everyone talking at once, excited voices competing to be heard. The sob howling inside me could come out, and no one would notice.

I swallow the urge to scream and plaster a smile on my face, nodding when everyone else does. They talk about the future while I finish my beer and push the food around on my plate. I try to be okay, or at least to *look* okay. But I'm not okay. I'm sinking. Deeper every minute, and the quicksand is nearly to my chin. As the world turns around me, I'm stuck, mired in misery.

It's too quiet. The dark house is too empty as I make my way to the kitchen by rote and stand against the sink. There's a bottle of Jack in the cabinet by my head, and I pour myself a hefty dram. Turning to face the gloom, I drink it all down, coughing from the burn. Another drink follows.

With my eyes adjusted to the dark, I can see everything so clearly. *Too* clearly. The house is so empty. *Too* empty. Ari filled every corner of this space with her aura and presence, and I'd never realized it until her aura and presence were gone. Same goes for me. There's a hole in my chest that she used to fill. When she left, she took a piece of me with her.

And that's pretty much all she took. My gaze lands on the keepsakes and knickknacks dotting the counters and shelves—the Spanish tile mosaic I bought her in Barcelona, the jade dragon from Taiwan, the print from Dubai—all left behind when she went away. But then, why would she take them with her? None of these keepsakes meant anything to her. The art and gifts—they were tokens of my travels. Rather than reminders of the special times we shared together, they're mementos of the times when I left her behind.

I always took for granted that Ari would still be here, waiting in this dark, lonely house for my return. It's no wonder she was miserable.

It reminds me of when I was a boy, and I tried to capture the sun in the palm of my hand. But when I peeked between my fingers, the light would escape, and all I saw was darkness. Is that what I've done here? Is Ari the beautiful butterfly I kept in a jar? Crushing her wings in the darkness of my grip when I'd take her out to play?

Well, regardless, she's gone now, and all I have is this empty whiskey glass. I fill it again.

Leaning against the sink, I pull out the cigarettes I bought on the way home and slide one into my mouth. With a flick of my new lighter, I hover the flame near the end but don't ignite it. I've never smoked in the house before.

Why do I hesitate? What harm's it going to cause now? It's not like Ari would notice. I could light a hundred cigarettes in this house, and it wouldn't matter. I could light the whole place up. Burn it all down.

Jesus. Where is my head tonight?

Wallowing in self-pity—that's what I'm doing. It's no wonder Ari left me. I'm pathetic. I'd leave me, too, if I could.

Finally, I light the cigarette and take a long, soothing drag. Glass of whiskey in one hand, bottle in the other, I move to the table and log in to my laptop. There, my determination fizzles out. I stare at the screen for a full cigarette and another dram of whiskey before I steady my shaking fingers over the keys and start an internet search for "Texas Uncontested Divorce."

It's surprising how easy it is to get a divorce. I used to believe there was something to marriage, a meaning larger than two people—larger than the sum of its parts. I'd been naïve. I'd been naïve about a lot of things.

I light another cigarette and pour another drink as I skim through the help documents, print off the forms, read them thoroughly, and then, by the light of my laptop screen and the smoldering tip of my fifth cigarette, I fill out the papers.

3

SUNDAY, AUGUST 21, 2005

Blinding daylight streams through the kitchen window and shines off the tiled floor, which makes my bed. Squinting, I drape an arm over my eyes.

Ugh. My head hurts. And why did I sleep on the floor? I don't know how long I've been down here, but the cool tile feels refreshing against my cheek, so I'll stay.

A loud knock thunders at the front door, and the disturbance elicits a whiny groan from me. Who would be knocking at this hour? What hour is this? What *day* is this?

The sound of a key sliding into the lock startles me from the fog. The door knocker has a key, which means it's one of two people—Ari or Jake—and I don't want either of them to find me in this sorry state.

I sit upright, and my head spins with the sudden movement, but I work through the pain and disorientation, scrambling to get my hair into some semblance of order. My clothes are rumpled, too, but it's too late to fix them now. I press my back against the kitchen cabinets and listen as the door opens with a creak.

"Greg?" It's Ari. Her voice sounds almost nostalgic to me now, like a favorite song I haven't heard in a while. "Oh my God, Greg!"

I look up at Ari in the kitchen doorway, and I'm stunned by the sight of her. Her chestnut brown hair—which I used to love to run my fingers through—falls in soft waves around her shoulders and shines like she's in a shampoo commercial. The feather-soft tendrils frame the delicate lines of her face. And her wide doe eyes, paired with the soft pucker of her pink lips, always give her a surprised expression, like she's in awe of the world around her.

Ari teeters on a set of crutches, her leg still encased in a thick plaster cast, now covered with graffiti. I flinch at the memory of that day—was it only a month ago?—when I'd stood helplessly on the driveway of this house as a car ran the stop sign at the corner and hit her. The image of her striking the windshield and falling to the ground like a broken doll still haunts me.

It was a blur of panic and shock—but some things I will never forget. The feeling of my heart pounding as I raced to her side. Yanking my tie off to make a tourniquet and stanch the bleeding of a deep gash in her arm. Her warm blood coating my palms and soaking into my shirt. And always, in the back of my head, the nagging thought: *I can't lose her. I'll die if I lose her*.

Ari lived that day, but I lost her anyway. She went into the hospital, and she never came home, opting instead to move in with Alex once she was released.

Lying here sprawled on the floor, I must look pathetic. Ari's expression shifts from concern to abject horror as she takes in the sight of me.

Ashamed, I want to hide from her. She sees too much; she always has. And now, those all-knowing eyes sweep around the room, no doubt noticing the empty bottles of Jack. I look around, too, seeing what she sees, and cringe. I've consumed most of what's in the liquor cabinet. On the table beside my laptop is an antique saucer full of blunted cigarette butts.

"Greg, are you okay?"

The concern in her tone cuts like a knife. And it's a dumb question. *No, I'm not fucking okay.* I twist my head to frown up at her and in a groggy croak, ask, "What do you want, Ari? Why are you here?"

She huffs and swings across the room on those crutches, so used to maneuvering with them that she looks almost graceful doing it. She pulls a chair out from the table and sits, leaning her crutches against the wall. "I was worried about you. I called, several times. You didn't answer."

"Why?"

"Why what?"

"Why are you worried? Why are you calling me, Ari?"

She blinks with surprise. "Because no one's been able to reach you since dinner on Monday night."

What day is it? I don't dare ask her; it will only bolster her concern. "Well, there's no need to worry. I'm fine." I force a flat, toothless smile at her.

Ari scowls at me. "You don't look *fine* to me."

"Well, so fucking what, Ari?" My tone is sharp, sharper than I intend, but I don't alter it. "I am no longer your concern."

Ari softens. "I still care about you. That hasn't changed."

I let out a bitter laugh. *I still care about you.* What a rich sentiment. That shit should be on a greeting card. I mumble, "Everything's changed."

"Greg." Her eyes glisten with unshed tears. "I'm sorry. I know I hurt you, and I'm so sorry."

If she starts crying, I'm done for. Nothing unhinges me quite like Ari's tears. I'd rather be the cause of her anger, so I lash out, aiming to hurt her. "For fuck's sake, Ari, it's not all about you! This might come as a great shock to you, but I will learn to live without you. What I can't live with is you coming around here feeling sorry for me. This"—I gesture at the stretch of space between us—"doesn't help me. You being here doesn't improve the situation one *fucking* iota. Seeing the pity in your eyes right now—it makes me feel pathetic."

Ari flinches. "I'm sorry—"

"Stop being so sorry, Ari." I push to my feet so I'm standing over her. Looking down at her makes me feel less vulnerable, and so does being cruel. "Stop trying to fix everything. Stop trying to fix *me*. I don't need you, I don't need your pity, and I don't want you coming around all the time. Just back off."

"Greg—"

"Here," I grab the pile of papers she's managed to ignore even though they lay right next to her on the table and push them toward her, "you saved me a stamp."

Ari glances at the papers, then—despite the bold print across the top of the first page, naming them—looks up at me and asks, "What is this?"

I clear the lump from my throat and answer with as steady a voice as I can muster. "A copy of my petition for divorce. You can keep that for your records. I'll file an identical copy with the county to start the process. I won't contest anything. Whatever you want, it's yours. We'll split the assets—"

"I don't want your money."

I keep talking, like I haven't heard her. "I'll prepare financial statements listing everything—"

"I don't want your *fucking* money, Greg."

Now she looks angry. Good, this is good; anger I can handle. "I'll hire a realtor. Once the house sells, we'll split the proceeds—"

"Why are you being like this?" Ari looks around the kitchen. I wonder if she, like me, is remembering when we tore out the old linoleum and replaced it with the tile now beneath our feet. Is she thinking of the meals we cooked together, all the laughs we shared over dinner and wine?

Does she remember the night of our fifth anniversary when we didn't make it to the bedroom before we tore each other's clothes off, and I had her right there on the table? And after, we'd sat naked on the floor, feeding each other dessert, drinking wine, and sharing memories until the sun rose. Because I remember. That's all I can see when I look around this house—the memories of when I was happy, which all feel so far away now, like I'm watching home movies of someone else's life. I rub my hands over my eyes but can't scrub the images away.

"I'm being like this because it's how I need to be." My answer is honest. "And now, I need you to leave." Looking for something to do, I grab a cigarette out of the pack on the table and light it, puffing a big breath of smoke into the air over her head.

Ari stands up right in my cloud of smoke, wobbling a little on her broken leg, anger flashing in her eyes. "Look, if you're mad at me, then just fucking be mad! But this stupid self-destructive shit only hurts you."

Ari stares, as if waiting for me to speak. But what would be the point? Talking about the pain doesn't take it away.

"Damnit, Greg. Why won't you talk to me?"

The longer she stands here, challenging me to get mad, the more my pain ferments into something vicious and mean. Anger tinges my tone when I ask, "What do you want to talk about, Ari? The weather? Or about how you still barge in like you live here? You *left* me, Ari, but you won't *leave*."

"You know what, Greg? Fuck you."

"Oh. Fuck me?" I let out a hollow laugh. "Is that still an option, or are you monogamous yet? Isn't his cock enough for you?"

The look on Ari's face rips a new hole in my chest. I want to undo what I just said, rewind and take it back. But I can't. A tear escapes the corner of her eye, and I want to brush it away, but I can't do that either. I'm not the guy who gets to touch her like that. Not anymore.

I stand there as she pulls her key ring out of her purse. Her fingers tremble as she fishes our house key off and gently sets it on the table. Clutching the divorce papers in her white-knuckled grip, she turns away from me to collect her crutches, and without another word, she leaves me.

The door clicks shut, and my emotional dam breaks. I let out a peculiar sound, like the pained cry of an injured animal, and throw that stupid fucking house key across the room with every ounce of strength I have in me. It lands with a clatter in the corner, and then there's nothing, just more of that awful silence she's left in her wake.

I startle awake...again. To find myself lying on the kitchen floor... again. How long have I been down here this time? I look toward the window, wondering about the time. It's dark out now, nighttime. But is it the same day? How many days have I lost?

The last thing I remember is reaching for a bottle of schnapps from the back of the medicine cabinet, er, the *liquor* cabinet. Heh. Nice

Freudian slip. The bottle sits empty and discarded on the floor, just like me.

Someone bangs on the door, the knock so loud and angry I flinch. When a key slides into the lock, I know I'm in deep shit. Now that Ari has returned her key, there is only one person this could be, and he's exactly who I don't need finding me like this. I struggle to sit up, but it takes too much time. In a matter of seconds, I'm lifted to my feet by the scruff of my shirt collar, facing off against a very pissed-off Jake.

With his long hair braided into tight stripes that hang almost to his waist, the lean lines of his face pulled taut with anger, his dark eyes filled with rage and burning black holes through me, he's like some foregone warrior stepped out of time from his fight against land-hungry marauders.

"What the fuck is wrong with you?"

It's a valid question. I blather a bit of nonsense in response, my eyes trained on his Cannibal Corpse T-shirt.

Jake opens his mouth like he has more to say, but a sour look comes over his face, and he grumbles, "Christ, you stink." Next comes a look of pity from him. That's the worst. I can handle his anger but not his pity.

I close my eyes.

Jake grumbles as he hauls me out of the kitchen. He drags me down the hall as my feet scramble and I try to hold my ground. It's no use. He's bigger than me, stronger, and he's sober—I can't compete, so I go limp.

Jake shoves me into the bathroom and pushes me into the tub. Trying to stand, I stumble and land in a sprawl in the bath. Jake hits the cold faucet, and in an instant the showerhead comes to life with a squeal, dousing me in a jet of icy water that zaps my brain back online. I yelp and scramble to get away, but Jake pushes me back into the tub until my resistance crumbles.

Jake knocks the toilet lid closed, sits, and stares at me. "Picture this: I'm about to lie down for a nice nap with my beautiful baby momma when I get a 911 text from Ari telling me you're drinking yourself into oblivion…AGAIN. What is this, the *third* time I've had to piece your

Humpy-Dumpty ass back together?" He smirks and looks me over. "At least this time you skipped the prostitute and blow."

Was it just a couple weeks ago when Jake was on the tour of a life-time and came looking for me in that New York City hotel room, only to find a coked-out monster instead? He tried to help me that day, and I attacked.

I'm lucky he's still my friend. The look in his eyes right now suggests I'm testing the bounds of our brotherhood yet again. "Enough with the silent stare, asshole. I'll ask you this one more time: What the fuck is wrong with you?"

I blink at him through the veil of water droplets, but there's no answer. If I knew what was wrong with me, I'd fix it. It's what I do. I've spent countless hours of my life poring over plans and design schematics, scrutinizing the nuances of structural designs, looking for fatal flaws. I, more than most, know how to find faults and how to fix them; it's why they pay me the big bucks. And yet, when it comes to the shambles of my own life, I can't even pinpoint the source of the problem, let alone fix it.

Like he can read my mind, Jake's expression tempers. "Please talk to me, brother."

This indignity is the worst kind of torture. My best friend—the man who's more of a brother to me than my own flesh and blood—shouldn't have to sit here and try to make sense of my downward spiral.

"Look, I get it. This shit sucks, and you're struggling. Let us help you."

"Us?" That word used to mean Jake, Ari, and me. What does "us" mean now?

"Yeah, *us*. A lot of people care about you, Greg. Pushing away the people who love you doesn't help anyone, least of all you."

I groan and lean back, letting the cold spray of water fill my mouth before spitting it out. I run my fingers over my face and through my hair, feeling chilled but cleaner and refreshed.

Jake hits the faucet, cutting the water off. He throws a towel at me, and I rub it over my head as my teeth start to chatter. Finally, after I'm a little more put together, I say, "I admit I could be handling this better."

That earns me a bitter laugh.

"All right, so what's the master plan here?" Jake claps his hands together. "Tell me how I can help you."

I groan and push to my feet, balancing carefully so I don't slip and fall as I step out of the shower. I toss the towel away and strip out of my shirt, shoes, and soggy socks; then I start to unzip my pants.

"Whoa there." Jake cocks his head at me. Like he's never seen it before.

I ignore him and drop trou, then wrap the towel around my waist and walk to the bedroom, where I pull on a dry shirt and a loose pair of athletic shorts.

When I'm dressed, I join Jake in the kitchen as he cleans up my mess. He tosses the empty bottles in the recycling bin and washes the saucer I'd used as an ashtray before setting it in the rack to dry.

"What day is it?" I collapse into a chair at the table, rubbing at the crick in my neck.

"Sunday."

"Which Sunday?"

Jake frowns. "The twenty-first."

"Shit." I've managed to lose a week to this funk.

When Jake finishes cleaning, he opens the fridge and pulls out a carton of eggs. He grabs a frying pan and scrambles them, heaping a pile onto a plate and serving it to me with a glass of OJ.

He does it all without saying a word—not passing judgment, just helping. I eat the food, and he sits across from me, pulling my laptop toward him and browsing through the webpages I still have open: the how-to guide for a quickie divorce.

"Well, it looks like you're already making plans."

I smirk between bites of egg.

"It's weird, how easy it is," he remarks, a sentiment that mirrors my own.

"Makes sense though. Why force two miserable people to stay together?"

I finish my food, and Jake washes my plate and fork. He refills my

OJ, then together we sit in a shared silence for a while. It's nice, companionship without the onus of conversation. I like that I don't have to plaster a smile on my face and pretend to be okay. Even at my lowest, Jake's here for me.

"When do you go back to work?"

I haven't thought about work in weeks. When Ari was hit by a car, I took all my accrued vacation, almost six weeks, under the guise of taking care of her. Then I turned my phone off and flew to New York with suicidal ideations.

"Tomorrow," I answer.

Jake considers, then slaps his hands on the table and announces, "Okay, this is how it's going to go. You're going to do a load of laundry. You're going to take a proper shower and shave and brush your teeth and floss. And then you are going to pack a bag."

"To go where?" I complain, exhausted by the idea of having to move from this chair.

"You're going to come live with Nicole and me."

"What? Why?"

"Being alone in this house is killing you. Look at you, drinking yourself to death and sleeping on the kitchen floor—"

"I'm fine—"

"You're not *fine*. You're about as far from *fine* as I've ever seen you." Jake scowls at me. "Look, the thing is, I could use your help. Nicole and I have our hands full with the pregnancy, and I'm taking on more students to pay for all the diapers and car seats and—"

"Aren't you a big-shot rock star now? Why are you still teaching guitar?"

"Rock stardom doesn't pay all that well, at least not until we record an album together. In the meantime, I'm working my ass off to save up. And I'm trying to keep Nicole off her feet as much as possible, so I could use some help with the mundane household chores."

"Okay."

"Really?" Jake seems surprised.

"Anything I can do to help." I like this scenario because it's about helping Jake, not about helping me.

"Cool. Thank you, brother," Jake says. Then, he slowly grins. "But I have one rule."

I cringe, waiting.

"Not a drop of alcohol. You drink even an ounce of booze around my lady and my unborn child, and we're going to have a problem."

I nod.

Jake adds, "Also, no smoking. That shit stops now. You feel me?"

"You said you have one rule. That's two."

"I have two rules, no drinking and no smoking, and brother, you've got to talk to someone. You've got to let this shit out, and let us in."

"That's three rules."

Out of the blue, Jake launches into Monty Python's "The Spanish Inquisition" skit, and, for the first time in as long as I can remember, I laugh.

4

MONDAY, AUGUST 22, 2005

"Greg?"

I glance up from the coffee maker. Kate stands in the employee break-room entrance looking sculptural, a marble beauty in a slate skirt and travertine top. She looks surprised to see me, which is fair, considering it's been weeks since I've reported to work.

"Hi," I say. It comes out sounding awkward. But that's not surprising. Everything with Kate is awkward now. Once upon a time, things were simple—I was her boss, and she was my assistant. Then we had sex...a lot of sex. I made the mistake of thinking we had love, too, and that's when everything imploded. Now here I stand, Kate's ex-boss and her ex-boyfriend, while the coffee machine gurgles and dispenses my drink.

"Hi?" She hisses in an angry whisper. "That's *all* you have to say to me?"

What else is there to say?

"You dumped me then transferred me to Brad Winters' team—"

Technically, she dumped me, but it was more or less mutual. As for the Brad Winters thing... "It was a promotion, I thought—"

"I know what you thought. It was still a shitty way to leave a girl,

Greg." She huffs, though she still keeps her voice low. "Then you vanished. I was worried something happened to you."

"I'm sorry, Kate. For everything."

"Hendricks," Kevin Crawford, the "Son" in "Crawford & Son," crows from the doorway. I glance past Kate and squint at the shine of his reptilian smile. I haven't missed him during my vacation. "Let's talk."

He doesn't wait for me to agree. He turns and swaggers down the hallway like a gunfighter at high noon, expecting me to follow. With a heavy sigh, I move to pass Kate. She surprises me when she reaches out and hugs me. I let go of a shaky breath as I wrap my arms around her.

"I'm sorry, too, Greg."

I grin, just a little, then follow my boss to his corner of the twenty-second floor.

Kevin's office is obnoxiously opulent, with mahogany bookshelves he never uses and, in an homage to the good ole boy world of yesteryear, a wet bar. I eye the decanter of bourbon and quickly look away.

"How are things at home?" Kevin kicks his cowboy boots up onto the corner of his desk and leans back in his chair like it's a chaise.

I panic, not sure how to answer. Is there some coded meaning to the question? How much does he know about Kate and me and Ari and Alex?

"Did Ari get the flowers I sent?"

Oh, *that* home. "They were beautiful, thank you." *They rotted on the kitchen table while I rotted in New York City.*

"Is she recovering well?" He pinches his face into some mediocre attempt at concern, but it makes him look constipated.

"She is." This is a surreal conversation. I forget that the rest of the world doesn't know my wife left me.

"Good." The all-American country boy gives me his patented cowboy grin—serpentine with a hint of aw shucks—but when he speaks, he effects an authoritative tone that reminds me of trips to the principal's office in high school. Considering Kevin is five years my junior and only my boss because of nepotism, it's a tone that chafes.

"Listen, Hendricks, I spoke to Dad about this, and we've decided to let you go."

I slide forward to the edge of my seat, my hands fisting the wooden armrests of the chair. "You're firing me?"

"We're letting you go."

"On what grounds?"

"AWOL." Kevin grabs his paperweight and tosses it from one hand to the other as he leans back in his chair. It's one of those scorpions frozen in a hunk of acrylic. A scorpion had to die for that paperweight.

Hang on. AWOL? Absent without leave? As if this is the military.

"You violated our HR-policy when you took extended leave without written notice," Kevin elaborates.

"I wrote—"

"There's a process for these things, procedures, and a one-sentence email written at three o'clock in the morning informing me you'd be taking your entire vacation starting the next day is *not* notice."

I chuff and lean back in my seat, taking in the strange shape of this new reality. I've never been fired before.

Without warning, Kevin's office door opens, and a large man in a dark green jacket steps inside, glaring at me. I glance from the big man back to Kevin, feeling some irrational sense of betrayal. "You called building security on me?"

The little shit smirks, and it's a good thing he called security because right now, I want to pick up my chair and throw it through the window, then push the asshole out.

Before I can do that, the Jolly Green Giant removes me from Kevin's office in some sort of wrestler hold. I struggle for a moment, but what is the point? It's just a job, and on the long list of things I've lost lately, it hardly merits a second thought. Former colleagues gawk from the doors of their offices and peek like prairie dogs over the walls of their cubicles to watch the action.

Halfway to the exit, I pass Kate, who is standing in the break-room doorway, a cup of coffee clutched against her chest, her eyes wide with shock. With an awkward nod, I say goodbye.

"Oh my God, your leg!" Sheryl shouts from the living room.

"Got the cast off today!" Ari replies in a sing-song voice.

I freeze for a moment, overwhelmed by the sound of her, then bend to look through the pass-through window that connects the kitchen to the living room so I can stare at her legs like everyone else.

Once Ari and Alex have made it through the gauntlet of hugs and chatter, Ari aims for the kitchen. I run my fingers through my hair and meet her at the doorway. She yelps with surprise at the sight of me, then her smile sinks. She takes a fortifying breath, and it breaks my heart all over again.

"I'm sorry," I say nervously. "Ari, I'm so sorry. What I said was so incredibly inappropriate and shitty. And I'm sorry."

Ari peers up at me through the fan of her dark lashes and blinks, then navigates around me so she can set her casserole dish on the counter. I hold my breath, not sure what to expect from her considering I basically called her a slut at our last meeting and served her with divorce papers. So it surprises me when she turns around and hugs me.

I nearly sob. I wish I didn't need this affection from her, but I do. I wrap my arms around her shoulders, not wanting to let go but knowing I'll have to. Any minute now.

When she does step away, cold washes over me. There's a strand of hair tangled in her eyelashes. I want to brush it away. I want to touch her, just one more time—

Alex steps into the kitchen, smiling as he offers his hand. There's none of the macho, hand-crushing squeeze I always half expect from him, though that's something he's never done. He crosses to the fridge and pulls out a pair of Lone Star tallboys for himself and Ari. He offers me one.

I must look like a madman as I vigorously shake my head. "No thanks, man. Day one of sobriety," I say.

When Nicole and Sheryl's roller derby friends Tynisha and Rachel arrive, the "family" is all here, so we start dinner. I settle into my meal in relative silence as the people around me chat, choking down food I can hardly taste, grunting at words I can hardly hear, my focus fixated entirely on the whiskey I can't drink, the cigarettes I can't smoke, and the wife I can't touch.

"How was your first day back at work?" Jake cuts through my fog with his question.

Uh. I glance around the table before sheepishly admitting, "Got fired."

Everyone speaks at once, asking why.

"I went AWOL."

Jake laughs. "What, like in the army?"

I shrug. "First time fired, and security escorted me out of the building."

"What will you do now?" Ari asks.

I shrug again.

Nicole answers her question. "I'm hiring him as a housekeeper. The dude cleaned every inch of this house today. Even the oven."

"We should go to karaoke to celebrate," Sheryl chirps with excitement.

"Celebrate what?" Tynisha asks her.

"Greg's Funemployment! Time to par-tay!"

"Clearly you didn't get the memo, Sheryl." I smile, make a joke, but I'm starting to shake as I speak. "I'm trying to stay sober now."

She shrugs. "You can party sober too."

"Y'all have fun with karaoke tonight, but Greg and I have somewhere else to be," Jake says.

We do? Jake pushes to his feet, pulls his keys out of his pocket, and twirls them around his finger. Curious, and a little nervous, I follow him out the door to his truck.

"Hi, I'm Greg." *What am I doing up here?* "I know this is the part where I'm supposed to say I'm an alcoholic, but… Honestly, I don't feel like an alcoholic. All my life when I heard the word 'alcoholic,' it was said with derision. That was the word used to pass judgment on the homeless winos begging for change on the corner. How could I be an alcoholic when they're alcoholics, and I'm nothing like them? I have my shit together, while they're a mess." *Jesus, I sound like an asshole.* "Of course, that's a bunch of classist, elitist bullshit. And it's a lie. I have more in common with those guys than I want to admit. And I don't have my shit together at all."

I take a deep breath of the stale rec center air and look around at the sparsely populated metal folding chairs lined up before me. Why did I volunteer to speak? The guy asked if there was anyone new, and I raised my hand, then kept it up when he asked if anyone wanted to talk. Now, here I am, leaning on the podium for support as I mount my confession.

"A few weeks ago, I hit rock bottom. My wife left me"—my girl-friend left me, too, but that's not relevant here—"and I didn't handle it well. I tried drinking myself into oblivion and snorting enough cocaine to kill a horse. When none of that helped, I flew to New York and rented a Manhattan hotel suite. It's a hell of a view of rock bottom from the thirty-fifth floor."

Not able to look Jake in the eyes for this next part, I glance down at the keepsake movie ticket I clutch in my hand. I rub it when I'm stressed, and lately I've rubbed the sheen and most of the letters off. Where it once read the full title of the movie Paradise Theatre was showing last December, now only the words "It's a Wonder" are legible.

I feel parched, an unquenchable thirst choking me. Clearing my throat, I admit, "I was going to jump. That was the plan, but then my best friend showed up. He was my guardian angel that day. He saved me when he screwed up my plans to kill myself. And I was angry at him for that."

Finally I get the nerve to look at Jake. His jaw is rigid, his posture steely, but his eyes are warm with empathy, a compassion I do not deserve. "I abused him verbally and physically. I hit him, repeatedly. Somehow I got a fork in my hand from one of the room service trays, and I stabbed him with it. Right here." I rest my fingers on my shoulder in the same place where Jake's new scar remains. "I literally stabbed my best friend in the back."

My sweaty palms squeak as I clutch the edges of the podium. "You'd think that would have shocked me out of my drunken stupor, but no. He had to save me from myself again last night. I've been dragging my knuckles against rock bottom for a while now. And I guess what I'm trying to say is: Hi, I'm Greg, and I'm an alcoholic. I've been sober for twenty-four hours. Working toward hour twenty-five."

To the sound of applause, I make my way back to my seat beside Jake. As the next speaker goes to the front of the room, he says quietly. "I'm glad you didn't jump."

My eyes water. For a moment, I let those words ring in my head like heavenly bells, then I look away, down at my lap. I can feel his eyes on me. I know he wants me to agree. I'm supposed to say, "me too," right now. And I want to. I *wish* I could say I'm glad to be alive, but the words stick in my throat, and I'm so thirsty.

5

SATURDAY, AUGUST 27, 2005

Cross-legged on the floor of my living room, I sort my once-wedded belongings into piles: his, hers, and trash. I expected this process of dividing assets to be more emotional, but treating it like another item to check off my to-do list dulls the ache.

It's been a whole week of soberly marking items off my lists. I've cleaned every inch of Jake and Nicole's house, groomed Gomez and Morticia—their dog and cat—updated my resume, and hired a realtor. Now, I tend to the minutiae of a breakup, sorting through twelve years of knickknacks and deciding what to do with the furniture neither of us want.

The droning voice of a television-news reporter helps chase away the silence of this space. I take a break from sorting CDs and glance up: a guy in a windbreaker fights high winds to report from a beach in Florida about a hurricane called Katrina. The Category 2 storm spins over the Gulf after killing seven people when she made landfall in Fort Lauderdale. Too soon, the news cycles to a story about President Bush, and I turn my attention back to my work, pulling a stack of books closer to determine whose is whose.

The day stretches long, and the piles grow into unstable mountains of stuff, looming large and threatening to crush me like Alpine avalanches. I take a break to drink some iced tea, my go-to beverage now that I'm a teetotaler.

On the television, there's more weather news. With increasing urgency in his tone, a meteorologist informs viewers the National Weather Service has updated their forecast model. "The storm has grown in intensity and shifted course in recent hours. Now a Category 3 storm, Hurricane Katrina could make landfall as far west as Louisiana. So folks in the New Orleans metro area need to—"

New Orleans.

Those words send a chill through me. My mind races as I imagine the worst and hope for the best. These forecasts are notoriously unpredictable, aren't they? What are they called, spaghetti models? Throw a bunch of spaghetti at the map and see what sticks? The hurricane is closer to Cuba than it is to New Orleans. It's too soon to worry, but tell that to my mind, which races with thoughts of Violet and her Paradise in the path of a storm.

It's late Sunday morning when Jake and Nicole roll up in Jake's old truck, ready for the big breakfast I promised in exchange for helping me haul unwanted items to secondhand shops.

"What's up, buddy?" Jake tries to sound unconcerned when he finds me in a valley among the mountains of junk, staring at the television from the floor. But I can see it in his eyes—he thinks I relapsed.

"Hurricane Katrina—it's a Category 5, and it's heading for New Orleans," I say, pointing at the television, trying to look as sober as I am. "Expected to make landfall tonight or tomorrow morning. They've issued mandatory evacuations for everyone except Orleans Parish, where it's voluntary."

Jake seems relieved that I'm coherent. He turns to the television for a moment, assessing the latest news, then finds a clear spot on the couch to sit. "How many people are in that city? Half a million? I-10 must be a fucking parking lot."

"Still. It's not enough. It needs to be mandatory," I grumble. "They need to go door-to-door to help people reach shelters or leave the city. They need to tell people who are living in low-lying areas to vacate their homes. They need…to do more," I finish, helplessly.

"Greg, you sweet lamb." Nicole cants her head at me as she sits on Jake's lap. "New Orleans is an old coastal town. I'm sure they know how to handle a hurricane. Didn't they just get hit by Cindy last month? This is old hat for them."

"Cindy was barely a Category 1, if that, yet it still flooded streets and knocked out power for days. Katrina is a Category 5. It's significantly more powerful. New Orleans sees lots of storms, sure, but they haven't been hit by a major hurricane since Betsy and Camille in the 1960s. Camille wasn't a direct hit, but Betsy was. That storm breached levees and flooded thousands of homes. There were people who drowned in their own attics because the floodwaters rose so quickly they were trapped."

"How do you know all that?" Nicole asks.

"It's what I do. I devoted my entire career to structural engineering, until my career ended this week."

"Your career did not end. You're between jobs," Jake says.

I roll my eyes at him. "I was in New Orleans last December to assess the structural integrity of a bridge over the Mississippi. The bulk of my work was identifying potential modes of failure when the structure was subjected to the stress of storms at varying intensities."

"They paid you to identify failure? And here I've been doing that for free all this time," Nicole quips.

I try to smile, knowing I'm probably boring them with the details. For me, this stuff is anything but boring. Growing up, I'd always been fascinated with structural design and architecture. Then Chernobyl happened. I vividly remember the look of devastation on my father's face. He was a nuclear physicist at Oak Ridge National Laboratory, and we were watching his worst nightmare come true.

That's when my interest shifted, and I became obsessed with understanding the limits of human engineering. I studied the mistakes caused by hubris or bad design and implementation. The Tacoma

Narrows Bridge snapped because no one had considered the effect of aeroelastic flutter in 1940. The Kansas City Hyatt Regency walkway collapsed and killed over one hundred people because of a load miscalculation. It was bad design—more than the iceberg—that sank the Titanic.

A gray image of the cyclonic circulation over the Gulf appears on the television. I focus again on Katrina and the damage she could do. "The thing about New Orleans is, it's sinking. A century of human engineering to dredge shipping channels and reclaim swampland for housing developments has dramatically changed the topography of the Mississippi Delta and the city itself. The dwindling Delta has made the city much more vulnerable to storm surge. And within the city itself, subsidence has dropped some parts of New Orleans as much as ten feet below sea level. Roughly half the city is below sea level now. They've built a network of levees and pumps to keep the water out, but the storm surge and rainfall from a Category 5 hurricane will put a lot of pressure on those systems."

"Shit," Nicole murmurs, and that about sums it up.

Suddenly overwhelmed with anxiety, I move to my feet and pace, trekking through the mountains of mess as I try the number for Paradise Theatre again—I got the number from the operator last night.

"Who do you keep calling?" Nicole asks.

"A friend," I answer, but do I have any right to claim Violet as a friend? I spent one evening with her, then walked away. Will she even remember me? My questions go unanswered when my call goes to voicemail. To the machine, I say: "Uh… Hi, this message is for Violet Devollier. This is Greg Hendricks, you might remember me… We painted together." This is so awkward. I clear my throat. "If you get this message, please call me." I leave my number and hang up, hesitant to look over at Jake and Nicole.

"You painted together?" Jake asks. "Is that a euphemism?"

On the television, the news cuts to a press conference. It's the mayor, surrounded by leaders of every agency involved in disaster management, issuing the first ever mandatory evacuation for the city of New Orleans.

"We are facing a storm that most of us have feared," the mayor says as he finishes reading the evacuation notice. He then goes on to add, "The storm surge will likely topple our levee system."

"He said it," Nicole whispers.

I nod. "He said it."

6

MONDAY, AUGUST 29, 2005

"What's the latest?" Nicole settles beside me on her couch, her attention on the television, where a radar image of a spinning cyclone makes landfall repeatedly, like a skip in the record.

"Unsubstantiated reports of a levee breach in the Lower Ninth Ward, near Florida Avenue. There may be others too. Parts of I-10 are under water right now."

Just as she's about to say something, the news channel patches through a phone call from the city's mayor, and Nicole grapples for the remote to turn up the volume.

"We're getting reports of issues with our levee system. We haven't been able to verify that the levees are being overtopped, but we have had many calls that people are on roofs—"

"It's happening," Nicole mutters.

As the phone interview continues, the mayor describes damage to the Superdome roof—the place that had been the city's "refuge of last resort"—and mentions reports of fires in the city.

I'm not sure how long we watch the horror unfold on television as increasingly worse images and stories start to come out of the city. A rotating slideshow of chaos and destruction—broken windows in downtown high-rises, water lapping the sides of cars parked in the city streets, people walking through the waist-high toxic stew that has engulfed their city.

Jake comes home from a guitar lesson to join us, switching between channels as every news and weather channel is running nonstop with the story now. When Ari and Alex and then Sheryl, Tynisha, and Rachel arrive, I remember it's Monday, Family Dinner Night. But the food cools on the kitchen counter as everyone pulls up a chair to stare at the television. There is no jovial chatter tonight. No one suggests karaoke.

Every bit of our focus is turned to the terrible news, as embedded reporters stand wearily against the foul wind and try to tell us about the developing crisis in the city—water as high as eleven feet in parts of the Lower Ninth, looting of a Winn-Dixie, levees and pumps failing throughout the city, no power for over half a million households in Louisiana, people on their roofs waving T-shirts like flags, desperate to be rescued from the rising waters.

One of the television anchors reads a memo from some agency: "—strongly urges anyone seeking refuge in an attic to bring necessary tools for survival with them, such as an axe—"

"Holy shit," Jake says under his breath. "It's like what you said about Hurricane Betsy. People are drowning in their homes."

I can't sit anymore, but I can't stand still either. The horrific images running through my mind are shadows I can't shake even as I start to pace from corner to corner. Talking to the television anchor like she can hear me, I ask, "How is that message supposed to help the people who need it? They have no power, no television. Hopefully they have battery-powered or hand-crank radios."

"It's the twenty-first century, and it's come down to hand-crank radios and axes," Rachel says.

Twitchy and shaking, I pace faster. I'm angry, and I don't know where to direct my frustration. I want to punch the walls and scream and yell. I want to do *something*, anything. Instead, I'm stuck here, hundreds of miles away, impotent and useless.

I pull my phone from my pocket and call the theater again. It doesn't even ring anymore, just makes a clicking noise, like the operator can't route the call because the number doesn't exist, like the phone fell off the edge of the Earth today.

"I'm going there," I say before I realize the words are out of my mouth.

"What?" Ari's voice cracks with the question.

"I can't be here. I need to be there. I need to be doing something. I need to help."

"Put your cape away, Superman. You've got work to do here first," Jake grumbles.

"What work? I got fired."

"Sobriety, you dipshit." Jake interrupts my thoughts, his voice pitched so loud I can't ignore it. "You think giving one good speech at an AA meeting has fixed you? No, recovery takes time, *and* it takes work."

I wave his concern away. "I can work on it there."

Jake leaps off the couch and stalks toward me. The look on his face is fierce, fiery rage burning deep in his dark eyes. In a voice that sounds deceptively calm, he asks, "Who do you think you're trying to fool? I know you, brother. I've seen you at your worst. So don't fucking stand here, twitching all over the place, and tell me you're fine and fucking dandy while you run off to the eye of the storm with another death wish."

I blink, a bit stunned, and look around the room. Everyone is watching us, jaws hanging open; they're stunned too. Jake doesn't move a muscle, waiting for my reaction.

"I'm sorry, Jake. I'm sorry I've given you so much reason to doubt me." I reach for him, hugging one arm around his neck. When he doesn't push away, I wrap the second arm around him, and he hugs me back.

I pull away enough to look him in the eyes, saying, "I love you, brother, and I promise you—New Orleans won't be like New York. It's not a death wish. It's where I need to be." I point at the television. "That's the work I need to be doing. I'm useless here, but I can help people there."

Jake grabs the back of my neck, holding me still. "Promise me you'll stay sober. Promise you'll get help if you need it. I can't help you if you're there, so you fucking promise me you'll find help if you need it."

I don't trust my voice to speak, but he deserves a real answer. I clear my throat and say, "I promise."

Suddenly, everyone has an opinion, all talking at once. But Ari's voice rises above the rest when she says, "Greg, a minute ago they were talking about looters on the news. You can't drive in there in the beamer—"

"He can take my truck," Jake says. "It's a beater. No one will look twice at it."

"I can't believe you're encouraging him!" Ari directs a deep scowl at Jake.

Jake ignores her, asking me, "You're going to look for Violet, aren't you?"

When I nod, someone asks, "Who's Violet?"

I pause for a moment, not sure how to answer that. Finally, I say simply, "Someone I care about."

Glancing at the chaos playing on the television, Sheryl asks, "It's a disaster. How do you plan to find her?"

I smile when I think of Paradise. "I have an idea where to start looking."

7

"Mind if I sit?"

A man stands at the side of my table, holding his tray of truck-stop food. He wears a Vietnam Vet ball cap pulled low over his graying hair. It slants a shadow across the weathered lines of his dark face, shielding his eyes from the bright fluorescents overhead.

"Of course not. Please join me." I gesture to the empty half of my wooden booth, and he slides onto the seat. I straighten my posture, a habit left over from my mom's training about showing respect for my elders.

"Willie Henderson, down from Bossier City. You?"

"Greg Hendricks, Austin, Texas." We shake hands. His grip is firm, his movements strong and efficient; he's a tough old man.

Glancing around at the other tables—they're all occupied by groups of two or three men, with only a few women in the bunch—I smile at my dining partner. "Full house tonight."

Willie stabs his spork into creamed corn, devouring his meal like it could be his last. Between bites, he says, "Hope all this waiting ends tonight. By the time they let us in, won't be nothin' left to save."

I take my cue from Willie, popping a bite of Salisbury steak into my mouth. If they do finally open the road to New Orleans and let us in, this might be my last warm meal for a while; I should eat before it gets cold.

"Where you headed?" Willie asks. It's become the customary greeting among those of us sleeping in our cars at this truck stop. It's assumed we're all here for the same reason: to get into New Orleans.

"Tremé, you?"

"Lower Ninth. My pop's got a place there."

I hiss through my teeth. All the televisions in this place flicker with bad news out of the Lower Ninth, but the rumors circulating from table to table are worse. A barge broke through the levee wall there, unleashed an explosion of water that blew houses apart and killed untold numbers of people. "Did he stay?"

"No, thank the Lord Almighty. He went with my sister to her son's place in Memphis. I got a brother and a couple of nephews bringing their boats up from Houston. Should be here soon. We're goin' in to see what's left. What about you? What's in Tremé?"

"A woman," I answer, probably a bit too quickly because Willie grins. I clarify. "A friend."

He chuckles. "If you're driving into the belly of hell for her, she must be a good friend. You on your own here?"

I wipe a napkin across my mouth. Full, I settle back in my seat after my meal. "Yes, sir."

Willie considers something, then leans in a little closer to share a secret. "Word is they're letting people through if they're hauling boats. We'll be lining up at the blockade at five in the morning. You're welcome to join us."

"I'd appreciate that, Willie. Thank you."

The bell on the truck-stop door chimes as a group of men step inside. They glance around a moment, then come straight to our table. One of the men looks a lot like Willie but younger, and he's flanked by two men who look a bit younger than me. Willie makes quick introductions of his brother, Reginald, and nephews, Jamal and Trevon. I shake all their hands, plan to meet them at the roadblock at dawn, and let them have the booth while I return to Jake's truck for a few hours' sleep.

I've filled the truck bed and every inch of the cab with supplies that could be helpful in New Orleans, stopping at every store along the way until there's barely enough room in the truck for me to drive. In the bed, I have cases of water and toilet paper, flashlights and lanterns, generators and fuel, a couple of box fans, and an assortment of tools. The passenger seat and footwell of the cab are crammed with nonperishable food, electrolyte drink mix, batteries, a first-aid kit bursting with medical supplies, and baby formula. Not that I expect Violet to need baby formula, but someone else might.

For security, Alex lent me a ratty old tarp to stretch across the truck bed and cover the supplies, and in the cab, I drape a blanket over the passenger seat so it won't be obvious from afar that the truck is filled with high-quality loot. Still, I don't leave the truck unattended for long.

I settle into the driver's seat and crack the window for a breeze. It's miserable here, so hot and muggy my clothes stick to my skin and the leather seat of the truck. But idling for AC is a waste of fuel, so I sweat when I should be sleeping. At least this truck stop has clean showers. I suspect that's a luxury I will miss when I get past the roadblock and into New Orleans.

At half past four in the morning, my phone chirps its alarm, and I groan awake from a fitful sleep. I head into the travel center to brush my teeth, take a pee and a quick shower, and grab a cup of coffee. I text Jake my morning message, letting him know where I am and that I'm still on the wagon. Then I crank up the truck and amble through the parking lot looking for Willie and his family. When I find them and wave, they nod and I get in line, forming a processional of five guys in four pickup trucks hauling two boats.

We wait for over an hour while Willie and his brother talk to a couple of the National Guard troops tasked with keeping people out of New Orleans. Eventually, someone gets approval over the radio that they're going to let our group through. I call Jake one last time, to give him an update and let him know I probably won't have reliable cell service where I'm going, then hang up as the guardsmen start to move the barricades.

Falling in line behind Willie and his group, our small caravan trickles into the city as a deluge of refugees floods out. We see buses leaving, one after another; they're full of the people who'd been trapped at their so-called "refuge of last resort" while the roof came off, the toilets stopped up, the electricity failed, and they ran out of food.

The buses move fast—in a hurry to get people to the relief of cities that still function—but our convoy is slow, like a funeral procession. Sad, solemn, and silent, we move in mourning as we enter this hallowed ground.

I wave to Willie as I split off from his group and take the exit to my destination, descending from the elevated highway down into the city below. It's not as bad here as I'd imagined, but that's not saying much. Closer to the lake, it's much worse, or so I've seen in the helicopter footage on television, but here in the center of the city, most of the buildings are intact, with a high-water mark on the walls showing how the water has receded as the city patches the holes in the levees and gets pumps back online.

In places, the roads are impassable; cars, tree limbs, and broken bits of homes are strewn about like a spoiled child's discarded toys, so I detour and meander in my truck, taking in the sight of so much devastation. Everything is coated with a layer of toxic mud that stinks of shit, pollution, and death.

The city is not deserted though. In places, people walk around, looking at damage, looking for food and supplies, looking shell-shocked and wary as I drive past. The closer I get to Violet's theater, the worse the damage, and my heart lodges in my throat when I come to her street. It's covered with water. The theater is still a few blocks farther, so I'll walk the rest of the way.

I struggle to get the booted waders on in this hot sticky weather, immediately feeling like I'll pass out from the heat of the plastic pants. But as I start forward, I'm glad I have them. What I'm walking through could hardly be described as water. It's a toxic soup of chemicals, waste, and iridescent oil that shimmers on the surface of the gravy-brown substance. It smells awful and is probably flammable. It's definitely not something you want touching your skin or an open wound. I shuffle my feet beneath the surface, afraid a misstep might dunk me into a manhole or cause me to break a leg on some unseen impediment. Any injury here could be fatal.

I parked the truck three blocks away, where the water laps at the shores of a higher elevation, and with each step I take toward Violet's theater, I sink deeper into the drowned city. A pit grows in my stomach as I dread what I'll find when I reach her place.

It's so quiet here, with only the buzz of insects and helicopter blades slicing the thick air above as coast guard units search for trapped survivors. It's eerie, to feel so alone in a major American city. Like I've stepped off the edge of the world. There is nothing here but heat, bugs, and misery. No power, no phones, no climate control, just destruction everywhere.

When I finally catch sight of Violet's theater, I breathe a little easier. It's still standing. The blade sign has sustained some wind damage, but nothing major. Here, too, is that ubiquitous high-water mark about a foot above where the water laps now, and her seafoam-green walls, along with everything else beneath that line, are stained and coated with a layer of God knows what.

Violet boarded over the front doors and ticket window with particle board, but they've come loose, and one of the doors hangs open and askew, leaving the place vulnerable to the elements and all other manner of threat. I hesitate to enter. It's a weird sort of *déjà vu* to step back into this space, still uninvited.

"Freeze."

The voice comes from behind me. It's thick with a Delta drawl and masculine. It exudes authority, like the teacher's tone my mom used when she'd scold me. And then—as if the tone of voice weren't frightening enough—there is the unmistakable sound of a pump-action shotgun locked and loaded.

I do as I'm told, freezing every muscle as still as stone. Even my heart and lungs seize up in my chest.

"Very slowly, put your hands up where I can see 'em." *That's not a teacher's tone; that's a cop's tone.*

Inch by painfully slow inch, I follow the command to raise my hands. I remain silent, too, though he hasn't read me my rights. Beads of sweat trickle down my spine as I wait for him to say something more. To tell me what I need to do so he'll stop pointing a gun at me.

"Turn around," he instructs.

Flinching, I turn, but there's no one behind me. The street is as empty as it was when I arrived.

Confused, I glance all around me, my arms starting to weigh heavy and sink down.

"Up here," comes the voice, and I look up at a man standing at the edge of the corner store roof. He's older than I expected, probably in his sixties, with trim, salty hair and dark, leathery skin, wariness worn into the wrinkles around his frown. His eyes are as hard as the gunmetal in his grasp, assessing me with cold dispassion as he holds my life in his hands.

His gun is a 12-gauge Remington 870 shotgun—my brother's preferred weapon during deer season back in Tennessee—a nice gun, which is *pointed directly at my chest*. After a moment, he pulls his aim off me and slings the gun over his shoulder. I let out the breath I'd been holding and blink as the man asks, "What you doin' 'round here?"

"I..." It takes me a moment to clear the lump from my throat so I can say, "I'm looking for Violet Devollier. This is still her theater, isn't it?"

"How do you know Violet?"

It's a reasonable question, but one I'm not sure how to answer. "She, uh, I helped her once, and she gave me a ticket to come back and see a show—"

"Theater's closed at the moment," he says.

"Yeah. I just want to make sure she's okay."

He pulls a walkie-talkie off his belt and says, "Uncle Sam calling Sweet Vee."

"Come in Uncle Sam." The voice crackles over the radio, and I know in an instant, it's Violet. She's okay. That's one concern addressed. I glance over my shoulder at the gaping door into the flooded theater, home of so many other concerns.

"I've got a white boy here, says you gave him a ticket for a show."

"Say again."

"My name is Greg—" I try to clarify, but the man talks over me.

"A ticket for a show," he shouts into the receiver. "That's what he says."

There's dead air for a moment before Violet responds. "Don't know what you're talking about."

Desperate now, I reach for the ticket in my pocket, my proof. But my jean pockets are buried beneath the plastic waders, and I end up slapping my waist uselessly.

"I was here the night before her opening. She was showing *It's a Wonderful Life*, and I helped her paint the—"

"Yeah, yeah." Gruffly, Sam waves his hand toward the south. "Go over there and tell her yourself."

"Over where?"

"She's about five blocks thataway and two blocks over," he gestures in no particular direction, "above the Beaux Ballroom."

"The drag bar?"

"Yeah, the drag bar," he affirms, like I'm an idiot.

"Thank you." It feels odd to thank the man who held a gun on me. Sam just waves me away as he steps back from the edge of the roof.

From the outside, Beaux Ballroom looks much the same as I remember. The streets here are dry, and there's no high-water mark marring the walls of the building. But inside is another story. It's daytime, yet dark. The twinkle lights draped from the ceiling don't glow, and the disco ball doesn't spin. There was no flood here, but there's no power either.

The crowd is different too. Gone are the dancing denizens, partying the night away. Instead, there's a handful of people dotting the bar stools and table chairs, humming along to the refrain of Billy Joel's *Piano Man* that a guy plays on a piano in the corner.

"Hey there, hot stuff."

I turn to the bartender, a middle-aged man with feathery blond hair in cut-off jeans and a Southern Decadence shirt.

"How can I help you?" he says.

My attention goes to the picked-over wall of mostly empty liquor bottles behind him, a bottle of Jack perched about midway up the mirrored wall. I panic, and before I can stop myself, proclaim, "I'm a recovering alcoholic."

"Noted," he says with a flirty grin.

That was awkward. "Actually, I'm looking for Violet."

He pulls a walkie-talkie from behind the bar and says into it, "Sweet Vee, you have a suitor. He's sexy in a grungy sort of way"—I look down at my rumpled clothes—"and he's sober."

There's a clicking sound over the walkie, then Violet's voice sounds again, crackling with static. "What the hell are you talking about, Paul? What suitor?"

The bartender sets the walkie-talkie aside and turns his attention back to me. "While you wait, I have plenty of nonalcoholic options such as warm bottled water and an assortment of warm fruit juice cans. Of course, this is a barter bar, so what can you give me in exchange?"

"Uh…"

"What suitor?" Violet's voice sounds over the radio again. And then, like some sort of strange dream, the voice comes to life. There is no static or crackle this time when she steps into the bar and asks, "Paul, what the hell?"

I turn toward her; she's standing in an open courtyard doorway, a shadow silhouetted by the harsh daylight outside. She takes a step into the dim room, and I can see her better now. Like everything else in this place, she looks the same but different. Her hair is a little longer, the controlled curls from before now a cloudy puff, like a dark halo around her head. Her complexion is paler, her expression tired, and the twinkle in her eyes doesn't spark today. Still, to me, she's a ray of sunshine.

She frowns. "Honey Eyes, are you kidding me?"

I'd forgotten that nickname. "Hi."

"What brings you here after all this time?"

"I was worried about you."

Her frown deepens. "I don't see or hear from you for, how long has it been, nine months? But when the devil drops out of the sky over my head, here you are, strutting back into my life like Walker, Texas Ranger."

"Violet, I'm sorry. My life got…complicated—"

"I thought we made a connection, but after months with no word, I figured our friendship was of the one-night variety. Now you're back to, what, save the day? Listen here: I don't need a savior. And if this is some kind of fucked-up tragedy tourism—"

"You're right. I walked away and didn't look back, and I regret that because I did feel a connection with you, and I'd like for our friendship to be more than a celibate one-night stand."

She stares at me, seeming to fight the urge to laugh.

Seizing the moment, I ask, "May I hug you?"

She considers, then reluctantly says, "Yeah. Okay."

Walking with quick strides, I cross the distance between us and hug her. She stiffens for an instant before relaxing the tight coils of tension in her posture and melting against me. I tighten my arms, feeling such profound relief at the warmth of her against me.

I read somewhere that a hug lasting at least twenty seconds can decrease the stress hormone cortisol and increase the happiness hormone oxytocin, so I aim to hug Violet for as long as she'll let me. We could both benefit from an extra-long hug.

At about the twenty-second mark, she releases a heavy sigh against my chest and links her arms a little tighter around my waist. I squeeze my arms around her shoulders, holding her tighter too. She strokes a hand on my back after what's probably thirty seconds, and I do the same. At roughly the forty-second mark, she lets out the sweetest sigh and softens against me, nuzzling my shoulder, her breath warm on my neck. It's like some of the pain and frustration of the last few days seeps out of her. I feel it, too, like there isn't enough room inside me for the pain when this connection with Violet is creating so much contentment.

As our hug approaches what I guess is the one-minute mark, Violet whispers against my neck, "I'm sorry."

"For what?" I whisper back.

"For griping at you." She sighs. "I'm taking things out on you that aren't your fault. It's coffee withdrawal. We ran out yesterday, and either everyone else is out, too, or they're hoarding—"

"I brought coffee."

"*What?*" The excited tone of her voice makes me smile wide.

I clasp her hand in mine and tug her toward the door.

An extremely tall Black man with a shiny bald head stands from a stool at the bar and hollers, "Everything all right, Sweet Vee?"

Violet nods as I lead her out to the sidewalk and over to Jake's truck parked at the curb. With the blazing sun beating down on my head, I unstrap a corner of the tarp covering the truck bed and flop it over. She gasps and steps closer to look at the bounty I've brought. I pop the lock on the passenger door, and she reacts with even more excitement at the sight of all that food. I grab one of the cans of instant coffee, handing it to Violet. "For you."

Violet squeals and hugs the coffee against her chest. "Hell, Greg, you're better than Walker, Texas Ranger."

"What do you want for it?" The sound of a gruff voice makes me nearly jump. I look to the doorway of the bar, where the bartender leans against one side of the doorframe, and the tall Black man stands with his arms crossed, leaning against the opposite side. His bald head is so smooth, it reflects the sun, which forces me to squint.

To the bartender, I answer, "You said this is a barter bar. This is what I have to offer."

8

The two men take charge, commanding the group of people sitting around the bar to pitch in and help bring the supplies inside. Violet guides me to a stool at the now empty bar, and the two men join us there. The bartender hands me a bottle of lukewarm water. It tastes spectacular in this heat. I drink the whole thing in a few gulps.

"I'm Andre, Violet's cousin." The bald man offers his hand, and I shake it.

The bartender introduces himself next. "And I'm Paul, Andre's *much* better half."

Andre pretends offense for a moment, then winks at his partner.

"Y'all have met before," Violet informs us. "But you boys were in different outfits."

"Well, then," Andre says and changes his voice, sounding much more feminine when he says, "Miss Bea Haven, glad to make your acquaintance. Are you a fan?"

"Oh." I see him with new eyes, remembering his drag performance to Kylie Minogue. "Yeah, you were amazing."

"Well, thank you." Andre returns to his original tone of voice when he adds, "It's too hot for hair. Get used to bald and beautiful for a while."

Paul clears his throat and offers his hand like he expects me to kiss it. He affects a syrupy southern drawl as he says, "And I am Miss Jezebel Jewel."

I remember him as the Dolly Parton drag queen who'd been behind the bar all those months ago. I kiss his knuckles. "Nice to meet you, again."

"Enchantée."

"And this is Greg Hendricks, the guy who helped me paint the theater the night before the opening," Violet says.

Paul laughs. "Yes, darling, how could we forget your Texan cowboy?" To me he adds, "Your clean-cut Monty Clift look was something special, but this beard, oh heavens me."

I reach up and scratch the week-old scruff on my jaw. "I haven't had a chance to shave."

"Don't you dare." Paul gasps and holds his hands over his heart.

"Andre's point about bald and beautiful is appealing. It's too hot for hair."

"Violet, honey." Paul talks to her now, clearly frustrated. "Use your feminine wiles and talk some sense into him."

"Tell me, Greg," Andre says as he sits on a nearby barstool and assesses me, "why would anyone in their right mind come here *now*?"

I'm a little lost with the rapid change in subject. It's a good question, one I was starting to wonder myself as I waded through water over my knees an hour ago. "I'm here to help in any way I can. With the theater, with the flood damage. I want to be useful."

Andre frowns at me. "Not much usefulness around here at the moment. Water's still up at Vee's place, we got no power here, and who the hell knows when we'll get any of it back."

I nod. "However long it takes. I've got nothing better to do."

Andre considers, then points to where the last of the people are carrying loads to the overflowing storage room. "Obviously, you've earned yourself a lot of credit here. What do you want in return?"

"I…uh…would appreciate a portion of the food and a place to sleep, if you have room."

Andre says, "Done."

"Andre, darling, my brother-in-law is on the couch until we find Louie," Paul interjects.

Andre waves away his concerns. "Greg can sleep in Violet's room."

"Uh… I can sleep on the floor."

Andre looks horrified and raises his voice to say, "Well, of course you're sleeping on the floor. I'll set up an air mattress for you."

Someone comes through the door carrying a cured ham leg over one shoulder and a wheel of cheese under the other arm, hollering, "Lunch is served."

The newcomer sets the gourmet food on the bar, which starts a new flurry of activity. The piano man and another move into the courtyard, where they start heating charcoal briquettes on a backyard grill. One man pulls a cast-iron skillet from a pile of cookware, while the other brings over a couple dozen eggs, which they scramble. Someone else chops onions to toss into the eggs, along with cubes of ham. Another plates everything and grates copious amounts of the cheese to melt over each pile of ham and eggs.

I join them in the courtyard with the camp stove I brought, a can of coffee, and a pot of water to make "cowboy coffee"—as Paul calls it. Once it's ready, I serve it up to anyone who's interested and has a cup to carry it. Someone hands me one of the first plates of food, and the smell of the piping hot meal has my mouth watering. I try to pass my plate to Violet, but she declines. "You earned that with the haul you brought. Eat. You look like you could use it."

I don't argue, but I wait until she's served before diving in. I'm famished. From the silent way everyone in the place eats, I'd say we all are. When I'm finished, I glance around at the others and ask Violet, "What's the story here?"

"Neighbors and friends," Violet says between bites, glancing around the room. "We all pool our food stores and make a big communal meal each day. It's easier for all involved than scrounging for scraps. Tony—the guy who brought the ham and cheese—he owns a deli, so he brings food each afternoon in exchange for whiskey each evening. Galen over there at the piano is a concert pianist. He rolled that thing eight blocks to bring us entertainment. The guy sitting next to Galen is James, his partner. They've been together twenty-five years. Their anniversary was this week. We made them a cake yesterday in a cast-iron skillet. Some serious frontier shit happening here." She grins around a bite of food, then continues telling me the names and stories of each person. The names I forget almost immediately, but the stories stick with me. Musicians, artists, restaurateurs, political activists, and community leaders, and here I am, an unemployed alcoholic.

Violet and I carry our plates out to the courtyard, where a civil rights lawyer and her partner wash dishes as their contribution to the collective. In the corner, Violet introduces me to Federico, who is hunched over a cloudy pink puff of fabric and an old foot-pedal-powered sewing machine.

"What are you making?"

"This is mosquito netting, Sweet Vee."

"Out of chiffon?"

"Darling, chiffon is the only thing we have in abundance around here. And I'm not dying of malaria because some bug bit my ass while I was trying to sleep." He turns back to his work, pushing a pair of bifocals higher on his nose as he flutters his foot on the pedal, and the machine whirs into action. It reminds me of Grandma Millie at her ancient sewing machine, making shirts for my brother and me to wear on our first day of school every year when we were boys.

I like the ingenuity of this group, using these old human-powered machines now that the electricity has failed. In this time of crisis, old has become new again, and those things we used to ignore are needed once more. Maybe that will be me too. Old and replaceable but handy and good to have around in these trying times.

Violet leads me to a porch glider in a shady part of the courtyard. The movement of the chair cools us a little, making the late day more bearable. But Violet collects a couple of bamboo fans from a nearby table and hands me one. It makes all the difference as I fan air at my face and feel instant relief from the heat.

"I like your friends."

"They're a special bunch."

We settle into an easy sway on the swing, our fans cooling our skin as the others gather around the piano or the bar, singing and chatting and whiling the hot hours of the day away. We've sat in comfortable silence for so long that it surprises me when she speaks again.

"You seem different, Greg."

Different is an understatement. The last time she saw me, I was clean-shaven with well-trimmed hair and sported an expensive suit. Now, I'm in a twenty-year-old Slayer T-shirt and ratty jeans, I can't remember my last haircut, and I haven't shaved in days. My fingers go to the bare spot on my ring finger, stroking the pale strip of skin that had been sheltered beneath a gold band for so many years. "Yeah. I'm different all right."

Violet notices the gesture. I suspect she notices everything. Eyes of a fox, fast and smart and always watching. "No offense, but you seem a bit…broken."

I can't help it—I laugh.

She gives me a pitying look. "What happened?"

I don't know how to answer that question. Where do I start? Do I tell her how my marriage fell apart? Do I tell her about the drugs and alcohol, the suicidal ideations? Do I tell her about the end of my career?

In the end, I tell her everything, every ugly detail, because while I care what she thinks of me, I also care about being honest with her. When I finish talking, Violet stares at me. In the waning sun, she's more shadow than light, her profile backlit by the candles Paul's set out on the bar through the doorway beside her.

"I was right, then. You are broken. And you've come back to the last place where you felt whole so you can put yourself back together again."

"No." I frown. "I came here because I want to help."

Violet folds her arms over her chest and stares at me, looking skeptical. "Look, Greg." She says my name with a heavy sigh, like it exhausts her. "This is going to sound shitty, but I need you to listen. Okay?"

Sweat beads and drips down my back, and I'm not sure if it's the heat or the anxiety. I'm terrified of what she's about to say.

"I'm sorry about all you're going through, and I'm glad you're getting back on your feet, but I can't be your crutch. Okay? I've let myself be that before, too many times, and I won't do it again. Especially not right now. You've come to the land of the lost to find yourself, but your loss is not special here. We're all lost here. We're all broken, and I don't have the capacity right now to tiptoe around another shattered life.

"If you've come here because you want to help, that's wonderful and much appreciated. But if you're here to find a woman who makes you feel the way you used to feel about yourself, I can't be that for you. Do you understand?"

It's probably the most honest thing a woman has said to me in a long time, and I appreciate that. There is no ambiguity, no need to interpret the meaning of her words. Ari was never like this. She was honest to her core, but she kept a lot to herself. And since I'm terrible at reading people, I never understood what was going on with her until it was too late. Kate, on the other hand, would say one thing and mean the opposite. It was exhausting.

This, with Violet, is refreshingly clear. I know exactly where I stand with her; I can practically see the boundary she's placed between us.

I smile. "I understand."

9

SATURDAY, SEPTEMBER 3, 2005

The sun begins to set, and the group of bar patrons singing along with the piano man dwindles as people return to their own shelter for the night. Someone mentions a curfew, but I don't know if it's a formal curfew so much as common sense. Helping Paul and Andre barricade the door behind the last of the daytime visitors is an unnerving reminder that I've come to a powerless, lawless, forgotten place.

We blow out the candles in the bar and carry a few of them upstairs to the apartment above. In the courtyard, the darkness around us is total, but the stars above are on full display, a celestial celebration of light. It seems cosmically cruel that a city with the spirit and personality of New Orleans should be doused in darkness while the sky above sparkles and shines. It fills me with loneliness as I stare up at all that space, the cosmos shining with the light of the living and the dead stars alike.

Inside the apartment, I take a moment to appreciate the decor. It's a wild mix of colors, all the shades of the sunset in one room: pillows, drapes, walls, and furniture in bold shades of golden yellow, neon orange, ruby red, hot pink, and vibrant violet. Everything sparkles, too, with shimmery beads draped over the windows and doors. And nailed to the far wall, beside a small television, is a sequined dress with a cardboard cutout of Dolly's face and bust attached at the neckline.

"Wow." I blink at the sight of it all. It's a lot to process.

"Paul is a little obsessed with Dolly," Andre explains.

"Who isn't a little obsessed with Dolly?" I ask without thinking.

Paul chuckles behind me. "Oh, I like this one."

We whisper because someone is sleeping on the 1970s vintage golden ochre couch in the main room, but I nod to Andre and Paul as they turn left into their bedroom, then follow Violet to the right. The apartment is shotgun-style, and we walk through a kitchen that opens into the hall off the bathroom before reaching Violet's bedroom at the back. French doors open to the balcony on the right side of every room, and the barely moving breeze cools the space as much as it can in August. In Violet's room facing the windows is her bed, a queen covered in white sheets and surrounded by a billowy cloud of pink chiffon mosquito netting stapled to the ceiling above. And in the corner near the balcony door is another curtain of pastel chiffon.

Violet stands there, staring, then starts to giggle. "When Andre said he would set up an air mattress for you, I was skeptical. Didn't think we had an air mattress." No longer concerned for the sleeping man in the living room, she turns toward the door and hollers, "This is not an air mattress, Andre! It's a pool float."

"Beggars can't be choosers, darling," Andre hollers back.

Violet smirks at me. "Well, it ain't the Ritz."

I look down at the hot pink pool float and shrug. "It'll be more comfortable than sleeping in the truck like the last few nights."

Violet turns to me, scrutinizing my expression like she's trying to read something written on my face. Finally, she says, "In all my belly-aching and boundary-laying before, I can't remember if I thanked you for coming here. So thank you for coming, Greg."

"You don't have to thank me."

"I know I don't." She shrugs and moves across the room to her bureau. "I'm going to get ready for bed."

She collects some clothing and a candle and leaves for the bathroom. I take the moment alone to look around her room. Despite her invitation and my spot on the floor, I don't belong here—I'm invading her privacy—but I can't help my curiosity, so I step closer to the bureau and look at the photos pressed into the frame around her mirror.

There are a few photos of Violet with Paul and Andre and with their alter egos in sparkly dresses and bright wigs. But many of the photos show an adorable little girl with her family. In one, a mother and father, a small girl, and teenage boy open presents around a Christmas tree. In most, it's the girl and her father. They look happy. I recall Violet telling me about her father's recent death, her reason for buying the theater.

When she returns, I want to ask her about him. But one glimpse of her in sleep shorts and a tight tank top gets my dick hard. I turn away, embarrassed by my reaction. I can't rightly talk about her dead father while sporting an erection. But she doesn't need me to inquire; she sees me staring at the Christmas photo and explains as she slips a hot pink satiny sleeping cap over her head. "That's Andre, Aunt Niecy, Dad, and me."

Talk of her family life helps me with my problem, and I can relax as Violet answers my unasked questions. "Andre's dad was never around, and my mom died when I was little, so Dad and Aunt Bernice moved into the adjoining sides of a duplex and raised us like we were one big happy family."

"Sounds nice."

"It was."

Was. Past tense.

Like she's reading my mind, she says, "Then Aunt Niecy died, and Dad died a year later. Now Andre and I are orphans, but we still have each other. He's got Paul and this place, and I've got..."

Her voice fades, and sadness sinks into her expression. I wish I knew the right thing to say, but like an idiot, all I can manage is, "I'm sorry."

Violet considers for a moment, then takes a deep sigh and turns away from the family photos.

I go to my duffel bag, digging for basketball shorts, my toothbrush, and razor. As I move toward the bathroom, Violet snatches the razor away from me. "Don't you dare. I agree with Paul—you've got a good thing going there."

It's way too hot for a beard, but… *She finds it attractive?* I nod and enter the bathroom, where I stare at myself in the mirror. It's the first time seeing my reflection since the truck-stop bathroom at dawn. Was that just this morning? It feels like a lifetime ago and a world away. I scratch at the scruff on my face as the candlelight dances over the walls around me. I can't help the smile that comes over my face. Violet likes my beard. I guess I'll keep it then.

After taking a sponge bath with a bottle of water, a washcloth, and a bar of soap, I brush my teeth and use the toilet but don't flush. Paul explained the bathroom routine to me before bed: without running water, the toilet doesn't flush, so they collect gray water all day while cooking and washing up, then pour it into the toilet tank at the end of the day. The last person to use it each night flushes. Does the rest of America know the state of life in New Orleans right now? We were served up images of people on their roofs, desperate for rescue from the high waters, but even the dry parts of the city are a primitive, smelly hell.

Back in Violet's room, however, is heaven. Candlelight dances on the walls. A pastel puff of mosquito netting billows in the slight breeze, and inside that pretty pink curtain is Violet, a vision of beauty.

In the months since I met Violet, I haven't forgotten that she was beautiful, but when I met her before, I was in a different headspace. Still so focused on my wife, I hadn't fixated on every detail of Violet's expressive face. Then, I didn't long to touch her like I do now. In this candlelight and steamy heat, it's all I can think about. How soft her skin would feel against my palms, against my body, how warm she'd be, her skin slick with sweat, her mouth—

Fuck.

Turning away, I cross the room to settle onto the lumpy air cushion. I'm not tired. I'm restless.

I came to New Orleans to help, and so far, all I've done is wade through murky swamp water, eat their food, and ogle Violet while she tries to sleep. I can't get comfortable, and every time I move, the pool float makes rude noises. The third time I try to turn onto my side, Violet giggles at the sound.

I try to remain still, silently staring up at the candlelight flickering on the ceiling. How can the air be this wet and it not be raining? I'm shirtless and coated with sweat. The pool float sticks to my damp skin now. The sudden buzz of insects makes me wonder if they've found their way inside my chiffon protection. It's like torture as every drop of sweat feels like those insects crawling over my skin. I need to scratch them off. I need to move. I want to scream.

"This is ridiculous. Come into the bed." After so much silence, Violet's voice startles me.

My voice squeaks like the pool float when I ask, "What?"

"I can hear you twitching as you try to keep still. Just come up here on the bed. There's room for the both of us, and maybe you'll be able to relax enough to actually get some sleep."

Given my body's reaction to seeing her in those sleep shorts, that's unlikely. I stammer and wipe some of the sweat off my brow. "Violet, the floor is fine. You don't have to—"

"I know I don't have to. Now get up here."

"But—" Does she realize I'm fighting against a raging hard-on eight feet away from her? Being that close to her, in a bed…

Like she can read my mind, she says, "We're both adults who can recognize and respect boundaries, right, Greg? I trust that we can sleep together without *sleeping together*?"

"Of course."

"Then stop stalling and turn out the light on your way."

I come up onto my elbows, enough to see her shift to one side of the queen mattress, making room for me. Noisily, I get to my feet and cross to the bureau to blow out the two candles. I try to calm my breathing as I wait for my eyes to adjust to the darkness.

With the waxing moonlight and stars to guide my way, I carefully part the curtain around Violet's bed and crawl across the top of her sheets to settle beside her. Only the buzz of the bugs outside our curtain disturbs the silence, and the shimmer of moonlight in her eyes pierces the dark.

I know I should close my eyes, try to sleep, but my body is wound tight, and my mind is racing. All I can think about is Violet, so close I could reach out and touch her.

I consider what to say, but the only thing that comes to mind is, "Are you still celibate?"

Violet barks out a loud laugh, and someone groans in complaint from somewhere else in the apartment. "Yes, I'm still celibate."

I nod, like I understand, but I don't. "What does that mean, *exactly*?"

Violet moves onto her elbow, casting her face into shadow. I can't see the shine of her eyes anymore when she asks, "What are you asking, *exactly*?"

I grasp for words, trying to keep my voice low as I elaborate. "Does it mean you don't experience the desire for sexual release? Or is it that you choose not to experience sexual release at all? Or do you choose not to experience sexual release with another person?"

"*Sexual release*." Violet chuckles. "You talk like a textbook."

"Sorry, I mean, for instance, do you masturbate?"

Violet laughs again, covering her mouth to try to keep quiet in the silence of the dark. Finally, she whispers, "Yes, I masturbate all the time."

I'm glad we're having this conversation in the dark because her admission is having a powerful effect on my body.

She lays her head back down, and I can see the lines of a smile around her eyes when she answers, "I'm celibate, not asexual. I abstain from sexual *intercourse*, not sexual *release*. I simply prefer to handle that stuff myself, without all the bullshit that comes with other people."

"What about intimacy?"

She makes the sweetest little sound, like a sigh, and says, "You can have plenty of sex without intimacy, and it's just as possible to have intimacy without sex."

She's right, of course. I think about the last miserable months of my sex life and the prostitute I hired in New York. I'd been so lonely, and I thought a professional could help me fill the void left in my heart. She couldn't. What I'd needed was intimacy, and all I got was sex. Sex can be intimate, sometimes, but sometimes it's just fucking.

"I guess I do kind of miss that part of things," she says with a wistful tone, and it sends a little tickle up my spine. Because, right here, right now, curled up with Violet, in her bed, in the dark, whispering secrets—this feels intimate.

I keep the thought to myself, though, and we lie there, staring at each other in the darkness for a while. "Well, if I accidentally cuddle with you, I apologize in advance."

Violet laughs, and the sound draws me closer, like I'm a puppet, and she pulls my strings.

I keep talking, making little sense as I clutch my fists in the sheets to keep from reaching for her. "Cuddling is sort of my natural state of being. I don't sleep well with other people unless I'm cuddling them. I sort of starfish all over them."

"That's one of the weirdest confessions I've ever heard. See if you can restrain yourself from 'starfishing' all over me."

"I'll do my best."

Violet yawns and whispers, "Goodnight, Greg."

I yawn, too, then I whisper back, "Goodnight, Violet."

10

SUNDAY, SEPTEMBER 4, 2005

Something smells good, fresh like flowers and…coffee? I flutter my eyes open. The hot pink satin of Violet's sleep bonnet is so close it tickles my nose. *Oh shit.* At some point in the night, I cuddled up against Violet, playing the big spoon to her little. I freeze every muscle, the air going stale in my lungs as I assess the situation. I'm all the way into her space, my head halfway across her pillow, my hips nestled up tight to hers, and my palm rests possessively on her thigh. *Jesus.*

Slowly, like I'm playing that old kid's game Operation, I try to extricate myself without setting off the buzzer. I lift my hand from her thigh and when I do, Violet chuckles. "Good morning." *Buzz,* I've lost the game.

"I am so sorry," I say as I rush out of the bed, only then realizing how hard my dick is. I turn away from her to hide it. But I'm sure she already knows; she probably felt it poking her ass.

Still, Violet says nothing about it, instead chiding me for something else. "You need to stop apologizing for everything. Trust me—if you'd touched me in a way I didn't like, I'd have let you know. Anyway, it was nice. I like cuddling. It's like what we talked about last night, intimacy without sex."

Tell that last part to my dick. It didn't get the memo.

As if I spoke that out loud, she says, "As for that thing you're trying to hide from me? That's biology."

I nod at the wall, shuffling toward the door, muttering, "I'm going to take a turn in the bathroom."

Out in the hall, I'm greeted by Paul, nursing his coffee and staring curiously at the tent I've pitched in my basketball shorts. "Well, good morning to you too, Greg."

I groan as I disappear into the tiny dark bathroom and try to piss my problems away. When I come back out, the whole house is awake. The sound of raised voices filters from the kitchen, and I freeze.

It's Violet who says, "You're the one who put him in my room."

"But not in your bed, Sweet Vee." That's her cousin, Andre.

"Calm down."

"Oh honey, don't tell me to calm down."

"Look, I trust him. Okay?"

"Why? What has he done to earn your trust? Other than bring us a lot of stuff. Is he buying your trust?"

"Don't fucking go there. And so far, he's proven himself to be a lot more trustworthy than most of the guys I've actually slept with in that bed, so I don't know what your problem is."

I'm not sure what to do. Do I walk into the room where they are clearly talking about me, or do I remain here, lurking and listening?

"Don't take it personally," says Paul, still lingering by the door, watching the drama. He's in jorts again but wearing a different Southern Decadence T-shirt today. "Andre's just playing the part of the overly protective brother. It's one of his favorite roles. Honestly, you're positively perfect for our little Miss Vee. I'm already planning the wedding."

I blink at him.

"Come on, honey, time to make an entrance." Paul grabs my arm and pulls me into the kitchen with his elbow through mine. To Violet and Andre, he announces, "The topic of conversation has arrived."

Violet smiles at me, and Andre stares, expressionless. Is he upset because I slept with Violet—or rather slept *beside* Violet—and woke up spooning her with a massive erection? On second thought, I can see why he'd be a bit bothered.

Paul pushes me down into a chair at the table. Andre scowls at me from the other side. Beside him is a middle-aged white guy I don't recognize. The lump on the couch the night before, I presume. The reason I slept in Violet's room to begin with. Violet sets a cup of campfire coffee in front of me before taking the seat at my side. Paul leans against the sink, his coffee cup cradled at his lips, hiding his expression.

A heavy silence falls over the room, and I'm probably the only one who can lift it, so I say, "Andre, I'd be lying if I said I don't find Violet attractive. I do. She's stunningly beautiful, both inside and out. But I honestly came here to help. Back home, my life is in shambles, and maybe I'm using this as an excuse to run away from my own problems, trying to help others piece their lives back together while mine sits waiting. I don't know. I'm not that self-aware. What I do know is construction and safety, and so I'm here to share that knowledge in the best way I know how."

Paul tries to stifle a laugh, saying, "My lord, Violet, if you don't marry him, I will."

Andre turns his scowl on Paul for a moment, but I can see his expression has softened a bit.

"I want to be honest and forthright," I add.

"And we appreciate that," says Paul. "Don't we, dear? Plus, let's not forget our Miss Vee is a grown woman of *undisclosed* age. She can have all the hot Texan cowboys in her bed she wants."

Andre huffs. Violet is barely keeping it together, covering her mouth to keep from spitting out her coffee.

The white man across the table puts his hand out for me to shake it. "Hi, I'm David, Paul's brother-in-law. I'm here until we find Louie. If you're here to help, we could use it."

I shake his hand. "Absolutely. Who's Louie?"

"My mom's cat," Paul explains. I expect more detail but get none as Paul takes a long sip of his coffee. Violet passes around a box of the protein bars I brought yesterday, and my stomach growls. Everyone grabs a bar, and we tuck into our meager breakfast, savoring the first food we've had since yesterday's lunch feast. From down in the street comes the tut-tut of a car horn, and everyone gets up to go downstairs.

They're already dressed for the day, and I'm still in my basketball shorts.

Hustling into Violet's room, I grab a pair of jeans and a T-shirt from my duffel and dress, stumbling down the stairs and outside as I'm tugging on my boots and tying the laces. Everyone mills around a waiting pickup truck. The bed is crowded with several of the people we'd spent the day with yesterday. Andre, David, and Paul pile in, which doesn't leave much room for Violet and me.

"We can follow in mine," I say as I gesture to Jake's truck.

It's easy to follow the others; the roads are too scattered with debris for either vehicle to get above fifteen miles per hour. Overhead, choppers have come out with the sun, circling the city. Inside the truck, I max the cold air, and Violet and I sigh with relief at this brief respite from the heat.

As we meander through the streets, getting closer to the lake with each block traveled, I ask, "What's the story with Louie?"

"Louie is Paul's mama's cat. They call him that because he sounds like a trumpet when he meows, like he's the spirit of Louis Armstrong come back in the form of a cat," Violet answers.

"Louie's lost?"

"Yeah." Violet frowns as she leans a little closer to the AC vent and holds her blouse out to let the cool air blow over her chest. "Paul's mama's place flooded really bad. Fortunately, she had two stories. Some of her neighbors weren't so lucky."

"Jesus."

"A levee half a mile away from her place broke, and the water came in so fast she had to flee upstairs with Louie. For a whole night, the water lapped at her top step. Next day, a man with a boat came by, hollering for survivors. He got Mary Anne and Louie out through the bedroom window and delivered them to dry land. But Louie was in such a state that he clawed Mary Anne all to hell, jumped out of her arms, and ran off. Paul and Andre managed to get Mary Anne on a bus to Baton Rouge, where she's staying with Paul's sister, Beth. But Mary Anne is beside herself with worry about that damn cat, so Beth's husband, David, has come to aide in the search."

"Have you checked with the animal rescue groups?"

"They're on the lookout. If Louie shows up, they'll bring him to the bar."

The truck ahead takes a sharp turn left, and I'm faced with what appears to be a roadblock and a convoy of military vehicles. The cavalry has arrived, and they're blocking the road, so we take the parallel road until we reach standing water. It looks deceptively calm, like a quiet lake lapping at the higher ground, but everywhere are the remnants of its destructive power.

Sitting there, staring out at the water while we revel in one last moment of air-conditioning, Violet goes on: "The working theory is that Louie might try to return home, so we come back here to look for him. It's probably a waste of time. He's a cat, and he'll be found when he wants to be found. But it's not like we have anything better to do, so here we are."

"Which house is it?"

"You can't see it from here. It's two blocks that way. The water keeps receding, so we can get a little closer each day," Violet says as she gets out of the truck. Everyone in the other truck is already pairing off and fanning out, holding tins of cat food as they holler the cat's name and make that *pspspsp* noise cats like.

No one's going into the water, which is smart. But it limits our search options. I glance at the waders in the back of my truck, and with a grin to Violet, I settle onto the tailgate and slip the heavy plastic pants over my boots and jeans. "With these on, I can get closer to the house."

"What's your plan?"

"Walk two blocks that way"—I point with my chin as I pull the shoulder straps up—"look for a cat along the way, try not to fall into a manhole."

"Solid plan."

"What does Louie look like?"

"A cat. Orange. Fluffy." Violet shrugs, helps me straighten the overall straps, and stuffs a can of cat food into the front pocket. "Watch out for fire ants. They form these big balls and float around. Oh, and keep an eye out for gators."

"There are alligators in these waters?"

"Probably." She shrugs again.

My skin starts to crawl at the idea of everything in the water with me, wondering how deep it is two blocks up. I break out into a fierce sweat in the plastic pants, but with a deep breath, I take a couple of sloshy steps forward. The water here is darker and clearer than it was over by Violet's place—more lake water than city sludge—and oddly enough I can see fish school around me, curious little minnows nibbling at the plastic pants as I move forward.

Each step I take brings me deeper into the waters of Lake Pontchartrain, and each step is a terror. What if I step on something sharp or an open manhole or a body? I get as far as waist high—any deeper and the hem of the waders will be under water—then stop.

I turn back. Violet is standing on the roof of Jake's truck, a hand over her eyes to shield from the sun. I wave and she does, too, then I turn my attention to the houses around me.

Most are destroyed, hardly resembling houses anymore. Some look like they were totally immersed in water, and I fear there's far worse than a missing cat to be found here. Some houses have clearly moved off their foundations, looking much as they did before, but at odd angles and cluttered together against trees and cars and other houses.

Lifting the can of cat food over my head, I holler, "Here, Louie, Louie, Louie!" and pop the top open. But what's the point? How could any aroma compete with the fetid stench of death that permeates the air? The whole city is tainted with the smell, not from the hundreds of human deaths making headlines but from the millions of mice and frogs, squirrels and birds that died in the wind and water. Beloved pets and feral wildlife perished side by side in this place, and I've waded into the center of their watery graves.

I try to ignore the sickness churning in my stomach and cluck my tongue a couple of times to call to the cat. Nothing. No sound or movement.

The silence here is otherworldly. There's none of the normal noise of a city, no buzz of electrical lines or rumble of traffic, none of the white noise of radios, televisions, and conversations coming from every corner. Even the birds are silent. All we have are the water lapping, insects buzzing, and choppers chopping.

I call to the cat again, but if Louie is here, he's not ready to be found. Feeling a heavy sense of disappointment, I turn and carefully make my way back to higher ground. A few of the other groups of searchers have made their way back to the trucks, all watching me as I emerge from the water. No one says anything. We're all looking dejected, the heat of the day and disappointment of not finding Louie draining any of the good cheer we woke with.

I drip sweat as I strip out of the waders and toss them into the truck bed to dry before we make our way back to the bar. The ride is quiet; Violet and I soak in the cool air as we stare out at the wasteland around us. The city feels empty. Even with people walking around and the military showing its presence, the spirit of this city is missing. It's depressing.

When we walk back into the bar, Galen heads over to the piano to start up with Billy Joel again, a rusty repeat of yesterday's lazy day, and I feel thirsty for whiskey. It's the first time I've thought about drinking since I got here, and it scares me. I don't want to be so fragile, so close to the edge that one bad morning might dump me off the wagon.

I turn to Violet. "Now what?"

"Now what *what*?"

"Is there anything I can do?"

"Not really. Without power or running water, there's not a lot we can do but try to keep cool, fed, and rested."

I sigh with disappointment, trying to keep my attention away from that half-drained bottle of Jack on the wall behind Paul.

"But…" she says teasingly.

I latch on with hope, desperate. *But, what? But, what?*

"With those fancy pants of yours, we can get to Uncle Sam's place and the theater. If you don't mind carrying me."

Do I mind carrying her? I'm already halfway to the door when I say, "Let's do it."

11

SUNDAY, SEPTEMBER 4, 2005

I park the truck at the edge of the water, and Violet and I stare at the view in front of us. "It's gone down a little since yesterday," I say.

Violet doesn't respond, so I get out and start to dress in my waders. She shuts off the ignition and joins me, tossing me the keys, then she straps on a backpack filled with extra food, bottled water, and supplies. When I'm fully dressed and she's got the backpack strapped tight onto her like a turtle shell, I turn around and crouch down. "Saddle up."

Violet curls her arms around my neck to hop onto my back. I try not to notice the way her breasts feel pressed against me as I heft her up a little higher. I try, and I fail.

Violet spurs her heels into my hips. "Giddy up, Cowboy Greg."

I rein in my thoughts and gallop a few steps, hoping to get a laugh out of her. It works. She giggles and clasps onto me a little tighter. But as I near the water, I stop horsing around and hunch over to be sure I have a good grasp on her before we go in. I take each step like I'm walking a tight rope, feeling my toe in front of me before putting my weight on the foot. It's a long, slow slog, but eventually the corner store and the theater come into view.

Violet hollers, "Uncle Sam! Where y'at?"

After a moment, the man who aimed a gun at me peeks his head over the edge of the roof and grimaces at us.

"Howdy," Violet says in an over-the-top Texas drawl. "Cowboy Greg and I have brought provisions."

Sam lets out a hearty chuckle and says, "Come on up. I'll unlatch the trapdoor."

Violet pushes the front door of the corner store open, which is no easy task with it hanging off its hinges and partially submerged in water. A little bell tinkles over our heads as we move it aside. It's a strangely normal sound in this surreal reality, making me feel nostalgic for the world outside here.

Inside, the smell is awful: dank floodwater combined with the stench of curdled milk and rotten food. The shop is a wreck, with shelves strewn about, products everywhere. Some of the items on higher shelves are untouched, but the items on the lower shelves float around my knees or form new obstacles to every step I take.

Carefully, I navigate my way to the Employee's Only door Violet points out. The back room smells as bad as the front, with stacks of boxes and their contents rotting in knee-deep water. There is a set of stairs at the back, and we take those up to a landing that has a ladder fastened to the wall. At the top of the ladder, a shaft of sunlight is partially blocked by Sam's face as he looks down at us.

"Well, ain't you a sight for sore eyes, Sweet Vee."

"Good to see you too, Uncle Sam," she says.

I turn to let her off my back, and she climbs the ladder. Then I follow her up. The asphalt roof feels twenty degrees hotter than the ground below. It takes a moment for my eyes to adjust to the sunlight. When I can see, I follow Sam over to the shade of a pop-up tent. He settles onto a folding chair beside a plastic table strewn with a walkie-talkie, binoculars, radio, flyswatter, some bottled water, and his Remington shotgun.

Less than twenty-four hours ago, this man was pointing that gun at me. I shiver at the memory.

Looking away, I take in the view from this third-floor perch. You can see for miles up here, and everywhere I look, the sun shimmers off the surface of the water. I don't know how long it will take the aged and inadequate pumps to drain this city, but it's already taking too long. Every day that water stands, this city grows more toxic.

"What ya got there?" Sam asks, and I turn my attention to Violet as she unstraps the backpack and sets it on the table.

"Stuff." She pulls out a couple of eggs from a side pocket, where she'd carefully wrapped them, then it's all nonperishables and a few rolls of toilet paper.

"Sweet Vee, you know I've got more than enough of that here in the shop. I want for nothing except these eggs and a cool shower."

"Well, Cowboy Greg brought a ton of toilet paper, and I figured it couldn't hurt to bring some to you."

"Cowboy Greg? You're the one I damn near blew a hole through yesterday."

"Yes, sir." I squint at his bright smile and decide to put the gun incident behind me as I offer my hand. "Greg Hendricks. It's nice to formally meet you, Sam."

"My name's Clifton."

"Why does everyone call you Sam?"

"They call me *Uncle* Sam because I cash their tax refund checks every year."

"Ah."

Violet elbows me. "At least your nickname is your real name, right, Cowboy Greg?"

I like that she's making fun of me with that dumb nickname.

"Whatchu doing here, Cowboy Greg?"

I like the name less when Uncle Sam uses it. "I've come to help, sir. In any way I can."

Uncle Sam raises a brow at me and glances at Violet. She offers a half shrug, and he finally shakes my hand. "Well, that's nice of you, I guess. I'm sure we'll have a use for another pair of hands once this water goes down. And sorry if I scared you yesterday. Just keeping an eye on the block. Can't be too careful."

"Uncle Sam is former NOPD. To him, everyone's a suspect," Violet says in a dramatic voice.

"Everyone *is* a suspect right now," Uncle Sam says. "When civilizations crumble, civilization crumbles, you know what I mean?"

Nodding adamantly, I know exactly what he means. I like this guy. He has a calmness about him that reminds me of my dad. It's comforting. I like that he's Violet's neighbor and keeps an eye on her place. I feel safer with him around, which is odd considering he's the only person who's ever pointed a gun at me. "NOPD, eh?"

His expression animates when he senses my interest. "Twenty-two years on the force. Retired a couple years back and bought this place for a bit of the quiet life." With a smirk he gestures to the disturbing quiet all around.

"What about you, Greg? What do you do?" Clifton asks as he digs through the backpack Violet brought him, sorting out the items then opening a package of beef jerky and taking a sinewy bite.

"I'm unemployed at the moment, but I was a structural engineer."

"Sounds fancy, except for the part about being unemployed."

I shrug. "Between jobs."

"That's the spirit."

"So what's the news?" Violet gestures at the radio.

"The generators at the aquarium failed. A lot of the fish died," he says. "Fish dying in a drowned city... Who'd'a thunk it?"

Violet and I both frown at the sad news, but it's hard to care about fish right now, so it's just another tragic headline that will likely be forgotten.

"Otherwise, nothing new. Everything's broke, and no one knows when it's gonna be fixed." Uncle Sam elbows me. "Maybe they could use an unemployed engineer to help 'em out."

I chuckle as he wrestles off another bite of jerky. With nothing more to do, Violet and I say goodbye, telling him we'll be back in a few days and to signal on the radio if needed.

Uncle Sam nods as we reverse down the ladder. When he shuts the hatch above, I bend over so Violet can hop back on me, and we head down into the murky water. We take the extra few steps over to Violet's theater, but she shakes her head silently when I ask if she wants to go inside.

Back at the bar, everyone is pretty much where we left them, a still life in disaster. Violet and I guzzle lukewarm water as we wait for Tony to bring lunch. On the piano, Galen plays something jazzy and upbeat, but no one feels the spirit of the music today.

12

After so many days of nothing but the same, it's another day of the same. All we do is wait. We sit, and we wait. From time to time we stand, and we wait. We look for Louie, visit Uncle Sam, and wait, wait, wait. The longer this purgatory lasts, the stronger my craving for whiskey grows. I try to ignore it, but sitting in a bar all day every day makes it difficult.

A cigarette-lighter converter in the truck charges my phone each day, but there's no point—none of the cell towers around here have power. We're in a communication black hole. Jake must be freaking out. I'm freaking out. I need to talk to him. He is, after all, my sponsor in this whole sobriety thing, and talking with him could be a reminder of why I need to stay sober. It's been how many days since I had a drink? I've lost count. Maybe if I were counting the days, it would be better. I would have something to focus on during this endlessness.

At least the water is receding. I can wade all the way to Paul's mom's house now, and it doesn't come above my knees. The house is bent at an odd angle, like a cut flower wilting in the sun. The pale blue shiplap walls are discolored and coated with slime. I stand as close as I can to the second-floor windows and wave a can of cat food around, calling to the cat, but Louie never comes.

This routine, the constant nothingness of our existence, is soul suck-ing. We're zombies, shuffling around with nowhere to go and nothing to do but eat. I start to wonder, again, why I thought coming here would help anyone. So far, I'm just another mouth to feed.

"Uncle Sam to Beaux." The staticky sound of Clifton's voice on the walkie-talkie is barely audible above the sound of Galen playing some-thing by Beethoven, but I hear it and step behind the bar to retrieve the device.

"Beaux here. Come in, Uncle Sam."

"Hey, Cowboy Greg. City must have got another pump back online last night, cuz it dried out quick this morning."

Like waking from a coma, I come alive again, my heart racing in my chest, my lungs rasping with breath, and my arms prickling like the numbness of sleep is wearing off. "We'll be right there, Uncle Sam."

I glance up at Violet, who's been listening. She turns to the room and lets out an ear-piercing whistle through the cute little gap in her front teeth. "Everyone, the water has receded at the theater and Uncle Sam's shop. Who wants to volunteer for cleanup duty?"

Most of the people in the room come to attention and stand, a small army of anxious do-gooders desperate to do some good. We pack up the tools and supplies we'll need, then take the trucks over to where Uncle Sam is standing in the middle of the road, his shotgun on his hip, waving at us. Aside from the slippery sludge that cakes the ground, the road is dry and getting drier by the minute as the mud bakes in the summer sun. Everything still smells awful, but it's a vast improvement from steeping in fetid water.

"You been inside yet?" Violet asks Uncle Sam, her expression a strange combination of excitement and fear.

"Was waiting for you."

She glances at me, and I hand her one of the respirators I brought and put the other one on. I didn't bring enough for everyone, but several folks have their own masks or wear bandanas over their nose and mouth to try to mitigate the damage that the foul air might do to their lungs.

We stand there a moment, baking like the mud, waiting, almost afraid to step inside and see what's left after Katrina took up her long residence. But waiting won't make it any better, so I clasp Violet's hand in mine. She nods resolutely and takes the first steps. We all follow her through the broken door, slip-sliding a bit in the muck and clamoring carefully over the soggy remnants of the plywood she used to protect this place from the storm.

I trigger my flashlight to cut through the darkness and instantly want to turn it back off when we see the magnitude of destruction. Everything that had once looked so bright and shiny is destroyed now. The brass and glass concession stand is coated in mold and fungus from the rot of the sugary candy. The once vibrant red carpet is water-logged and coated in that slimy, sickening layer of goo. The bottom four feet of the walls are coated with the stuff too.

We go up to the balcony and open the door to the auditorium, but it's pitch-black inside and smells even worse. My flashlight hardly makes a dent in the darkness, but still we can see where the first several rows of red velvet seats are covered in mildew, as is the bottom few feet of the curtains that frame the screen. The lower portion of the walls I helped Violet paint are stained too. At least they are plaster. A hearty scrub, and they'll be good as new. The same cannot be said for most of the surfaces in this place though. To see the damage to all that Violet holds dear feels painful and personal.

I remember when I was eight, my aunt and uncle's house burned down. No one was hurt, but everything was destroyed. And as we helped them sift through the charred remains of their lives, my mom said, "It's just stuff. Stuff can be replaced."

I know she meant well; everyone who says things like that mean well. But the look on my aunt's face suggested it hadn't been a helpful sentiment. And now, standing here with Violet in the shattered remains of her dream, I see what bullshit those words are.

Yes, it's just stuff, but stuff matters too. It has meaning and memories attached, and it gives us comfort. To have that all stripped away… How do we move on from that loss? When everything was fine before, and now it's all gone, how are we supposed to start over?

Everyone stays quiet, like we're at a funeral mourning Violet's loss. We wait for her to speak, for her to lead us to help her. But the slant of her shoulders tells me that's too much weight for her. Tears wet the corners of her eyes, so I step up to do what I came here to do: I help. "We need to focus on remediation."

"Remediation?" Violet perks up.

I put a little volume in my voice and try to enunciate through my mask for the whole group to hear. "We need to air out the theater. Uncover and open the windows and doors. I have some box fans and generators we can use to get the air moving. We need to eliminate all sources of mold growth to salvage the building and its contents.

"Anything with paper or fiber in it—drywall, cork, particle board, upholstery, carpet—those sorts of materials will mildew and mold. If they got wet, they have to be removed and replaced. Plaster, concrete, solid woods, metals, glass, plastic—those sorts of materials will be fine. We need to spray them with bleach and let them dry. The good news is most of these walls are plaster. Only the walls of the bathrooms and office are drywall. We'll need to cut the drywall about an inch above the water line and spray the wood studs with bleach."

Violet nods, like she's glad for me to take over.

I am a boss at this sort of thing, so I'll be the boss here. "You two in the bandanas—those aren't going to do your lungs any good. You shouldn't be in here. Work outside. There's a drill in my truck. Use that to back out the screws holding the plywood on the doors, then set up the fans and generators to get the air moving. Let me know if you need any help. The rest of you, are your masks N95?"

A few inspect their face covers, and it looks like we're all wearing quality protective equipment. "Okay, good. Let's split up. Half of you can work with Violet and me on the theater, the rest can help Uncle Sam clean his shop."

Andre decides to take charge of the other group, naming about five people to follow him and Clifton to his store. For our group, I have a few guys retrieve box cutters and utility knives from the truck so we can cut the carpet out.

I use the pause in activity to take Violet's hand and pull her over toward the wall behind the concession stand. Right above the high-water mark, mercifully saved from the flood, is a black-and-white portrait of a handsome young Black man in a military uniform—

Vietnam era, I would guess. It's framed in brass, and there is an engraved plaque that reads, "Henry Clement Devollier: 1949–2003." It's Violet's dad, her inspiration for buying this place. Carefully, I take the portrait off the wall and help her hold it. A few tears escape the corners of her eyes and land on the glass.

"His portrait survived the flood," I say. "Paradise will survive too. We'll build it back, Violet. I promise you."

She looks up at me, her eyes shining with so much sorrow, and I want to hug her, but instead I squeeze my hand on her shoulder. "Why don't you take this out to the truck for safe keeping?"

She leaves, and I don't expect to see her back inside the theater for a while. I can only imagine the pain it will cause her to destroy the work she put into this place.

When she's outside, one of the guys brings me a utility knife, and we get started. First up is the carpet. With heavy gloves, bulky goggles, and our trusty respirators and masks, we use utility knives and—much to Federico's chagrin—fabric scissors to cut the ruined carpet away from the stairs and yank it from the edges of the walls. Sooner than I expected, Violet is at my side, one of the many who roll up the carpet so we can heft it outside.

"Lift with your legs, not your back." Galen's partner shares this bit of wisdom from the muffled confines of his mask as we grunt and struggle with the unruly roll of damp carpet, trying to get it outside, where it will no longer spoil the air in the theater. Our gloved hands grapple for a hold of the heavy fabric as we half drag, half carry the thing across the lobby and shove it through the door. I feel every muscle in my body scream and shout as I yank and pull. Finally, the theater disgorges its noxious contents out onto the steaming pavement. We drag the roll of carpet to the sidewalk a few buildings away, where the foul stench won't drift back to our noses. Now, it can take its time rotting in the sun while the city takes its time getting services like trash collection back up and running.

With that job done, we strip off our respirators and masks, like we've been underwater, to breathe in the fresh air. Working up a sweat in this heat is something else. I'm used to the baking Texas sun, sure, but this Delta heat will boil you alive. My skin is turning a shade of turgid red, like a crawfish tossed into a pot with Cajun seasoning. I step into the shade of Violet's blade sign, the word "Paradise" my only salvation from the sun. But the heat here doesn't need the sun to get you; it seeps into you from the shadows too. It's inescapable.

Andre brings us water from Clifton's shop and radios Paul that it's time for lunch. In minutes, he's there with a bottle of hand sanitizer and a hearty feast of beans and rice and cornbread, which we devour. Then the break is over, and we're donning our masks and gloves to go back in. I let some of the others work on cutting the drywall off the walls in the lobby while Violet and I take a team into the auditorium.

With a couple of lanterns, we can see better. It's so much worse here than in the lobby. Even with my respirator on, the smell is horrendous. I swallow a few times to keep from gagging. It's as if the darkness, heat, and toxic cocktail of chemicals and fossil fuels have borne some entirely worse species of mold. Today will be an extinction event for everything that's been thriving in this cave-like ecosystem.

The carpet is black everywhere the toxic sludge touched, which appears to be about the first five rows. The rich red velvet curtains that frame the screen look like they've been dipped in black paint. And the upholstery of the first few rows of seats is ruined, too, teeming with microscopic life.

I move down into the theater, my steps squishing on the wet carpet. The fabric is slick with new life, and I spread my legs and bend my knees for stability as I make my way to the fire exit door and push it open. The alarm is silent, disabled by the power outage, and I prop the door open with a brick from the alley.

Standing there in the doorway for a moment, I breathe the fresh air while I survey the vast amount of work in front of us. Violet is at the top of the auditorium, where that door is propped open too. It looks like she might be on the verge of tears again, so I put her to work. "Take some photos for insurance before we start in here."

She accepts a digital camera from one of the bar patrons and blinds us with the strobing flash in the dark room.

When she gives us the all clear, we begin the gory work of peeling the carpet off the floor, hacking the ends of the curtains off, and stripping the first rows of chairs. It's thirty trash bags worth of soggy stuffing and rancid fabric. Like a post-apocalyptic Santa Claus and his elves, we lug trash bags over our shoulders to toss into the dumpster at the end of the alley, each bag hitting with a dull thud that sends up a plume of flies, thick as smoke, buzzing all around.

In the break room we join the team handling the backroom mess. Some try to salvage old soggy paperwork while others bleach the cabinets and dispose of the fridge.

We've all smelled what festers inside Katrina fridges. It's the stuff of nightmares. We wrap this one with duct tape and a couple of people wheel it out to the alley.

Then we leave the theater to breathe and join the crew at Uncle Sam's shop. They're making a lot of progress: some roll the metal shelving racks out to dry in the sun while others bag the ruined food and products. Using milk crates to prop the freezer doors open, a couple of people spray down the units with bleach. They did the same to Violet's concession stand after they removed the ruined candy. I grab a trash bag, and Violet and I work to collect soggy boxes of cereal and waterlogged packs of toilet paper from one corner of the room.

The work is oddly cathartic. For me, it's a cleansing of more than the spaces. I feel cleansed too. Helping, doing something good like this, fills my spirit. And for the first time in a while, it's the exertion of my muscles, the ache in my back, legs, and arms, and the pounding of my heart that I feel more than the lingering emptiness in my chest and the thirst for whiskey. And it's not just me—this is an emotional cleansing for everyone here. This strength of community is a buoy in the storm.

Too soon darkness moves in again. As the sun lulls in the western sky, the powerlessness of this place becomes inescapable. As if the sunshine was the thing that tethered us to the rest of the world, the darkness sets us adrift once more, disconnected from the world around us, lost.

"Y'all best get a move on before last light," Uncle Sam says with a groan as he stands from where he's been sitting for another water break. He brushes the back of his britches clean then makes a point of thanking everyone individually with a hearty handshake. We offer for him to join us back at the bar for a warm beer or booze and a little companionship, but he kindly declines with, "This is my home, this is where I need to be," and heads back up to his bird's nest with his shotgun.

We pack the fans and generators and screw boards back on Violet's theater to secure it for the night, then return to the bar in silence, exhausted, like whatever fuel we'd been running on drained away with the light. It takes every ounce of my energy to make it up the stairs, wash from our day of sweaty, dirty work, and collapse into Violet's bed.

Violet hasn't said much all day. And I've been too focused on work to pry, but now as we lie side by side, staring at the ceiling, I ask, "Are you okay, Violet?"

She turns onto her side and stares at me for a good long minute, still silent, unmoving except for one lonely tear streaking down her cheek. "No." Her voice sounds watery when she says it, and then more tears follow.

My heart cracks open in agony. But I don't know what to say, so I say nothing. I move, hugging her against me. That's when the tears come in earnest. She sobs against my chest, clutching at my shoulders like she's desperate to hold onto something. I hug her tighter, kissing the top of her head and feeling my own eyes water as I listen to her heartbreak.

"I'm sorry," I whisper, like that'll help, like it will change anything. But it's something to say, to remind her I'm here, that she's not alone.

Andre appears in the doorway, clearly worried by the sound of her crying. I nod to let him know I have her. He watches me for a moment as I try to soothe her, then leaves us. And I curl tighter against Violet, letting her cry herself to sleep in my arms.

13

SUNDAY, SEPTEMBER 18, 2005

I wake to the smell of Violet's skin. Despite the lack of potable water, we still manage meager showers with our gray water, and I love the smell of her cleanser. I take a deep breath before I stretch my muscles back to life.

"Hey," she whispers. I look down at her deep dark eyes looking up at me. "Thanks for last night."

I touch her cheek, like I'm wiping the tears of last night away. "You don't ever have to thank me for that. I'm here for you in any way you need me."

She smirks at me for a moment, then slowly smiles. But it's a mask. There's tension in the tightness of her mouth and a new darkness in the depths of her eyes. I wish she wouldn't put on a false face for me, but if that's what she needs to do today, so be it.

Later, we pile into the trucks to look for Louie. The water is almost entirely gone from these streets, too, and my waders are no longer needed. Both trucks park in front of Paul's mom's house.

Violet looks antsy as we strategize our search. Then, to Paul, she asks, "Do you need us here?"

I feel a frisson of excitement at her use of the word "us" to include me.

"There is something I need to do this morning," she finishes.

Paul is already shaking his head. "You do you, baby girl. We're more than equipped to find this damn cat with the people we have."

Violet wraps her arms around her middle and starts to chew on a fingernail. I've never seen her this unsettled. I'm not sure what to do other than agree to whatever she asks of me. But she's not asking anything. As the rest of the search teams fan out, Violet paces in a small circle.

Finally, I offer, "Where do you want to go?"

Violet stops pacing but doesn't stop chewing on that thumbnail until she finally answers, "My old house."

I move toward the truck. She joins me, and silently we get in and crank up the air conditioner. "Tell me where to go" is all I say when we're strapped in and ready.

Violet's driving directions are curt and tense while she explains briefly that we're going to Gentilly, to the duplex where she and Andre grew up. When Andre's mom passed, followed a year later by Violet's dad, they sold the duplex and split the money. Andre's half went into buying Beaux Ballroom with Paul, and Violet bought Paradise. Still, the duplex holds a lifetime of memories for Violet. She wants to see how it fared. From the reports on the radio, I don't hold out much hope.

The roads are much more crowded than I've seen before. The National Guard roll their heavy trucks from neighborhood to neighborhood like patrolling police. Crews of electricians balance in bucket lifts between wires, trying to make everything work again. Pickup trucks trailing fishing boats, the so-called "Cajun Navy," head for the freeway to exit the city, leaving the remainder of the NOLA mission to the Coast Guard and National Guard. There are news trucks aplenty, animal rescue groups, and what look like a few disaster tourists as we turn into a neighborhood near the lake.

The road to Violet's former home is not easily navigable by car. Increasingly, we encounter debris strewn across the road. Homes and businesses on all sides show immense damage, their contents strewn all over. Search-and-rescue paint marks the walls of each structure. Katrina Crosses, they call them, the tale-tell signs of a living nightmare.

By now, we all have theories about the different initial codes spray-painted on the buildings of this city, but the search-and-rescue markings are standard and depressing to read. Top quadrant is the date when the search was completed. Left and right sections display the initials for the unit who completed the search and hazards found in the structure. I shiver as wall-after-wall have "rats" scrawled in this part of the cross. Lastly, in the bottom section are simple numbers, a benign display of a traumatic tally: the numbers of survivors rescued and dead recovered.

Squeezing my hands on the steering wheel, I focus my attention on the road. I don't dare look at the numbers. I don't want to count the dead.

"I hardly recognize— Turn right!" Violet shouts the order, and I follow, making a tight turn onto a road with very few houses on it, just slabs.

Violet moves for the door handle like she's going to step right out of the moving truck. I hit the brakes a little too hard, and the screech of tires sends a jarring jolt through us both. It's just in time. She's instantly out of the truck, jogging into a field strewn with slabs of brick and shards of wood. I park at the curb and follow.

Is this it? Is this where she used to live? There's nothing left. *Nothing.* If she'd still lived here, if she'd sheltered at home, there might be nothing left of her either. What remains of the family that did live here? All the families in this area? My heart breaks for her, for them, for this whole city.

I walk over to where Violet stares at what remains of a house. The numbers on the wall, two zeros, are good news. No living were found here and also no dead.

Muttering "my God" repeatedly, Violet turns in the center of the chaos, taking it all in. "When my dad died," she says quietly, and I strain to listen, "I couldn't be in the house anymore. It was too empty. And so…we sold it, Andre and me. His mom's place, my dad's place. We sold, and we never came back to this street again. It was too much, you know?" Her voice wavers, and she stops talking, instead turning to take in the sight of the other houses. "It's unrecognizable. Miss Pearl's house there…and Mr. Gibbons…"

I wince at the numbers on Mr. Gibbons's front wall, 0-1, and say a silent prayer for the man as my eyes begin to sting and my throat closes. Violet starts to walk away, and I don't know what to do. I hesitate to bother her, but I don't want to lose sight of her. Not here, not in this hell. So I follow. Half a block up, she stumbles. I run to reach her and barely catch her before her knees hit the ground. She lets out a heaving sob, and I hug her against me.

She hangs in my arms, boneless, and I slowly lower us both to our knees, like we're in church, but praying to what?

"I'm sorry. I'm so sorry," I say in a hushed voice, whispering like this is sacred space, hallowed ground, like it's a cemetery, and I don't want to wake the dead.

Violet doesn't react as I expect her to. She laughs. It starts as a bubble of nervous giggling but grows louder into something hysterical and out of control. She shoves my shoulders away and climbs to her feet. Shouting now, she says, "You're sorry. You're *sorry*? Stop saying you're fucking sorry. That doesn't fucking help, Greg."

I don't know what to do. I'm so confused. "I know. I'm sorry."

Violet shakes her head at me, then turns her face up to the sky. Staring at the burning sun too long, she shuts her eyes as tears streak down her cheeks, and she screams. After such a long stretch of silence, I startle at the noise. It is the most horrible sound I've ever heard. So much sorrow and hurt, like what lies in the heart and soul of her is crying out for an escape from this reality, or at least an explanation. *Why, God? Why me? Why us? Why here? Why anywhere?* All the questions that will never have answers are in that one harrowing cry.

When her scream peters out into a hoarse whimper, her shoulders slump. I want to pull her against me and hold her tight, desperately needing to fix this and somehow make it all better. Reaching for her, I stupidly ask, "Are you okay?"

Violet smacks my hand away. "No! I'm not fucking okay."

"I know. I'm sorry." Shit.

Violet cackles at me again, "*You know?* What do you know, Greg? What the fuck do you know about loss? Oh, you lost your wife? Well, I've lost *everything*! I have nothing left...nothing. Everything I built— it's nothing!

"Stop acting like everything will be okay, and we're going to tough it out. I'm sick to death of toughing it out. Everything is *not* okay. This is one big shit show that never ends, and I'm exhausted. Exhausted and angry. I'm fucking *livid*, and right now this rage is the only thing I have. So don't tell me it will be okay!"

I don't know what to say, rendered speechless and useless, overwhelmed by this tiny tragedy in the midst of such a big one. My ineptitude at making this better, fixing it, seems to frustrate Violet as much as it frustrates me.

I want to hug her. But when I reach out, she slaps my hand again. After a moment, she gives me an enigmatic frown and walks away. Instead of moving back the way we came, she walks toward a small parking lot, where a couple of cars were tossed into a pile by the water, and she keeps on walking.

After a moment, I move, too, following her. But she turns on me, scowling through hot tears, and says, "Don't follow me."

"But—"

"Give me some space, okay?"

Space. It's what Ari needed from me too. I bristle at the comparison between Violet and my wife. But... *Fuck!* What am I supposed to do now?

Violet walks away from me, and this time I let her go. I look around at the houses, all crushed and broken, and want to scream. What am I doing here? Why did I even come? I'm not helping. I can't help. I've been playing hero to a bunch of people who don't need saving.

My knees go weak, and I stumble as I settle on the curb. The concrete is coated with that dusty layer of toxic lake water, but I don't care. I sit there, my legs folded close to my chest, my elbows on my knees, my face buried in my palms as the sun bakes the back of my neck. Abandoned and alone, nothing more than an unwanted stray.

The sun moves through the sky while I wait, but I don't know what time it is. I could check the clock in the truck. I could go there, sit in comfort, blasting cold air on my face while I wait for Violet to return. But it seems wrong to feel comfort while so many others can't. What am I, a saint? As if being a hot and cranky martyr will do any good. But I don't want to waste the gas, and the truck is a hundred feet away

—a hundred feet I don't have the energy to walk—so I stay here and blister in the sun.

I'm so wrapped up in my little slice of misery I hardly notice when someone settles beside me on the curb. "You're turning into a real redneck baking out here, Cowboy Greg."

I lift my face to look at Violet. Her expression is a strange blend of sadness and regret.

"I preferred it when you called me Honey Eyes."

"Yeah, but your eyes changed."

"To what?"

"Sad eyes."

I nod and turn away to stare across the street.

"Greg, I'm sorry I walked away like that."

"It's okay."

"No. It's not. I'm extremely angry, but not at you, and it's not fair for me to make you the target."

"I get it."

"Oh my God, stop being so fucking agreeable, Greg."

"Sorry."

Violet smacks my shoulder. "And stop apologizing. Don't you ever get pissed off?"

"Of course."

"Well, then fucking feel it."

"I do feel it, but I understand—"

"Don't make excuses for me, Greg. Don't make excuses for anyone who treats you badly. Otherwise, why would they stop?"

What she says pisses me off, like she's suggesting it's my fault people keep leaving me.

"See, right there, I see it in your eyes. That spark of anger—feel it, Greg."

"I don't—"

"You do…feel it."

"I think—"

"Don't fucking think…feel."

"I—"

"Feel."

"Stop interrupting me!" I shout and push to my feet to get away from her aggressive barrage. I walk into one of the cracked shells where a home used to be, and the weight of that loss, the weight of all this loss—Violet's, the city's, my own—the weight of it on my chest, threatens to drown my lungs with rage.

Violet stands too. She stalks toward me like she's going to yell at me again, but instead she turns her face up to the sky and screams at the heavens. It's that same heartbroken sound she made before, and it cuts me to pieces. I wish she would yell at me instead of this painful primal scream. It's overwhelming, and it makes me want to scream too.

Clenching my fists at my side, I plant my feet on the dried earth, turn my face up to the brutal sun, and scream. I scream until my lungs hurt, my throat tightens, and my face burns with hot tears. I scream until the breath has run out of me, then take another and scream again. My voice cracks and chips away like shattered glass, and still I scream. All the anger and rage, all the hurt and betrayal racing to get out of me.

My scream blends with Violet's, a harmony of grief and pain. We touch, hugging, joining our bodies as our voices intertwine. We fall to our knees, neither of us strong enough to hold the other one up. When our voices run out, we heave silently with hot tears. Her sadness wets the collar of my shirt and mine drips into the soft curls of her hair. Eventually, the tears run out, too, but we stay tangled together, holding on.

It's a long time before either of us speak again. But somehow, we both know when it's time to leave. She clasps my palm in hers, and I lace our fingers together while we walk back to the truck.

During the drive, I keep her hand in mine and she lets me. But I restrain myself from tracing my thumb across her knuckles, reminding myself that the intimacy we've shared is supportive, not romantic.

14

SUNDAY, SEPTEMBER 18, 2005

The mood at Beaux Ballroom is bright and jovial, so different from the usual gloom since the storm. Someone has a battery-powered cassette player turned up as loud as it will go, and Prince's "Kiss" plays as several people dance. The moment we walk into the room, Andre swoops in and swings Violet into his arms. They dance and spin and air-kiss at the kissing part of the song. A smile lights up Violet's face.

As he comes away from the air-kisses, Andre scrunches his nose. "Darling, you smell dreadful." He spins away, sashaying across the room to dance with Paul behind the bar. Unoffended by the criticism, Violet comes to me, takes my hand, and pulls me into the dance. I go willingly.

People who don't know me might assume I can't dance—I'm socially-awkward in every other way, so it's a fair assumption—but in fact, I *can* dance, and when the opportunity affords itself, I *do* dance. My mom insisted all her boys knew how. It's a "life skill," she always said. And at this moment, I couldn't agree more.

I take Violet's hand and spin her around in a full revolution before pulling her into my arms and leading her in a simple swaying step. She giggles and grins, and I think I've surprised her with my grace. I aim to do it again with another spin, two revolutions this time, before tucking her against me once more.

Her laughter is as warm as her body, which fits so well against mine. The top of her head comes to just below my chin when we're close. And when she looks up and catches my eyes, the long, lingering look that stretches between us feels warm too. My breath shudders out of me as our bodies move together, our gazes locked.

When the song changes to something less danceable, we make our way to the bar, where Paul explains the obvious: "Hello, darlings, we're celebrating."

"I see that. *Why* are we celebrating?" Violet asks as we take our usual seats, and Paul serves our regular drinks: water for me and a vodka tonic for Violet.

"We found Louie!" Paul says in a boisterous cheer, and the room erupts in hoots and howls all around us.

"What? Where?" Violet asks excitedly.

"Well, while you two scampered off, we searched around Mom's house, and the little shitbag sauntered up to Justin, meowing rather demandingly for his tin of Fancy Feast." He pauses and points at us. "Say, why do y'all look so funny?"

Do we look funny? I brush my hair away from my face.

Paul gasps. "Oh my word! Did you two crazy kids have sex?"

"What? No!" Violet and I make our denials at the same time, too quickly, almost like we're guilty and lying.

Paul smirks and shrugs. "In any case, David took Louie to Baton Rouge, so the couch is free again, Greg."

I try not to look disappointed, but I've come to enjoy sleeping with Violet. Does she feel the same way, or will she be glad to have her bed back to herself again?

"Uh huh, that's what I thought." Paul winks at us and moves on to serve someone else a drink.

Elton John's "I'm Still Standing" erupts from the boom box in the corner, and everyone in the room starts to dance again. I offer my hand to Violet, and she takes it, following me to the dance floor. Everyone's dancing now, moving and sweating and ratcheting up the heat until it's practically boiling in here. No one cares; tonight is a night of celebration for our small victory, and nothing can bring us down, not even the damp heat.

We all find our own rhythm, our own joy. And my joy, every ounce of it, is in my arms as I spin and dip Violet at the end of the song. Everything feels right when she's with me; my anxiety drains away with every touch. Something changed between us today. Somewhere between the primal screams and here, we've come together on some new level.

I clutch her tight as I sing some of the lyrics along with the song. Everyone is, but it's me Violet smiles at. "You are full of surprises, aren't you, Greg? You can really dance, and you can sing too. I didn't know you had it in you."

"There's plenty you still don't know about me." I realize too late I'm flirting. I'm probably crossing all sorts of lines, but I can't help this closeness I feel with her and the relaxation it inspires in me.

There's flirtation in her tone when she says, "I look forward to more surprises."

The song ends and Louis Armstrong's "What a Wonderful World" starts. Violet's smile collapses as the first notes ring through the air.

"What's the matter?" I ask as her eyes glisten with unshed tears.

"This was my dad's favorite song," Violet says. Then she presses closer to me, resting her head against my chest as we slow dance to the saddest song about hope.

I wrap my arms tighter around her, hugging her as a lump forms in my throat, and I tear up a little too. When the song ends, our dance ends. We come to a stop in the center of the dance floor as the room keeps moving around us. I squeeze her a little tighter and whisper in her ear, "Would you like to head upstairs?"

Violet nods, and I curve my posture around her, like an umbrella shielding her from the storm, while we move to the private courtyard and up to the apartment.

We haven't talked about the change in our sleeping arrangements for tonight, so I'm surprised when she keeps her arm around my waist and brings me with her into her bedroom.

Once inside, she steps away from me, staring at her reflection in the vanity mirror and wiping away tears. She says, "Sorry about that. I know you didn't sign up for this wall-to-wall emotion marathon."

"You're in mourning, Violet. For your dad, for your city, for life as you know it. I understand. You don't need to apologize."

She scrutinizes my face, like she's looking for the lie. But after a moment, she huffs out a deep breath and grabs a change of clothes. "I'm going to get cleaned up. I'll see you in a minute."

Should I wait for her here or on the couch? What's happening between us right now?

Like she can read my mind, she says, "Wait here."

She vanishes into the bathroom with a candle from the kitchen. Pacing her room, I keep glancing into the vanity mirror. My skin is red from too long in the sun, my stubble is scruffy enough it can actually be called a beard now, and my eyes are bloodshot from the emotional outpouring earlier. I'm still trying to process everything that's happened between Violet and me when she returns. She smells amazing and looks edible in her tight top and short shorts.

"All yours," she says, and it takes me a moment to realize she means the bathroom.

I practically run to scrub myself clean and rinse off, then pull on some shorts and exit. I'm drawn to the flicker of candlelight through Violet's bedroom door. I lean against the entry frame as she looks up at me from the bed.

"Should I move to the couch—?"

"I'd like you to stay here."

"Oh."

"Or would you prefer the couch?"

I take a step into her bedroom, and it's like I've crossed some great chasm, a boundary. "I'd prefer to stay here."

Violet wiggles over to make more room for me.

I come around to what is becoming my side of the bed but hesitate. "It's just…"

"What?" she asks.

I stare at her a moment, then settle onto the bed beside her. It's confusing. She's sending mixed signals, and I'm afraid to ask for directions. Before, I thought sharing this bed was a means to an end. Now, there's another option, yet here we are. Every night we sleep together is more intimate than the last. Should I read anything into that? What are her feelings toward me? Have they changed?

"Greg? Would you like to cuddle?" She interrupts the maelstrom of my mind.

It takes me no time to consider my answer. "Yes."

Without a word, she moves closer to me, and we curl together. She rests her head on my chest, the satin of her sleep bonnet tickling the whiskers of my chin. I hug her a little tighter. It feels so good to be with her like this, but there is a voice in the back of my head, whispering to me: "You're falling for her. You're falling for a woman who won't love you back."

I can't sleep. My body lies limp and exhausted, the warmth of Violet against me so soothing. But my mind is on high alert, and it won't shut down as it cycles through a litany of pain, cataloging all the ways I can get my heart broken…again.

So I lie awake while Violet sleeps in my arms, and I stare at the stars, and the flashing lights—

Wait. What's flashing? It's like a strobe. Is it lightning? Is a storm approaching?

I try not to disturb Violet as I shift to sit up in the bed. From here I can see out the window, expecting to see some jagged flash across the sky, but instead it's the drapes of festoon lights that hang from one end of the courtyard to the other, flickering. On for a moment, then off again, on for a moment longer. Dimmer, brighter, too bright, a flicker and then a steady amber glow.

Holy shit. The power's back on.

Will it stay on? Is this a basic comfort we can rely on once again? I wait for a moment, almost expecting the lights to flicker back off, a terrible tease. But they remain on. And now I feel it, the cool comfort of climate control. The air conditioner that sat silent in a window of Violet's bedroom now rumbles to life, the cool breeze a miracle to behold.

Before I can consider whether to wake the rest of the house, Paul howls with glee, "Hallelujah!" I don't need to wake anyone. Paul will do it for me. He howls again, and Violet mumbles something in her sleep as she shoves a pillow over her head.

"Violet." I jostle her shoulder to wake her. "You're going to want to see this."

She comes out from under the pillow and rubs her eyes as she frowns at me. "What are you smiling about?"

"Electricity."

She shifts up and looks at the lights in the courtyard before slicing her gaze to the blinking numbers of her bedside clock. Then Violet jumps from the bed and extends her hands over the AC vent. "Oh my God."

I get up to close the French doors, which had been our only relief from the heat, and go out to the kitchen, where Paul is closing the rest. We stare at the burning bulbs like it's the 1893 World's Fair, and we're seeing electric power light up the night for the first time.

15

MONDAY, SEPTEMBER 19, 2005

The air is cool, the sheets are soft, Violet's neck smells sweet against my nose, and there's a robotic jangly sound that's pulling me out of this bliss.

"What is that noise?" Violet grumbles and stuffs a pillow over her head.

"My phone." I open one eye to watch it vibrate as it rings again.

"Answer it," she demands from beneath the pillow.

I am. It's weird to have it working again. After so long without power, without cellular service, it's a little jarring to be rocketed back into the twenty-first century overnight. It was literally last night when the lights came on, and now here we are savoring all the luxury and splendor we took for granted before the storm.

"If you don't stop that ringing, I will castrate you with my bare hands, Greg."

Okaaaay. "Hello?" I ask with a terror-induced frog in my throat.

"Holy shit! My call finally went through."

"Jake?" I sit up in Violet's bed and wipe the sleep from my eyes. The pink mosquito curtain paints the midmorning in a rosy hue.

"Dude. I've been calling you for days. And finally, *finally,* like a birthday miracle, I get through."

"Hey. Yeah. The cell towers have been down, along with all the other electricity in most of the city. Just got it back last night." I scratch my chin as I try to remember what day it is. "Whose birthday?"

Jake lets out a laugh so loud Violet pulls the pillow off her head and listens when Jake says, "Yours, you stupid idiot. Happy fucking birthday, old man."

"Oh." It's all I manage to say. Violet—who can hear every word Jake says—leaps out of bed and runs out of the room. Surprised by her rapid exit, I mumble to Jake, "Thanks."

"*Oh. Thanks?* Really feeling the love, brother."

"Sorry. I'm still half asleep. It's great to hear your voice."

"Yeah, yours too." He sounds so relieved, like he's truly been worried about me. "So how are you doing? You staying sober?"

I'm proud when I can honestly say, "Yep. One hundred percent."

"Did you find Violet?"

I look toward the door, where Violet is talking to Andre and Paul, but I can't understand what they're saying. "I did."

"And she's okay?"

"Yep."

"What's with the monosyllabic answers? Did I catch you at a bad time?"

"I'm sorry." I smile as I remember the impromptu dance party Violet and I had with Paul and Andre in the living room last night. "We had a late night."

"We?" Jake's tone turns suggestive.

I quickly change the subject before he starts asking probing questions. "How's Nicole?"

"She's good. She glows. It's the most beautiful thing I've ever seen."

"I'm happy for you, brother."

"And I'm happy you're doing okay. You sound better than I was expecting."

"What were you expecting?"

"Not much."

I laugh. I hadn't realized I'd been missing Jake until this call. The sound of his voice is heartening.

"Well, I'll let you get back to sleep or whatever you were getting up to. Call me when it's a good time. Love you, brother."

"I love you too."

I hang up the phone, and Violet comes back into her bedroom, asking, "Who are you saying the *L* word to from my bed, Cowboy Greg?"

I grin at the oddly possessive tone of those words. "My best friend, Jake."

She claps her hands. "Well, get your ass up, birthday boy! We've got a lot to do today."

It only takes me a moment to do what I'm told and get my ass up.

Apparently, the first thing on our to-do list for the day is to do copious loads of laundry and take long, warm showers. When the electricity kicked on last night, the water treatment plant came back online too, so we have lights *and* water this morning. There is a boil notice before drinking the water, but no one cares about that. We're just glad to be able to shower and flush the toilet again.

I reach for my razor before going into the bathroom, but Violet protests. Instead, Paul offers to trim my new beard into shape if I promise not to shave it off. When he's done, it looks good, I admit. And it feels good to have clean hair, clean clothes, and a nicely manicured beard that Violet enjoys touching.

When that's all done, Violet and I go to the theater. Uncle Sam radioed that the power is still off on their block, but we went anyway to retrieve some prized items and Uncle Sam himself. Violet sends me on a mission up to the theater's projector loft to collect the dissembled parts of the popcorn popper, which she stowed there for safekeeping. It's a lot of stair climbing, and I'm sweating in my clean clothes by the third trip. But I'd rather have this job than Violet's: convincing Uncle Sam to come back to Beaux Ballroom with us for some air-conditioning, a shower, and a soft couch to sleep on. You'd think the stubborn old man was glued to that roof.

"You're coming," Violet says.

"Who will watch the place?" Uncle Sam says defensively.

"Clifton, face it," Violet settles her hands on her hips, "no one's coming. No one's coming to rescue us same as no one's coming to steal from us. We've been forgotten. So come get a good night's rest."

When I have all the pieces of the popper loaded up into the truck bed, I join Violet at Uncle Sam's shop, where she's convinced him to lock up and come over for the night. He twitches with nervous energy the whole trip back to the bar.

Inside is a frenzy of activity—everyone is working on something. Some lean on ladders to string up more lights, some dust off the tables and mop the floor, while others boil water to make bar ice. When Violet whistles and asks for help, several people come to unload the popcorn popper and start assembling it beside the bar.

"All right, Uncle Sam, go get a nice shower and nap. There're laundry machines up there too." She points at the courtyard and the stairs. Without a word, he moves that way. I go to the bar and order a cold bottle of water.

"What's going on here?" I ask Paul.

"Oh, you'll see."

"I'll see what?" No sooner have I taken my first sip than Violet takes me by the hand and corrals me toward the door, toward my truck. "What now?"

"We need to scout for food and gas, and I want to see which other neighborhoods have power. We should find a gas station that's running, see if they have word on when delivery trucks will start coming back in."

I nod. Serious stuff. I guzzle what's left of my water and drive as she directs me around her city. Increasingly, there are signs of life. More people are on the streets, moving around, cleaning up the roads, and gutting the houses. Electrical linemen are attached to every pole, reconnecting the city to the power grid, block by block. There are even a couple of kids playing ball on one of the streets we meander down. The few gas stations we find open have lines wrapped around the block. We turn off the truck's AC and roll down the windows, knowing we still need to conserve as much gas as we can before regular services, fuel, and food fully return.

We pull up to a shop with an attached house. Violet knows a few people milling around, and I follow her over to talk to them. My phone rings. Still not used to the sound of it after so many days of silence, I look at it for a moment. It's Ari.

Violet glances at the screen. "Your wife?"

"My ex-wife… Well, almost ex."

She shoos me away, and I answer as I walk over to where it's quiet. "Ari?"

"Oh my God, it's good to hear your voice. We've been worried."

We? Worried? "I'm fine. No need to worry."

"Well, Jake said his call went through this morning, so I figured I'd give it a try too. I wanted to call and wish you a happy birthday."

"Oh." This feels so weird, talking to her like we're barely even acquaintances. I hate that it's like this between us. I think I could be the one to make things better, but I don't know how. "Well, thanks for calling. It, uh, means a lot."

Ari pauses like she's searching for something to say, settling on: "Is it safe there?"

"Well, I've only had one gun pulled on me so far."

Ari gasps, and I try to explain about Uncle Sam, but she's too distracted with worry. "Sheryl is going there next week."

"Why?"

"Animal rescue stuff. The shelter there is overloaded, so they're bringing some of the animals to Austin to find foster and forever homes for them."

"Cool." This is awkward.

"Yeah. So, how are you?"

"Good. Things are looking up. We have some power and water back. Violet and I are driving around looking for gas and food right now, so I should—"

"You found her?"

"I did."

"I'm glad."

There's an awkward pause, which I could end by saying something, but I don't know what to say. I'm saved by the bell when my call waiting sounds. It's my parents. "Hey, Ari, my parents are on the other line, so…"

"Oh, okay, well, happy birthday, Greg. Take care of yourself."

"Thank you. You too." I switch over to my parent's call. "Hey."

They don't respond with words; instead they sing. It's their tradition. They call on the exact minute I was born and sing "Happy Birthday" to me. It's corny and sweet, and they've been doing it since I was in college. When they finish, I laugh, and it feels good. They ask how I'm doing, and that makes me feel bad. I told them I was going to New Orleans, and then I disappeared off the face of the Earth. I hadn't expected to be cut off for so long. And my long silence since being in NOLA is probably not their only worry about me. I haven't shared the darkest details of my downward spiral with them, but I know they've seen I'm not myself lately.

"I'm doing well," I tell my parents when they ask. Glancing over to Violet, I watch her finish talking to a couple of people and make her way over to me. "New Orleans is in a tough place, but we're getting things back together."

"Jake told us you went there to help rebuild. I'm proud of you," my dad says.

There is no better compliment. My dad is my hero, my first role model for how to be a good man, and, maybe someday, a good dad. For him to be proud of me puts a lump in my throat. "Well, thank you, Dad, that means a lot. Listen, I need to get moving again. We're driving around looking for gas and food."

"Oh, well, be careful please. And know that we love you so dearly," Mom says with tears in her voice.

It chokes me up a little too. "I love you too."

When I hang up, Violet raises a brow. "Did you just tell your future ex-wife you love her? No wonder you're so confused."

I glance at the phone in my hand. "That was my parents."

"They called you too? Aww, isn't that sweet? You are very loved, Greg."

I blush, knowing she's right. I hadn't seen it before, but I do now.

After driving for another half hour or so, we return empty-handed, but at least we have some information about the state of the crisis. I'm exhausted by the time we pull up to the curb outside Beaux Ballroom. There's still a flurry of activity inside; everyone's rocking out to Elton John on the other side of the French doors, but the view is obscured because someone has painted the glass panes to look like banks of snow and snowflakes.

Violet directs me to a different door, a side access into the courtyard that takes us directly to the base of the apartment stairs. "Let's get cleaned up first."

"First?"

She pushes me up the stairs and toward the shower. Thirty minutes later, I'm smelling fresh and clean in my newly washed favorite T-shirt and jeans. And Violet looks breathtaking in a gold-sequined dress.

I stutter for a moment before I manage to say, "Beautiful."

"You like?" She twirls in her dress.

"I like." *Understatement.* "But I'm underdressed, and this is the nicest thing I packed."

"You look mighty fine in those Wranglers, Cowboy Greg."

"These are Levi's."

Violet laughs at me, and I love every second of it. I don't care that it's at my expense; if she's laughing, I'm happy. She clasps my hand in hers and leads me down the stairs and across the courtyard. When she opens one of the doors into Beaux Ballroom, I gasp at the sight of the place.

The bar has been transformed to some sort of winter wonderland. Faux Christmas trees with glittery blankets of snow dot the corners. Boughs of holly drape from the ceiling. And in the middle of the room, the chairs sit facing a screen set up on the stage. Around us, people mix and mingle, all of them wearing some sort of Christmas-themed attire: from ugly sweaters to red and green gowns. By the bar, Uncle Sam is in a Santa hat, scooping popcorn out of the big brass machine I hauled over here this morning.

I've always loved Christmas. The lights, the presents, the food, the family, the snow in the mountains. Mom and Dad would decorate every inch of the house, and everyone would gather to watch Christmas movies, piece together puzzles, and eat our weight in food. The bar right now reminds me of home.

"What's going on?" I ask Violet as Paul approaches me. Only it's not Paul—she's Miss Jezebel Jewel, and she's wearing a green sequined gown with a slit up the side to showcase her strong legs and mile-high stilettos. She's got to be almost eight feet tall in those heels and the matching wig, a green beehive decorated with ornaments and topped by a gold star.

Miss Jewel stops in front of me and strikes a pose, then starts to sing "Happy Birthday" Marilyn-Monroe style. But instead of "Mr. President" she calls me "Cowboy Greg." When she's finished, I'm stunned speechless while the entire room erupts in applause.

What. Is. Happening. Right. Now?

"Happy birthday," Violet says, and then she smacks a quick kiss on my lips, and my brain fritzes out. It's a chaste kiss, nothing sexual. Still, it's amazing to have her lips against mine, to know their softness and the subtle taste of strawberry from her lip gloss. I teeter on my weak knees. Violet fishes her arm through mine and guides me to a pair of barstools near the back.

"You guys did all this for me?"

Violet smiles warmly, and she laces her fingers with mine. "We take birthdays very seriously around here."

"Why?"

Violet looks at the people who mingle and drink around us. "Not everyone has such a loving and supportive family like you. For a lot of people who come here, they lost their family when they came out of the closet, or maybe they never had a family at all. The reason doesn't matter, but the point is, when we have a birthday in this family, we celebrate it."

"I'm part of the family?"

She frowns and rests her hand on my cheek. "Of course you are."

My heart swells like it might burst. I want to kiss her again like she kissed me, but Miss Bea Haven comes out onto the stage, looking stunning in a white gown that sparkles like fresh snow and with a snowflake-shaped halo over her bald head.

With a wide sweep of her arms, she declares, "We have our power back!"

Everyone cheers the double meaning of her words. I do too.

"In celebration of the wonders of electricity and in honor of the birthday boy, we're doing something special tonight. Sweet Vee told me that the night she met Cowboy Greg, his deepest desire was to watch the movie *It's a Wonderful Life*. So tonight, that's what we'll do. Happy birthday, Cowboy. Enjoy!"

The Christmas theme makes sense now. With another sweep of her arms, Miss Bea Haven exits the stage, and the screen lights up, flickering with the first images of the black-and-white Jimmy Stewart classic.

Emotions swirl inside, and I get a little teary-eyed as George Bailey ponders suicide, only to be talked away from the ledge by an angel who shows him what his community would be like without him. Memories of my moment on the ledge, my own guardian angel storming in to pull me back from the edge, swirl in my mind. And a new memory swims into my consciousness: my first AA meeting, when I couldn't reply "me too" when Jake had said he was glad I didn't jump. I didn't feel relief to be alive then. Now, though, I do. Sitting here, experiencing this film with this wonderful group of people gathered to celebrate my birthday—a celebration of my *life*—God, I do!

"Me too," I say.

"What?" Violet asks from my side.

I stand and tell her, "Give me one second. I need to make a phone call."

She nods, and I leave to go out to the courtyard and dial Jake.

"What's up, birthday boy?" Jake answers.

"I never thanked you for New York."

"What?"

"You saved me, and I never thanked you. Instead, I hurt you. I've apologized for that, but I never thanked you, so… Thank you."

Jake doesn't respond. He doesn't say a word. I know he's still there—I can hear him breathing, and he sniffs, like he's fighting tears. When he does finally speak, he says, "Promise me, if you ever get to that place again—"

"I won't shut you out. I will seek help. I promise." Tears fill my eyes as I imagine the pain and worry I put him through. I wipe my eyes as I say, "I love you, brother."

"I love you too." He sniffs again, and his voice changes, getting lighter when he asks, "What are you doing for your birthday?"

"We're watching *It's a Wonderful Life*. I stepped away for a minute to give you a call."

"Has it come to the Charleston contest swimming pool scene yet? I love that part."

"It's coming up."

"Well, don't let me keep you." Jake hangs up.

When I'm off the phone I return to the bar and take my seat beside Violet.

"Everything okay?" she asks.

"Everything is great."

Violet clasps my hand in hers. "Do you like your birthday surprise?"

"I love it." I imagine having missed this birthday entirely. The thought that I might be gone right now, had I jumped, terrifies me almost as much as it fills me with gratitude for the life I still have. I smile wide when I say, "It's my best birthday yet."

Violet looks like she has more questions, but the man in the movie announces the Charleston contest, and we turn our attention back to the movie.

"I love this scene," she says.

"Me too," I say, and I mean it in every possible way.

16

TUESDAY, SEPTEMBER 20, 2005

"I have an idea," Andre announces as he comes into Violet's room wearing a hot pink robe that barely closes over his muscular chest. He sits on the corner of her bed, and I scurry away from Violet like we've been caught by her dad. Andre chuckles. "Honey, the cat's out of the bag on this little cuddle-buddy situation y'all got going on. Now listen."

We stretch and yawn and listen as he explains, "The movie was a hit. Let's do it again, turn it into an event. We all need a Christmas miracle right about now. We'll make it a fundraiser. Take donations at the door. Paul already has a name for it."

"The Angel Wings Fund," Paul says as he leans against Violet's doorjamb in his matching hot pink robe, sipping coffee.

"The fund will go toward the theater rebuilding effort. And if we get enough, we'll help Uncle Sam, too, and others. All these hot, sweaty construction workers in town, looking for something to do with their money after dark. Let's give them something to spend it on," Andre adds, and Violet leaps into his arms, kissing her cousin all over his face and head, clearly loving the idea.

I'm beside the bar, scooping popcorn into bags, when the last person I expect to see leaps on me, wraps her arms around my neck and her legs around my waist, and plants a kiss square on my mouth. The popcorn scooper flies out of my hand, and popcorn rains down around us as Ari's strange little friend Sheryl squeals, "GREG! OH MY GOD! Of all the gin joints in New Orleans, what are you doing here?"

"Uh…" I stand there, stunned and struggling to breathe as the surprisingly strong woman squeezes me in her full-body embrace. "Hi? What are *you* doing here?"

It's a dumb question. One look at Sheryl's outfit and it's clear she's here for our nightly Christmas in September celebration. She's sporting green fishnet hose, red sequined hot pants, a tank top that reads, "Spank me, Santa. I've been naughty!" and her hair is dyed an electric shade of green.

It's been a week and a half since Andre's big idea, and word has gotten out. Christmas in September has become the hottest show in the city. Every day—while Violet and I check on Uncle Sam or hunt for supplies—a team of set designers adds more twinkle lights, more sequined snow, more Christmas cheer, and every night we host an increasingly absurd and wonderful event. People sing and quote along, wearing ever more outlandish costumes; it's like the *Rocky Horror Picture Show* but with Jimmy Stewart.

It's a beautiful thing to watch each night as a community comes together in support of their own: George Bailey and Violet Devollier, his bank and her theater. The Angel Wings Fund has already raised several thousand dollars in donations.

"Cowboy Greg, who is this fetching creature crawling all over you?" Miss Jewel asks with a big wink.

Sheryl leaps down from me, a smile beaming across her face as she introduces herself. "I'm Sheryl Novak, here with the Austin Animal Alliance. We're helping the local shelter workers and animal rescue groups evacuate distressed animals to temporary shelters west of the city. From there, they go to foster homes around Texas and Louisiana until we can find their families."

"Aww, aren't you precious?"

I must admit she is precious. Sweet beyond measure and the most intensely charming person I've ever known. Miss Jewel takes an instant liking to Sheryl, tapping her on the nose with a bedazzled press-on nail. How she bartends while wearing those is beyond my comprehension.

"And how do you two know each other?" Miss Jewel asks.

I answer without thinking. "She's friends with my wife."

"Wife!" Miss Bea Haven gasps behind me. "You're married?!"

Shit. Miss Bea Haven scowls at me, but it's Andre's voice she uses when she speaks. "Are you telling me that all this time you've been sleeping with my cousin you've been married?"

Uh. Technically. "Ari and I are separated. She lives with her boyfriend now. I filed for divorce before I came here. And Violet and I aren't *sleeping together*, we're just…sleeping together."

"Violet!" Sheryl squeals. "OH MY GOD, you found her?"

"My ears are burning. Who said my name?" Violet joins us all in the tight little nook between the bar and the popcorn popper.

Sheryl careens into Violet with one of her crushing hugs. "He found you! Oh, my God, it's so romantic!"

"What is happening right now?" Violet asks, her posture stiff as a board, Sheryl wrapped around her neck like a red-and-green scarf.

Sheryl pulls away, beaming and blathering. "Greg was a man with a mission, all broody and pacing around Nicole's living room, insisting he had to come here and find you. The news was so scary, we were all trying to talk him out of it, but he was fearlessly determined. And look, here you are together. It's like a fairytale come true… So romantic. And can I say, Violet, you have the most amazing aura. You totally glow!"

"Oh." Violet looks overwhelmed by Sheryl—welcome to my world—and says, "Well. Thank you."

I open my mouth to explain that Violet and I are just friends, but Miss Jewel grabs a big brass bell off the bar and starts clanging it loudly to get the room's attention. We all turn to her as she announces, "People, people, show time is upon us. If you haven't already done so, please donate to the Angel Wings Fund before you find your seat." Miss Jewel pauses while a patron drops a dollar into the donation bucket, then rings the bell again, and in a syrupy-sweet voice quotes Zuzu's famous line about angels getting their wings.

While Miss Jewel clangs at a few more donations, Violet and Miss Bea Haven move toward the stage and up into the spotlight. Violet shines like the North Star in her gold lamé dress, her wig of long dark curls sparkling where she's woven in strands of gold tinsel. I've never seen a more beautiful sight. Maybe I can see her aura too.

Like she can read my mind, Sheryl elbows me in the side. "She's amazing. Tell her how you feel."

"What are you talking about?"

She rolls her eyes at me. "Greg, don't be stupid."

"Sheryl." I try to whisper as the crowd hushes for Violet and Miss Bea Haven. "I don't know what you're talking about."

"You came here looking for love, and you found it. Don't let it get away."

I frown at her. "I didn't come here looking for love. And Violet's not looking for love either. We're just friends."

"Tons of people aren't *looking* for love, but they find it anyway. And you two aren't 'just' anything. Get your head out of your ass."

I sputter, but there's nothing I can say to that. From the stage, Violet looks out across the crowd, and when she sees me, she winks.

"Oh." Sheryl elbows me again. She's going to leave a bruise. "She's definitely looking, and from the looks of things, I'd wager she's found what she's looking for." Sheryl waggles her brows at me as she drops a twenty into the donation bucket and finds a seat near the front of the crowd, leaving me frozen, my head spinning.

What is she even talking about? Sheryl walked into this room ten minutes ago, and she thinks she knows it all? I roll my eyes and focus all my attention on the show.

Miss Bea Haven towers beside Violet, looking resplendent in a vibrant red gown with a white faux-fur collar, like a sexy Mrs. Claus. She clamps the microphone between inch-long press-on acrylics similar to her partner's and says, "Thank you, thank you, thank you for coming. I won't take long. I know we all want to dive right into the movie, but before we do, allow me to introduce you all to the beneficiary of this event. My cousin, my favorite woman, and my heroine, Miss Violet Devollier. Miss Violet bought and renovated the Paradise Theatre. She brought that theater back to life with more than wood, brick, and screws"—she does a little hip pump when she says "screws" and the crowd goes wild—"she built it with hope, love, and dreams. She spent her life savings and her blood, sweat, and tears on her dream." With a hand on her hip, Miss Bea Haven turns indignant. "Then this bitch Katrina comes in here trying to destroy it? Not on my watch, sister. No ma'am!" She whips her long platinum-blond ponytail over her shoulder. "Tonight, like every night, we will raise the money to rebuild Paradise. Thank you for coming. Come again, and bring your friends."

Everyone applauds, and Miss Bea Haven hands the mic to Violet. She gives her cousin a wide smile and says, "Well, goodness, yes, what she said. Night after night, I am truly honored and feel such sincere gratitude to you all for your amazing generosity and support. I love this community. I love this city. I love you all. Merry Christmas in September, New Orleans!"

Applause fills the room, and Violet raises her arm to present the start of the movie. Uncle Sam, our projectionist, clicks a switch on the projector to get it started as Miss Jewel lowers the house lights. The black-and-white images of Bedford Falls light up the screen, and the audience is transported to a different time and place. All the chairs are taken tonight, and the smell of beer bothers me, so I go out to the courtyard and sit on a table, watching the movie through the filmy glass of the French doors.

"What are you doing out here?" Violet asks when she comes out and sits beside me on the table.

"Taking a little break from the crowded room. Don't let me keep you. I'm fine by myself."

"Well, do you mind a little company?"

"If that company is you, then I'm happy for it."

We watch the movie, laughing when members of the audience wearing angel wings reenact one of Clarence's scenes.

"So Sheryl, she's…something else," Violet says.

"That's one way to put it." I chuckle. "She was right about your aura, though. You shine."

Violet's expression changes to something I've never seen before, something bordering on bashful. I think she liked that compliment.

"How do you know her?"

It takes me a moment to remember we're talking about Sheryl. "She's Ari's new best friend. She's a veterinarian, here to rescue animals."

Violet nods, and we fall into another deep silence. After so much quiet between us, it surprises me when Violet says, "Do you still love her?"

"Sheryl? I never—"

"Your wife."

"Oh. Uh…" I consider how to answer that. "I think part of me will always love her," I admit. Violet turns away, and I follow her gaze inside, where George Bailey spends his honeymoon money to fund his community following a run on the bank. After a few moments, I find the words. "But there's another part of me that grows bigger every day that is past loving her. I was stuck in the past for a while, stuck loving a woman who didn't love me back, but I think I'm past that now."

"Past the past."

I smile.

Violet smiles too, and it's so beautiful. "You know, that first night I met you, you made an impression on me."

"Oh yeah?"

"Oh yeah. When a handsome guy in a tailored suit wanders into your life, rolls up his sleeves to help you paint, then takes you out for drinks and tells you all about his messed-up marriage… Well, that's a guy you don't soon forget."

Handsome? I'm stuck on that one word.

"There was a minute, that night, when I thought I might kiss you."

"Yeah?"

"But your phone rang, and you left and never came back."

I swallow the lump in my throat. "Until now."

She slowly nods. "Until now."

"I sincerely regret taking that call." *On every level.*

Violet leans closer to me, closing the distance between us, and her lips brush against mine. For a moment, I freeze, as if I've forgotten what to do next. And then, like a lightning bolt jolts through me, I remember. I move my lips against hers and moan at their softness. I reach up to clasp my fingers on her neck, pulling her closer, holding her there so I can taste her and feel her and connect with her on a level I never imagined I'd have the privilege to reach.

She feels so good, tastes so good, and when she moans against my mouth, I go lightheaded. I move closer, wrapping my arms around her to pull her tight against me. It's like I'm a teenager again, making out with a beautiful girl in the back row of the movies, learning her, feeling her, tasting her, falling in love with her in the dark.

When she pulls away, pressing her forehead to mine, catching her breath, my mind swims with questions. All I can manage to ask between ragged breaths is, "Why'd you do that?"

"Because I wanted to."

"But… Why?" I groan, frustrated that I can't express myself better. "I'm sorry, Violet. I don't know how to do this anymore."

"Do what? Kiss?"

"Read people. Read signals. Understand what you want."

"I thought I was pretty obvious about what I want."

"But before, you set a clear boundary—"

"And I'd like to move that boundary."

"To where?"

She frowns at me. "Greg, I kissed you because I wanted to kiss you, and I thought you wanted to kiss me too."

"I did. God, I do." I can't leave well enough alone. "But Violet, I'm broken. I'm a mess. And you said you didn't want to be my crutch, or tiptoe around my shattered life—"

"You remember everything about that conversation, don't you?"

"You made an impression." I serve her words back to her.

She chuckles. "Greg, I didn't know you when I said those things, not like I know you now. I was broken, too, then. I mean, I'm still broken, we both are, but… You give me hope, every day, even in all this bleakness. When I wake up in your arms, I know I will have a better day with you in it. I like you, Greg."

I'm stunned. No one has ever said anything so romantic to me before. "I like you, too, Violet."

This time it's me who leans in; it's me who kisses her. I wrap my arms around her, hugging her tight as I savor the taste of her sweet lips. She lets out a little gasp, and I slide my tongue along hers when she lets me in.

The crowd cheers at something in the movie, and we come apart, a bit dazed. I raise my hand to her cheek, caressing her soft skin, and she lets her eyes drift closed, like my touch soothes her. There's an intense power in that. To be the man who can soothe this incredible woman, and I can't imagine a greater honor. I want that desperately; I need it with an intensity that nearly knocks me over. It's terrifying.

Violet reads the change in my expression. "What's the matter?"

I'm afraid to let myself get any closer to you. When I fall in love, I fall hard, and if we keep kissing, I'll fall and never get up again.

But would that be so bad?

"Nothing at all," I say as I kiss her again. And this time I really kiss her. I wrap my arms around her waist and pull her onto my lap. Her skirt teases up her thighs, and I'm instantly, painfully hard.

Violet wraps her arms around my neck, hanging onto me as much as I'm hanging onto her. Her mouth is like heaven, so soft and warm, and I want to taste her for hours. We make out for the entire film, not stopping until the crowd inside starts singing along with "Auld Land Syne." Miss Jewel recruits Sheryl to perform Zuzu's precious moment of the bell ringing and an angel getting its wings.

Violet slides off my lap, and coldness creeps over me now, even in the dank New Orleans heat. She grins as she wipes her lipstick off my face, then clasps my hand and drags me back into the bar.

Sheryl hugs Miss Bea Haven and Miss Jewel, then bounces over to us, her eyes focused on where Violet's hand is clasped with mine. She knows something happened between us. She probably thinks she's the kewpie cupid who brought us together. And maybe she did, a little. She beams at Violet and says, "I'm glad he found you." Then she smacks a kiss on my cheek before saying, "I can't wait to tell every-one!" And with that, she leaves.

"Who's everyone?"

"Uh, our little family in Austin." I start counting people off on my fingers. "Jake, Nicole, Ari, Alex, Tynisha—"

"You count your ex-wife and her new boyfriend as family?"

"Well, yeah, I guess so."

"You just gave me another reason to like you, Greg."

17

As we lock up behind the movie guests, I grow increasingly nervous about my courtyard make-out session with Violet. What does it mean for us? Will we pick up where we left off? Or should I slow down? I don't remember the pace and rules of regular courtship. Kate and I drunkenly jumped into bed the first night we kissed. And with Ari, well, that was a long time ago.

I don't know what's expected of me now. Are we friends with kissing benefits, or are we something more? Will she tell me if I'm something more, or do these things work themselves out naturally?

I'm probably overthinking it. Why am I like this? At work, being analytical was a plus. At play, it's irritating. I need to go with the flow, follow Violet's lead, and enjoy myself along the way.

"Uh oh, the hamster is on its wheel again," she says as she comes in from her shower, joining me on her bed. She curls up to face me, tucking her hands beneath her chin. It's adorable. It makes me want to kiss her. Though tonight, everything she does makes me want to kiss her.

"The hamster?"

"The hamster in your head, running on its little wheel. That's what

I imagine is going on in there when you get that far away look in your eyes."

I laugh.

"What are you thinking about?"

I want to say, "us," but that sounds premature, like suggesting there is an *us* might ruin any possibility of there ever being an *us*.

"Nothing." I can tell she knows it's a lie, but she doesn't push.

"Do you want to know what I'm thinking about?"

"Absolutely."

"I'm thinking about how you took my breath away with a kiss."

Her words leave me breathless too. She licks her lips, and I suck a jagged breath into my lungs. Together, we close the gap between us. She brushes her mouth against mine, and I hiss like her kiss burns.

Her breath tickles when she speaks again. "I'm thinking about how good your touch feels, and how I want your hands on me again."

My hand reaches for her, following her lead. I rest my palm against her neck and ask, "Where's the boundary now?"

She takes my hand in hers and guides it down until I'm clutching her waist. Above the belt. Okay, I can work with that. Then, my hand still in hers, she guides my touch to her breast.

Oh fuck.

I respond like a hungry beast, devouring her mouth while my hand roams. I roll her onto her back so I can get both hands on her, touching, squeezing, caressing. Her breasts are magnificent, so soft except where the strokes of my thumbs harden her nipples.

She breathes the sexiest moan into my mouth, and I'm lost to her. Any hope of sparing myself the fate of another painful heartbreak is gone. From this moment forward, Violet has me—

The irritating sound of a ringing phone jolts us apart.

"It's yours," Violet says.

I roll onto my back with a groan and grasp for my phone on her nightstand. Caller ID tells me the cockblocker is Jake. I answer, "Hey."

"Praise Jesus."

"Since when did you start praising Jesus?" I settle onto an elbow, grinning at Violet.

"Since you landed yourself in the crosshairs of another major hurricane, and it's hit or miss getting a call through."

"*What*?" I sit up a little straighter, the humor gone from my tone.

"Rita."

"Who?"

"Not who, what."

"Jake," I grumble. "What are you talking about?"

"Hurricane fucking Rita! She's bigger than Katrina, and she's headed your way."

The blood in my veins freezes, and everything sort of stops for a second before I get my senses back and say again, "What?"

"Do you not have access to a goddamn radio? Pay attention! Rita is already a Cat-fucking-5 storm, and she's aimed right at Louisiana and Texas."

"You're shittin' me."

"I shit you not."

"Fuck." I frown and look over at Violet. She frowns too. Jake's loud enough that I'm sure she can hear every word he says. She scrambles from the bed, practically running for the door. I follow her out to the kitchen, where she clicks on the transistor radio and arranges the antenna until the sound is clear.

"*Hurricane Rita, a Category 5 storm, expected to make landfall somewhere between Houston and New Orleans on Saturday morning.*"

"Another one?" Paul asks as he walks into the room. Andre follows, and we all stand there listening to the weather report. On the phone, Jake is silent, listening with us, letting the news sink in. The radio announcer lists parishes along the coast issuing evacuation orders. It's difficult to process, absurd really. In my lifetime, New Orleans has never been hit by a storm as large as Katrina, and now to be in the path of another…within a matter of weeks?

Violet chews her fingernails, clearly nervous. Downstairs, someone pounds on the door to the bar like it's a police raid. We all jump, our nerves frayed, and drift into the living area, looking down the stairs toward the bar as if we can see that door from here. Andre grabs a baseball bat and heads downstairs to find out who's trying to get in.

In my ear, Jake coaxes, "You need to come home, brother. Ari is trying to reach Sheryl to tell her the same thing."

Well, speak of the devil, and she appears. I nearly laugh out loud when Andre comes up the stairs with Sheryl behind him.

"She's here," I say to Jake.

"Yeah, I meant to tell you but couldn't get a call through. She's in New Orleans too."

"No, I mean, she's right here standing in front of me."

Sheryl steps into the narrow living room and announces, "There's another hurricane coming."

"We know, precious," Paul says.

To Sheryl, I ask, "Are you planning to leave?"

"My hotel is shutting down. Apparently, all tourists are ordered to evacuate. What are you planning to do?"

She looks at me expectantly, like I'm a tourist too. But my time here has changed me. I'm not a tourist anymore. I've adopted this city as my home, and the people in this room have become my adoptive family. I won't go anywhere without them.

To Paul and Andre, I ask, "Do you have a vehicle? I have room for Violet, but—"

Andre's voice is resolved when he says, "We're staying."

I look at Violet, silently pleading with her.

She smirks. "Welcome to life on the Gulf Coast. There's always another storm."

"This one is stronger than Katrina."

Violet shrugs. "I'm staying, Greg. I'll understand if you want to leave, but I'm not going anywhere. This is my home, and come hell or high water, I'm staying here."

"Violet, we're talking about hell *and* high water."

She smiles at me, but I can see in her eyes she will not budge. And I can hardly blame her. After all the work we've put into this community in the weeks I've been here—and for Violet it's been a lifetime of living here, helping her neighbors, being helped by her neighbors—it will take more than another storm to make her leave. As I consider my options, I realize there's only one: Where she goes, I go. If she stays, I stay.

I turn to Sheryl. "We're staying."

"Are you fucking kidding me?" Jake squawks in my ear.

Still talking to Sheryl, I ask, "Are you driving back to Austin?"

"Hell no. Houston is evacuating too. The roads are a nightmare. I'm heading to the animal shelter in Gonzales."

It's Paul who says, "You're welcome to stay here, honey. We have a couch that Greg's not using. And we're on high ground; Katrina proved that."

Sheryl declines. "Someone's gotta keep the fur babies calm during the storm. I have a very soothing presence."

We laugh, but I think she's serious. She gives hugs all around, and I read her my phone number so we can stay in touch as Rita comes to town.

Once she leaves, I turn my attention back to Jake, preparing myself for him to argue with me. Instead, he says, "Give me the address where you're staying as well as the names, descriptions, and phone numbers of everyone staying with you. In case we need to report you missing with the Red Cross."

It's a sobering thought. But I know it's important for someone to know where we are, so I hand the phone around, and we all give our information to Jake. When the phone returns to me, I say, "That's everyone."

"Okay." He exhales a heavy sigh. "Be smart, be safe, be careful."

"You know me," I say, and oddly, for the first time in too long, I feel like the smart, competent, level-headed Greg I used to be.

When Violet and I return to bed, we've lost any interest in making out, too distracted by what's coming. She curls into my arms and lets me hug her as she tries to sleep. But I can feel the tightness in her body, hear the edginess in her jagged breath, and see stress as she continues to bite her nails. She's having an anxiety response to the news of another storm.

I wish she'd let me take her out of here, but I know it's no use arguing. If I can't evacuate her to keep her safe, then I will do what I can to help her remain safe and calm here. To start, I'll distract her.

"I've never been in a hurricane before." Odd subject to choose, I admit, but perhaps addressing the elephant in the room could help take away some of its power. We can always change the subject.

But she answers, "It's intense. Are you sure you're up for it? There's still time to leave."

"Do you want to leave? I will take you out of here in a heartbeat."

"No. I'm staying."

"Then I'm staying too."

She turns her eyes up to me and holds my gaze for a moment, the silence stretching between us. I think she's measuring my resolve. It's full; my resolve is full, and it's overflowing. Still, to distract her again, I ask, "If you could go somewhere, anywhere, right now with a snap of your fingers, where would you go?"

She smirks and turns her gaze away, settling more comfortably against my chest, and lets out a sigh. "The mountains."

"Oh yeah? Which mountains."

"I don't know. Any mountains. I've never been out of the bayou. I'd love to see the opposite of briny swamp water for a change."

"I grew up in the mountains."

"Right down the road from Dolly Parton, right?"

"Yep."

"What are they like?"

"The Partons?"

She smacks my chest. "The mountains."

I take a deep breath and let it out, picturing my home near the Smoky Mountains. "Tall."

She laughs, and some of her tension uncoils.

"They're beautiful. Full of trees that whisper in the wind. Some days, you can hike up into the clouds, and it's like heaven. It smells like pine, but not the fake scent, the real deal. And in the winter, it snows."

"Do you miss it?"

"Sometimes. Mostly, I miss the snow. Not much of that in Austin."

"Not here either. Though we got a few snowflakes last winter, and it was so quiet, like silence itself fell over the city for those few minutes."

I nod. "The hush of snowfall is probably the thing I miss most about home."

"I'd like to see real snowfall and smell a real pine breeze. It's hard without a car though."

Someday, I'll take you. I almost say it out loud, but it's too soon for talk of *someday*.

"Do you stay through the storms because you don't have a vehicle?" *Because I have a truck, and I will fit all three of you in it, if need be.*

"I stay through the storms because this is my entire world, and to leave it would be to leave a part of myself behind. New Orleans isn't the sort of town you just live in—it's the sort of town that claims a piece of your soul. I can't leave her.

"All those people who had to flee Katrina or who were bussed out from the Dome, and now they can't get back home; I know they're hurting. They're missing a huge piece of themselves. I can't do that. I need to stay."

It's understandable. I've been here for only a few weeks, and I feel connected already. Violet was born and raised here, and this city's energy courses through her veins.

"But I do want to travel. I've always wanted to travel, just not right now."

"Traveling is most exciting when you have a home to return to."

"I'll bet you miss Austin right about now. A little too much excitement in the Big Easy, eh?"

Does she think that's what this is for a me, a bit of excitement before I return home? Have I ever given her any reason to think otherwise?

"No. Austin's not my home anymore."

Violet looks up at me with a glint in her eyes, like that one sentence tells her everything she needs to know. And that's good, because the truth is, Austin hasn't felt like my home for a while now. Sure, people I love are there—Jake, Nicole, the rest of that misfit family—and I technically have a house. But once I sell that house, I'll be homeless, free to go where I want, stay where I want. And the longer I stay in New Orleans with Violet and her family, the longer I want to remain.

Violet nestles tighter against me, and I savor the sensation, the rightness of this connection between us. Every time I hold her, I feel more comfortable about holding her, like we're easing into something, slow and steady and oh so perfect.

"Where all have you been?"

I've forgotten what we were talking about, caught up in the smell of her neck and the softness of her body. I clear my throat and answer, "Everywhere."

"Well, where *exactly* is everywhere? How many continents have you visited?"

"All but Antarctica."

"Really? You've been to Africa?"

"Egypt, South Africa, Morocco, and Kenya."

"Wow."

"Always for work. Someday, I'd like to travel for fun."

"Of all the places you've been, what was your favorite?"

"Iceland."

"Iceland?"

I nod. "It has everything—fire and ice, volcanos and glaciers, black sand beaches and the Northern Lights, these tiny little ponies with emo hair, and tons of sheep."

"Emo hair?"

"Seriously, you have to see them. I took a photo of a horse there, and it looks like an album cover."

She laughs again, a full-throated laugh. I smile at the sound. It's working, my distraction technique. She's stopped chewing her nails.

"There's this one village on a fjord I liked called Seyðisfjörður. I want to go back there."

"Say-dis-fuer-dur."

"See, you're already learning the language."

She chuckles. "What was so special about this village in the fjord?"

"It was quiet. This quaint little town surrounded by mountains, and it's on the east side of the island, so the waters were calm too. It had this gentleness to it that I hadn't experienced before. I want to go back, spend time there, and take a break."

"That sounds lovely."

Squeezing her tight, I want to ask if she'll come with me. Everything inside me is screaming that question, but I hold back.

"If you could go anywhere in the world, where would you go?" I ask her.

She doesn't hesitate, immediately answering, "Rio de Janeiro for Carnival."

I chuckle. "Really, out of everywhere in the world you could go, you choose a larger version of Mardi Gras?"

"Yes! I want to samba," she says and shimmies her hips against me. *Damn, I want to samba too.*

18

This is the most useful I've been in years. Instead of demolition work, which, while important, has a demoralizing effect, this work feels like progress. Fortifying our structures against the coming storm reminds me of the work I did in the early days of my career, back when I loved my job.

I'm hanging off the roof of the theater in a makeshift repelling harness with a guy named Caleb, who's strong and spry and probably into parkour or BASE jumping or something—he gleefully volunteered for this job. We dangle on either side of the neon blade sign over the theater marquee. Violet stands on the ground, hollering encouragement and instructions as we adjust the leaning sign. It came partially unmoored during Katrina, and a strong gust from Rita could rip it down, so we're strapping it to the building.

"On three," I say, and Caleb gives me a thumbs-up with one of the hands he has on the sign. There are two guys on the roof, too, tying straps off there as well. Everyone waits for the count, as I yell, "One, two, three!"

We groan from the effort to heft the sign back toward the building. When it's in the correct position, I signal with a whistle. Caleb and the other guys hold it steady while I fasten the connector of the safety latch. Then they all fasten their ends too.

"You got it!" Violet cheers.

Caleb and I hoot and high-five, then we hang there for a moment, catching our breaths as we stare at the bands of dark, heavy clouds blowing in off the Gulf.

Rita's track has drifted to the west, but they're still forecasting a lot of wind and rain for us. No one's talking about it much, concentrating on the work instead of speculating about the weather, but the dread is palpable in these quiet moments when we have time to look at the sky.

"Gonna rain soon," Caleb says, and I nod. We climb our way back up the ropes to the roof, where our helpers get us over the parapet wall, and we disconnect our harnesses before heading back inside.

I take one final pass to double-check the windows and doors are protected. Satisfied that the theater is as secure as we can make it, we leave through the alley. There, Andre stands, ready to board up the last exit.

In Uncle Sam's shop, Violet is trying to convince Clifton to come stay with us, offering the couch, but he's having none of it. We put fresh batteries in the old man's walkie-talkie and flashlight, make sure he has plenty of water, food, and toilet paper, then board up the windows and doors on his bottom floor. He's Rapunzel in his tower now, trapped until we return.

At Beaux Ballroom, the French doors of the bar and apartment still have the original storm shutters, which are easy to close and latch as we hunker down. It's just the four of us now. Everyone else has gone to their own shelter. We sit for a bit downstairs, watching the television behind the bar. It's déjà vu all over again, staring ceaselessly at a cyclone rotating over the warm waters of the Gulf of Mexico, except this time I'm at the center of it.

Outside, the rain starts in spits, and the wind howls in fits, nothing too dramatic yet, but it's early still. We secure the bar and drag ourselves up to the apartment with heavy feet. There comes a moment in every crisis when there is still time to turn around, to escape whatever terrible fate awaits. That time has passed. All we can do now is settle in for a long, anxious night.

Paul and Andre watch coverage of the storm in the living room. I've seen enough of hurricanes on television, and Violet seems uninterested in that dreadful entertainment, too, so we get cleaned up and retire to her room.

I'm not one of those people who claims to feel storms in my bones, but with this storm, I can feel it. Rita is a presence within us all, a heavy dread weighing us down, a nervous electricity keeping us wired and twitchy.

Violet shivers, and I suspect it's not just Rita affecting her. Katrina left a piece of herself in Violet too. I wrap my arms around her, and she clutches at me, holding tight like she's afraid the storm will take her if she lets go.

Outside, the wind bellows and moans louder. A shrill gust howls through the empty streets, shivering against the shutters and rattling the old windows. The rain comes heavier now, thick lashes that pelt the walls from every direction; intense and fickle, it goes where the wind blows. Strobes of lightning flash and flicker through the striped louvers of the storm shutters, and thunder rumbles the foundation of the city. Somewhere in this squalling tempest glass shatters, and the start of some irregular banging echoes as something comes loose and takes a beating from the storm.

"It's okay. You're safe here. I've got you, Violet." I don't know how safe we are, but my words seem to soothe her. I pull the blankets up tight around us, cocooning us together in some sort of illusion of protection.

Lightning flickers, and another crack of thunder slices through the silence. Violet startles with a yelp then grumbles, "I used to love the rain. I'm going to be so pissed if these storms make me afraid."

"I don't think you're afraid of anything." I brush my fingers across her cheek. "Just jumpy."

Violet smiles and tangles her fingers in my hair, like she's tying herself to me, her anchor in this maelstrom. In a sultry voice that zings straight down my spine, she says, "Give me something else to think about, Greg."

Since Jake's call about Rita cockblocked me a couple of days ago, Violet and I have been too busy with storm prep and storm fret to pick up where we left off, but it's been on my mind constantly. She gazes up at me as she rubs her body against mine, and I know exactly what she needs, what we both need.

I kiss her. It starts soft and simple, but when she moans against my lips, everything changes. Pulling her against me, tangling my body around hers, I take her mouth with deep, slow strokes of my tongue. There is a desperation in my kiss, and in hers, too, like it's the air we breathe, vital to our survival.

The tension loosens from her body, while my body, on the other hand, coils tight, coming to full attention. Scorching fire burns through my veins at the powerful effect she has on me. I'm tense with need but try to ignore the painful throbbing in my stiff cock. This isn't about me. It's about her.

Though, I'm getting as much from this as I'm giving. I can pretend this is some noble cause to help Violet forget the storm that rages around us, but I need it too. Desperately.

I kiss her with every ounce of passion I feel for her, tasting her lips like we have all the time in the world, like nothing else is happening, like it's just us here, connecting. I move my hand to her breast, palming its weight, pinching and rolling her nipple between my fingers. When she gasps into my mouth, I pinch it again, a little tighter.

"God, yes, Greg. More," Violet says as she reaches for her shirt and pulls it off over her head. She's not wearing a bra, and… I'm on her in an instant, my hand clutching one breast while my mouth takes the other. She moans and mewls, and my kisses turn to soft bites, teasing her nipple with my teeth now, the soft bites getting harder as she laces her fingers through my hair and holds me against her.

She takes my free hand in hers and pulls it to her mouth, sucking on one of my fingers. The sensation sends a rush of blood and total fucking madness to my cock. *Fuck. Me.*

I press a second finger against her tongue, while I turn my attention to her other breast, sucking that nipple too. Running my teeth across the excited flesh, I bite. Violet moans and bucks against me. I move an arm beneath her, hugging her close as I lave my tongue down the center of her chest and circle her navel.

"Greg."

Is there anything sexier than the breathy way she says my name?

"I want to move the boundary."

"To where?" I hardly comprehend our words, totally fixated on the softness of her skin.

Violet takes my wet fingers and moves them down her body to press between her legs. "I want to *remove* the boundary."

Oh. Kay. This is happening…fast. We've gone from a breezy flirtation to a whirling hurricane of lust in an instant. I'm frozen, my mind and body unable to work together.

I want her. My body is desperate to strip off the rest of her clothes and press deep inside her right now. But what then? Is this boundary coming down just for tonight, an emergency distraction from the storm, and tomorrow we'll find ourselves in some awkward in-between space? I don't think I could handle that. But if I don't take everything I want from her tonight, will I ever have another opportunity?

Why can't I shut off my brain for one night?

We tried that once with Kate, my brain reminds me. *It didn't end well.*

Violet isn't Kate, I remind my brain.

Holding Violet's gaze, I search for my answers there. Looking for her to assuage my anxiety without me having to give that anxiety a voice. And, incredibly, she does.

There is certainty in her gaze. She knows what she wants, and it's me. I'd expected to see her own anxiety reflected at me—after all, she's talking about breaking her celibacy. But there is no uncertainty in her eyes, only desire, and her heated expression is so sexy.

My hesitation is gone in an instant. I won't deny her. If she needs a distraction, I'll give her the best fucking distraction of her life. But I'll save her chastity for another time. When we cross that boundary, it won't be a hurricane hookup, it won't be a distraction. Sex can wait until after the storm.

But there are plenty of other ways to give her what she needs right now. Focusing my attention on the waist of her sleep shorts, I pull, and she lifts her hips to let me slide them down her thighs and off. Even down here under the tent of bed covers, I can see her clearly, so beautiful in only a pair of lacy purple underwear.

Slowly I kiss my way up one leg while I tickle my fingers up the other. And when I've reached her center, I press my mouth to the lace, planting a kiss there. She bucks and moans, and it's music to my ears, but it's too soon for that.

I kiss my way up her abdomen, plant wet kisses on each breast, and climb back up to take her mouth again. When she moans, I pull away and press my forehead to hers. Tracing two fingers along her bottom lip, I whisper, "Get them wet for me. I'm going to make you come with my fingers first." Then I press them into her mouth.

Violet sucks my fingers between her lips, twirling her tongue around them. When she has my fingers nice and wet, I pull them out and slip my hand beneath the fine purple lace to touch her clit. She gasps, and I take her mouth again, devouring the sounds she makes.

She writhes in my arms, mewling and sighing so sweetly as I touch her and smooth my fingers in circles over that sensitive spot. I pull away to watch as her excitement grows, savoring the sounds she makes and the flutter of her eyelashes. I bring her close to the edge, but never over, enjoying this slow seduction and the desperation in her words as she begs me to make her come.

I could do this for hours and never tire. But Violet vetoes that plan when she reaches down between us, wraps her fingers around mine, and uses my hand to get off. It's hot to feel the force of her touch applied to mine as her hips buck. She arches her back and moves our hands faster. I can feel it coming. She coils tight, arches her back, and spasms in my arms as she soaks my fingers and the fabric of her pretty purple panties.

"So demanding," I tease as I stroke her still, delighting as my touch elicits cute little aftershocks that send her into spasms.

"Yes, I am," Violet agrees. "Now do it again with your mouth."

She spreads her legs, and *damn*, this is hot. I'm pretty sure she's as debauched as me. At least, I hope so.

I like that there is no shyness with her. She knows what she wants, she knows I want what she wants, and she's making it abundantly clear she wants me to give it to her. There is no ambiguity in this, and I love that. I kiss my way down to the lace of her underwear and take a moment to gaze at her. But I can't see enough. I need to see all of her, now. I shove the covers off the bed and settle between her legs. I can see the slick evidence of her desire, and I need to taste her. I get close, letting my hot breath warm her, then press a kiss against her core. She bucks and moans, so tender to my slightest touch.

I can't stand the fabric in my way. Pressing her legs together, I tug them off then dive onto her and take my first taste. Like nectar of the gods, she tastes delicious. I want more, so I take more, moving my hands to cup her ass, and I pull her closer and drink deep of her ambrosia. She's so responsive, stroking my ego with every gasp and moan she makes. She bucks against my face and clutches my hair as I fill her with my fingers and tease my tongue over her clit. Her legs tighten around me, and I can sense when she's going to come again, moving my tongue and fingers harder and faster until she erupts with a scream, which she tries to stifle with a pillow.

Violet is great for my confidence. I just gave this incredible woman two orgasms. I did that. Me. It feels good, some of the most satisfying sex I've ever had, and my dick's not even involved.

I want more. I want to keep her coming for hours, days, forever. So I keep going, eating her out as she rides the waves of another orgasm and another. When she's had enough, she yanks my hair until I move back up her body to kiss her. She licks into my mouth as if the taste of herself on my lips is what she craves.

When she teases her fingers over my chest to the waist of my athletic shorts, I consider stopping her, but there is nothing in me that wants to stop this. My hesitation is fleeting and dies with a whimper when she takes my cock in her hand and strokes me. *Oh. God.* I choke as I huff and try not to come right then and there.

She sits up on her knees, and it's the first time I'm really seeing her naked. I freeze and stare at her like I'm some great artist, preserving her image on the canvas in my mind. If I'd thought she was beautiful before, I've run out of words to describe what she looks like to me now: goddess-like, a fantasy my mere mortal eyes can hardly behold.

I reach for her, wanting another taste of those tits, but she pushes me onto my back and tugs my shorts off. She takes a moment to drink in the sight of me, and I wonder how long it's been since she had a man naked in this bed. I'm honored that I'm the one she's chosen to break celibacy for—even if it is just a means to an end, a distraction from the storm now howling hauntingly through the eaves, pelting the roof tiles, and clattering the shutters against the glass of her French doors.

Violet crawls onto all fours, moving down my body, and sucks my cock deep. My whole body seizes up in some strange combination of agony and ecstasy. I wouldn't have called myself celibate, but it's been a while for me too. I haven't even jerked off since New York, and the feeling of Violet's soft lips and hot mouth on me, her throat tightening when she swallows around my length, makes me nearly come apart. I hold on, not wanting this to end anytime soon.

But, damn, she's good at giving head. She can take all of me, deep to the back of her throat, and when I start to move my hips and fuck her mouth, she lets me. I beg her when she pulls away, teasing my balls with her tongue, then thank her when she sucks me in again. She watches me watching her, her eyes twinkling with humor as she tortures me at the edge, pulling back before I fall over.

Finally, after what feels like hours of her exquisite torment, she takes me in her hand and asks, "Do you want to come?"

"Yes," I pant.

"Beg."

"Ah God, please Violet, make me come."

"Tell me what you want me to do."

"Suck me deep. I want to fill your throat. I want you to swallow it all."

She grins, and then she does exactly what I've asked. She sucks me deep and holds me there, swallowing so her throat tightens all around my cock, and I can't hold on. I come, hard, as her tongue coaxes more out of me. And she swallows every drop.

I am helpless to her now, spent and vulnerable and desperate for more. Sex has never been as good as that blow job. I will do anything she asks for more of that. She must be reading my thoughts because her smile is cocky as she settles on the pillow beside me.

I take her in my arms, hugging her close. Still not able to form words, I wonder if I can convey my emotions with touch. I stroke her cheek and kiss her. Now it's me who tastes myself on her tongue, and I like how our flavors blend together in our mouths.

I like everything in this moment. It's bliss, and nothing else matters. We've forgotten the storm. We hardly notice its impotent rage, swirling around us as we connect on this new level.

There's a knock at the bedroom door, and from the other side Paul says, "I've left a big box of condoms outside your door, honey pies. Sounds like you might need them."

Violet bursts into laughter. "Thanks, love."

When he walks away, she hops up naked and opens the door to collect our gift. She returns and drops the box labeled "Condiments" between us on the bed. I'm truly in awe at the massive assortment of individually wrapped glow-in-the-dark and flavored condoms.

"They put these in the bathroom dispensers downstairs," Violet explains.

Oh right, that makes sense.

Violet reaches into the box and pulls out something with an impressive amount of ribbing, but I hesitate. I want to tell myself that my hesitation is some noble protection of her chastity vow, but really, it's my own. With the blood back in my brain, I'm thinking again. And I'm afraid that taking this any further tonight will be a step too far. What if I fall in love with her while I make love to her, then what? Will she feel the same way? If she does, then what? And if she doesn't…? I set my hand on top of hers and say the words I dread saying, "Can we wait for that?"

"Wait for what?"

"Sex. Can we wait until it's more than just a distraction from the hurricane?"

She frowns. "Greg, you're not a distraction. Is that what you think?"

Well, yes. Or have I yet again missed some social cue? Regardless, I need to say this, so she completely understands. "I have strong feelings for you, Violet, and I've worked hard to shut off the sexual component of those feelings because you expressed a desire to remain just friends. If we change that now, if I let myself feel those feelings for you…I'm going to fall in love with you. It's in my nature. I can't do casual. I tried once and failed at it. If we're going to be together, I need it to be more than a distraction."

Violet looks oddly touched by my awkward admission. She rests her palm against my cheek and smiles. "Yes, we can wait."

When she kisses me, there's so much loaded into that kiss, so much emotion shared between us. It's then I realize my mistake. Sex isn't the boundary that will stop me from falling in love with her. I've already fallen.

19

I stir awake to the sound of Clifton's voice, staticky as it comes over the walkie-talkie on the kitchen table. "Uncle Sam to Eagle's Nest, come in Eagle's Nest."

"The eagle has landed. How are you holding up out there, Clifton?" asks Paul.

I stretch and blink my eyes open to the spiral of hot pink chiffon overhead, trying to reorient myself. Oh right, there's a hurricane. Or is it over? Between orgasms and sleep last night, Violet and I lost track of the storm. Rita could have blown the roof off, and we wouldn't have noticed.

I roll to my side so I can stare at Violet, gloriously naked and curled against me. I try not to wake her as I stroke my palm down her side, listening for some sign of the storm outside. But it's quiet, having gone from a fury to a flutter, and all I can hear is the dribble of water from the eaves of the building.

"Good morning." Violet stretches beside me. She rolls onto her back, and my hand slides across to her breast. I take the opportunity to squeeze, and she giggles like she's ticklish. She wasn't ticklish last night. With a growl, I fall across her, kissing her awake. Someone pounds on the bedroom door, and we groan as we come apart.

"What?" Violet asks.

"Good morning to you, too, love birds. I'm here to inform you that Uncle Sam is reporting blue skies to our south. He wonders if we might swing by with food and a means to extricate him from his locked tower."

We're already out of bed and tugging on our clothes before Paul finishes talking. The storm has passed, and it's back to normal life again—whatever "normal" is in this place. Once dressed, Violet opens her French doors and unlatches the shutters to push them aside. It's still cloudy here, but Clifton has a better view of what's coming, and it sounds like the storm's outer bands have passed us.

We head into the kitchen, where Paul and Andre stare knowingly, salacious smirks on their faces. "You two enjoy yourselves last night?" Paul winks.

"I'm sure my cousin does not want me to answer that question," Violet responds.

"I'm sure I don't." Andre agrees.

"Well, I do." Paul sits down and crosses his legs, nursing his coffee as he readies himself for gossip. "Girl, tell me everything. I want all the details. Does he have a nice dick?"

"I'm standing right here," I grumble.

"Yes, honey, but you're too shy to tell me about your dick," Paul explains.

"I, for one, do not want to know anything about his dick," Andre chimes in.

"Thank you," I say to Andre.

He turns and scowls at me. "Oh, don't you thank me. You're fucking my cousin, young man. Don't be thanking me."

"We're not fucking," Violet weighs in. And while that's technically true in a vanilla heterosexual sort of way, her audience this morning is not buying it.

"Well, what I heard last night did not sound like the buzz of your vagina monologue, sister, so spill it," Paul demands.

"Will you all *please* stop talking about my baby cousin's vagina and the boy who wants to get inside it? I am trying to cook some eggs over here, and I am struggling," Andre pleads.

"Fine." Paul pouts, then stage-whispers to Violet, "We'll talk later."

"No, we won't."

Thankfully, my phone rings. I dart back into Violet's bedroom; it's my guardian angel, saving me again. I answer Jake's call with a smile in my voice. "Blue skies and still alive, brother."

"Excellent news!"

"Yeah, I think it mostly missed us. We got some wind and a lot of rain, which we didn't need. Violet and I are about to head out and see how the theater and the rest of the city fared. Have you heard from Sheryl? How'd she do hunkered down with the animals at the shelter?"

"Nicole talked to her. Turns out the 'shelter' is a giant horse barn, go figure, but she and the animals are safe and sound."

I nod. "And how are you? How's Nicole and the baby?"

"All systems go."

"What is she, the USS Enterprise?"

Jake fakes a Scottish accent when he ad-libs from *Star Trek*: "She can't take much more, Captain."

In the background, Nicole laughs and hollers, "Dork."

Jake gets a bit more serious. "How about you? Still stone-cold sober?"

"I am. Thought living at a bar would be a problem, but after announcing my sobriety within a millisecond of walking in the door, they've been great supporters."

"You live in a bar?"

"Above it."

"I'd like to take a quick moment to point out the number of times you've said things like 'we' and 'us,' and now you're talking about the place you're staying as where you 'live.' "

"What's your point?"

"No point, just an observation." Jake pauses, but only for a moment before adding, "But it sounds like you're planning to stay."

"Hmm." That's all I can manage, though Jake's right: I have mentally moved in here.

When I came to New Orleans, I don't think I consciously considered whether the trip would be temporary or permanent, but obviously it has to be one or the other. In all my time here, I've never once considered returning to Austin. I told Violet that Austin isn't my home anymore, but does that mean New Orleans is? Maybe I need to slow down, take a breath, and ask Violet if she wants me around for the long haul. Lending me half her bed while I'm here to help with Katrina cleanup is one thing; moving in permanently requires further conversation.

"Anything you need to tell me?" he pries.

"Not at the moment," I answer.

"If you say so."

"I'll call you later. Heading over to the theater now. Love ya."

"Ditto. Stay safe."

"Let's go," Violet says to me as soon as I return to the kitchen. "Paul's got his *Gossip Girl* hat on today. He's driving me crazy." She shoves a hot thermos into my hands and grabs a bag of food as she heads to the door, expecting me to follow. I grab my tool belt and do exactly that.

"XOXO," Paul says and blows me a kiss as we leave.

Out on the street, Jake's truck is right where I left it—against the curb in front of the bar. Everything is soaked from the downpour. One shop has a torn awning, and another suffers a pair of loose shutters, but otherwise the area is unscathed.

I toss my tool belt in the back, and we head over to Uncle Sam's corner, driving slowly to scout for damage and flooding along the way. By the time we reach our destination, we're feeling cautiously optimistic. This area, which had been submerged under four feet of water post-Katrina, is mercifully dry. Puddles collect in the potholes, but it's nothing a pair of sturdy boots can't surmount.

We were lucky with this one. *There's that "we" again.*

Clifton sees us coming and waves from the roof. I strap on my tool belt and use my cordless drill to back out the screws we used to seal Uncle Sam's front door with plywood. While I'm working, Violet hollers, "How's it look from up there?"

"Drier than the last one!" Clifton states the obvious.

I get the plywood off the door, and Violet helps me carry it to the back of the shop before we head up the stairs to join Clifton on the roof.

He's happy to see us, especially when Violet hands him the thermos of hot coffee and container of eggs and boudin Andre made. He shoves his binoculars at me as he settles onto the one chair he's brought to the roof—we'd cleared off the pop-up tent and the rest of his rooftop gear before Rita—and tucks into his meal.

I scan the horizon, looking for any signs of levee breaches or other distress in the city. There is some helicopter activity to the east, but the area immediately around us is remarkably dry.

Between bites, Clifton says, "It's about the same as it was before. But for a while there, once the rain and wind let up and before the helicopters took to the air, it was too quiet."

Violet and I both nod.

"When I retired from the force, I said I was doing it for the peace and quiet. But you can be damn sure this ain't what I meant. Never thought of myself as much of a people person till all the people up and left. Now I'm talking to myself most days just to hear a voice. It's like the whole city went and died on me. I miss its life."

From the edge of the building, I'm inspired to speak. "The quiet is its own sort of being. Like a ghost, it haunts you."

Violet and Clifton stare at me, curious to see where I'm going with this.

"A few months ago, I was in New York, standing on a balcony on the thirty-fifth floor, and all I could hear was the wind. But after a while, I couldn't even hear that anymore. It was just silent, like the silence was eating away at…everything."

"That's dreary," Clifton gestures at me with his fork, speaking to Violet, "maybe you should get him away from the edge of the roof."

I cringe, regretting every word I've said. Oversharing 101: that was it. I could overshare some more, explain that a jump from this height is unlikely to kill me, but that hardly seems helpful. I force out a frail laugh. "I'm fine. Just maudlin. But…I have hope too. People will come back, Clifton. I have faith in this place. New Orleans is a city that comes back swinging."

Clifton chuckles and fills his mouth with more food. Violet eyes me with concern, but it's clear she's saving her thoughts for when we're alone. Right now, she turns to Clifton and tries to convince him to come stay with us. "It's not quiet over at Beaux. We have musical theater most nights."

Clifton waves her away. "Paul told me what you two been gettin' up to. If I come stay, am I gonna have to listen to you humping all night?"

Violet and I glance at each other. "Probably," I say. "Yes," says Violet at the same time.

Clifton's lips quirk into a smile. "Think I might prefer the quiet."

"Tell me about the balcony," Violet says the minute we return to Beaux. Paul and Andre are down at the bar with our friends and neighbors, setting up for tonight's showing of *It's a Wonderful Life* after the hurricane hiatus. Violet and I have the apartment to ourselves. We settle at the kitchen table and eat our breakfast. "When you first arrived, you mentioned you'd had suicidal thoughts, but will you tell me the details now?"

I swallow the bite I'm chewing, using the time to collect my thoughts. I hate having to tell her this stuff, but if the thing we're exploring is actually a *thing*, then she needs to know it all.

"I hit rock bottom in a lot of ways," I start, and then I tell Violet everything—every detail, every emotion, every mistake and shitty word and deed.

When I'm through, she considers, letting it all sink in. "Are you still at rock bottom?"

"No. Not even close." I'm not sure how to articulate this, but I try. "Being here…helping, it's like I have a purpose. A reason for being. A reason to live. I don't mean to suggest that *you* give me a reason to live —I don't want to lay that heavy burden on you. If you reject me, it's not like I'm going to kill myself. Feel free to reject me." *Uh.* "I mean that, in the time I've been here, I've felt like I'm doing something good. I'm helping to build something bigger than me. And I guess I need that."

Violet listens intently, then asks, "Do you know what I love about you, Greg?"

Love?

"Your honesty. You're oddly blunt, and it's incredibly refreshing."

Okay. Cool. But…love? That's a hell of a word for her to choose in that moment. I don't want to read too much into it, but she could have said "like" just as easily. Same number of letters, equal amount of effort. She chose "love" though. Why?

"You talk a lot about what you need, Greg, but what do you want?" Violet asks.

I consider her question. Since I arrived in New Orleans, I haven't given much thought to what I want. *Want* feels like a luxury in this place, like air-conditioning and hot showers. I'm just glad to have what I need, and it would be greedy to want for more. But would it hurt to consider what I want?

Well, I want to stay and help Violet get the theater up and running.

I want to stay and help Violet.

I want to stay with Violet.

I want Violet.

"Uh oh, the hamster's on his wheel again. I'm going to have to name that hamster in your head."

"My head hamster's name is Herman."

Violet laughs, and I mean she really laughs. It reminds me of the way she laughed back in December, before the storm. God, I love that sound. Her eyes twinkle, and her smile warms her whole face.

"I want you," I say, giving a voice to every ounce of longing built up inside me.

Violet surprises me when she stands from the table, her food forgotten, her chair scraping loudly across the floor. She comes to my corner of the table, and I push back in my chair like I'm going to stand, too, but she sits on me, straddling my lap. Clasping my face in her hands, she commands, "Then take what you want, Greg."

I do. I take her with a kiss. She gives me exactly what I want when her sweet lips part for me. Our hot breaths meet, the kiss goes deeper, and her tongue dances with mine as her fingers tangle in my hair.

What were we talking about? I can't remember. All that's in my head now is the word "want" shouting on repeat from the prehistoric part of my brain. I *want* this. I *want* more. I *want* everything. Clasping my hands on Violet's ass, I stand and carry her to the bedroom, kicking the door shut with the heel of my boot.

"That's my boy," Violet says in a voice that practically purrs. "Take what you want. I want it too." She spears her fingernails through my hair, scraping my scalp, and I growl like an animal.

I push through the chiffon and drop us both onto her bed, taking her mouth again as my hands reach for her clothes, desperate to get her out of them. She helps, stripping off her shirt and then pulling mine off too. I untangle myself from her legs to stand long enough to get out of my jeans, and Violet yanks her own off.

When we're naked, I stand and stare at her. Violet's body is a masterpiece of fine art. The soft weight of her breasts, tipped by dark, dusky points I want to tease with my tongue, swaying enticingly with every movement she makes; the round flare of her hips calling to my hands to caress; the little triangle of curls like an arrow guiding me to where I need to be.

She gives me a wicked grin and spreads her legs in invitation. What a gorgeous sight. I crawl up the length of her body, prowling like a predator, and settle my weight in the valley where she's welcomed me.

I take her mouth again, but this time I slow everything way down. As much as I want to tear it up with her, this will be our first time, and I need it to be special. We can get down to the dirty, hardcore fucking next time—God, I hope there will be a next time—but right now, I want to make love with her.

Clutching her tight, desperate for everything she's giving me, I close any space between us and kiss her senseless. She feels perfect against me, the curve of her breasts smashed against my chest, her thighs wrapped around mine, squeezing. But before I can get too comfortable in this position, she pushes against my chest, and to my surprise, rolls me onto my back.

She sits on top of me, and the view is exquisite. I could lie here and stare at her for hours, days, a lifetime. But I have other priorities right now. I touch her everywhere. Stroking my hands up her thighs, I clutch her hips and grind my stiff cock against her warm, wet center until we're both groaning from the sensation. Still moving underneath her, teasing her clit so she gasps and arches her back, I caress the curves of her ass and tickle my fingers up her spine, guiding her down to me. When she's within reach, I clutch the back of her head and pull her down for a kiss, flexing my fingers to hold her tighter as I take the kiss deeper.

But she has her own ideas. Taking her mouth away, she kisses down my body as she slinks lower. I brace myself for what I know is coming. She branded me with her hot mouth during the hurricane, and I'm practically hyperventilating now as she teases closer to my cock, planting soft kisses down my chest and abdomen.

Her tongue slides over the head and along the ridge of my cock; I groan, and the sensation sends a shiver through me. She swallows me whole, and I yell out, relieved the house is empty. She cups my balls as she does it again, and I have to stop her, or this will end before her celibacy does.

As gently as I can, considering my desperation, I pull her back up and push her onto her back, taking my turn to linger kisses over the swell of her breasts and her soft abdomen. At her core, I tickle her clit with my tongue before I take a taste. She moans and spreads her legs wider for me. I settle in for a feast, tasting and teasing.

Violet twists her upper body to the edge of the bed and grabs the box of "condiments" from the floor. Gasping for breath now, so close to coming, she blindly pulls a condom out and drops the box back toward the floor. It lands on its side, and condoms spill everywhere as I push my fingers inside her and tickle her clit with my tongue. She comes with a gasp and a cry, twisting all around me.

There is nothing better than bringing this woman to orgasm. She's so beautiful when she lets go and lets herself feel it. I glance at the mess we've made of the floor, condom wrappers everywhere, and grab the one she's placed on her abdomen.

"Strawberry Sundae flavored, *and* it's vegan," I inform her.

She opens one eye and then the other, and a wicked grin slides across her face. She comes up onto her elbows, then sits up with me as we stare at the condom between us. I don't make any move to open the package or wear it. I'll let Violet pace this. I want to be certain she's ready to end her celibacy with me; there can't be any ambiguity on that matter.

Violet takes the wrapper and tears it open, pulling out the little latex strawberry sundae, and licks the tip. "Hmm, not as good as the real thing."

I groan when her hands grab my cock, and she carefully rolls the condom on. Once she has a hold of me, she doesn't let me go, pulling me closer to her by my leash. She brings my cock to her entrance as I kneel between her legs, and from there I take over, pressing forward, feeling her warmth envelop me, inch by inch. She gasps and arches her back as she takes me in, making such sexy sounds.

When we are fully connected, I stop and revel in the sensations of her: the heat, the soft grip, the way her body flushes and her breasts rise and fall with her breath, her little gasps as she shifts her hips to feel me fill her, like she's coming to remember what this feels like.

It takes me a moment to remember, too, but this feels different. This isn't just sex and breaking the edge of celibacy. This is deeper; this is intimacy. I feel as close to her emotionally as I am to her physically. She hasn't just taken me inside her. I've taken her inside me too; she's a part of me now. It's scary but exhilarating at the same time.

After a moment, I move, sliding almost all the way out and then easing back inside. Violet moans, and her back arches up off the bed. Balancing on my knuckles, I do it again, reveling in the agonizing ecstasy as I tease us both with the slow build. I'm the one moaning now; she feels so good, soft, warm, wet, and essential.

Violet wraps her arms and legs around me, pulling my weight down onto her, my cock slipping even deeper inside her. Into my ear she whispers, "Greg, take what you want."

I am. She's what I want. This place right here—this is where I want to be. I'm obsessed with Violet, desperate for her, perfectly happy with her. So, I take. I take everything she'll give me. I move inside her, groaning with the sensation of the friction between us. She moans and presses her breasts up against me. I curl my back so I can take one of her nipples into my mouth, sucking and fucking and taking, taking, taking.

My breath catches in my lungs as I move inside her, so deep in the blissful warmth of her body, diving even deeper into the dark pools of her eyes. When I move, she moves with me. We dance together, and we're better together here than we are on our feet. It's incredible, a symbiotic connection I didn't know I was missing.

Violet is taking what she wants now, too, and pushes me off her and onto my back. Then she mounts and rides me. I give it all to her. Anything she wants from me—she can have it. That's what I want: for her to take me, all of me, completely.

I'm in awe. She's the most beautiful sight I've ever seen. Last night, a storm raged all around us, but today this woman is a force of nature like none other. Her power and splendor captivate me.

This is too much for any ordinary man to take, and I'm going to come soon. Desperate for her to lead the way, I grab her ass and slam my body up to meet hers. She gasps and purrs and matches my rhythm with her own, arching her back to let out the sexiest moan. I love the sounds of our union, flesh meeting overheated flesh as we break out into a sweat, her moans and gasps coming with each thrust.

We both take now, moving in a desperate frenzy. I can feel her ecstasy build; I can see it on her face, the way her lips stretch taut with her gasps, and her pupils turn her eyes blacker than night when they dilate. She claws her nails into my chest as I reach between us, playing with her clit while she rides me deep and hard.

That's what she needs, and she takes it as she goes over the edge with a gasp, saying, "Oh God, Greg." Her body spasms around me, and I breathe it in, inhaling that ecstasy inside me, consuming it, taking. When I orgasm, I shout so loud I think it rattles the windows. Unable to stop myself, unable to do anything but give myself over to the power of this woman, I pound up into her one last time and collapse, sprawling across the bed, exhausted.

Violet crumples on top of me, and I weakly clutch her in my arms as I catch my breath. She brushes some of my hair out of the way and thumps my forehead. "How's Herman the head hamster doing?"

"Dazed and confused," I say with a sigh, so content I can hardly move. But I manage to hug her a little tighter. Slowly, my mind comes back online—Herman spinning his little wheel—and I start to wonder if I've made a mistake, if this was too much, too far, too soon. I'm afraid to ask, but I need to know. "Are you okay? Did I—?"

"Gregory… What's your middle name?"

"Christopher."

"Gregory Christopher Hendricks, if we're going to make this a thing, I'm going to need you to quit that shit."

"What shit?"

"All the apologies and 'woe is me' shit. Constantly worrying you've overstepped some boundary I removed long ago. It's tiresome, so stop it. All you've done is taken what was freely given."

I'm stunned.

"I know you think you're a burden. You're not."

"But—"

"Let me finish." She shifts off me and onto an elbow at my side, looking me in the eyes as she works through her rant. "I've had it with this broken-boy crap of yours. You're not broken, Greg. You're bent, sure, but you're straightening yourself out. And you're not a burden."

She touches my cheek, maybe to add a gentle element to this strange postcoital conversation.

"You seem to appreciate my forthrightness, so I'm going to be real fucking forthright right now. I like you. No caveats, no buts. I like you, Greg, and I like having you around. I like looking at your handsome face and your sexy body. I really like having sex with you, and I want to do it again as soon as you're ready to go. But more than that, you're funny and kind and handy and smart. You have a good head and a strong heart, and I don't know what your plans are going forward, but I won't mind if your plans include me."

"They do. They are. I mean, I don't have any plans—it's only you. You're my plans." I'm not making much sense, but I can tell Violet understands me. And, God, that's refreshing. No one has ever understood me the way she does. I want to hold onto her and never let her go. I'm already hard for her again, and my hands can't help but smooth across her body toward my favorite parts of her.

That's when my phone rings.

20

It's Mom. I sit up in the bed and grab the sheets, draping them over my lap, feeling way too naked to talk to my mother. Violet follows my lead, covering her nudity too. It's a thoughtful gesture.

I update Mom that Rita has passed us by and we're okay. Noticing as I go that I'm saying "we," "us," and "our" again. It's becoming habit. I look over at Violet, ready to tell my mom all about her.

"That's good. Listen, honey, I'm afraid I have some bad news." Mom takes a deep breath and lets it out. My mind scatters like marbles on the floor, panic rushing through me. I know what she's going to say before she says it. "Your Grandma Millie passed away. She went peacefully in her sleep last night. I went to wake her this morning, and she was gone."

I'm swamped with sorrow and concerned about Mom having to find her. "Are *you* okay?"

"I'm okay, and thank you for asking. It's been a sad morning, but I know she's in a better place now. She's with your grandpa again. That's what she wanted. But it's hard, of course."

"How is Dad handling it?" He's an orphan now, like Jake. How strange that must feel. The thought of losing my parents brings tears to my eyes, and I wipe them away.

"Oh. Well, you know him."

I do. Dad's always been one of those stoic sorts of men who never cry, never show the cracks in their strength. And here I am, the opposite, my strength covered in fissures and seams where I broke into pieces and had to put myself back together again. My brother, Matt, is like our dad in that way. Until recently, I thought I was too.

"He's talking with his brothers now. They're heading over to the funeral home later this afternoon to start planning the service."

"When will it be?"

"I know you're busy down in New Orleans"—I nearly chuckle at the idea of being *busy* in New Orleans when I glance at my lap and over at Violet—"but we were hoping you'd be able to attend the service on Monday."

"Mom, of course I'll be there." It stings that she thinks I'd miss it. Have I been so self-centered my family can't count on me anymore? "I have Jake's truck, and I can be in Knoxville by lunch tomorrow. Help you guys organize things."

"Oh, Greg, that would be wonderful. It will do your dad good to have his boys back home. Which reminds me, I need to call your brother. Will you reach out to Jake?"

"Yes, of course."

"And…" My mom pauses, lets out a breath. "I know Ari was close to Millie, but I'll leave the decision in your hands if you want to invite her or not."

"Oh. Okay." Oddly, I'd assumed Ari would attend, but of course everything's different now. "Yes, I'll let her know too."

When I hang up the phone, I look over at Violet and gaze into the depths of her obsidian eyes. She reaches for me, lacing her fingers through mine and squeezing my hand. It's so sweet it pitches the crooked floor of my mind once again, scattering my marbles everywhere. I lie down and pull her with me, wrapping her in my arms as I stare up at the constellation of pink chiffon overhead.

"Who died?" she asks in a whisper.

"My grandmother."

"I'm so sorry, Greg." She strokes my bare chest.

I take a deep breath and start telling her about my family as I trace little patterns on her back. "My Grandpa Chuck died less than a year ago, and now Grandma Millie's gone too. They were together for seventy-one years. Can you imagine?"

"That's beautiful."

"They were so in love. Always dancing together, even in their nineties. They'd get up and bust out a foxtrot if the mood was right. And they laughed together so much." I choke up a little, the reality of loss finally starting to sink in. "And now…they sort of died together too."

"I read about that once. Couples who've been together a long time will often die close together. Like they can't live without each other." Violet pulls away and grimaces at me. "I'm sorry. That's morbid, isn't it?"

I shake my head. "I think it's kind of romantic, like a geriatric Romeo and Juliet."

Violet grins. I kiss her and hug her tight, and before I think too much about it, I ask, "Will you come with me?"

She seems surprised, and I wonder if I should backtrack, rescind my invitation. Maybe this is moving too fast. I mean, Violet and I just had sex, which is pretty intimate. But inviting a woman to a family member's funeral is a whole other level of intimacy. I've probably violated some postcoital protocol, but the etiquette of fucking and funerals is a mystery to me.

"Yes."

"Really?"

She climbs out of bed. "Yes, Greg, I'll go with you. I'll pack while you make your phone calls. Remind your wife to pack a suit for you."

Well, that's an odd sentence, isn't it?

"She doesn't have a key to the house anymore, but Jake does," I say more to myself than Violet as she yanks a suitcase down from the top of her closet. I'm stunned by her get-up-and-go energy as she dumps clothing and about two dozen condoms—plucking them from where they're scattered all over the floor—into her bag. She collects my duffel from the corner and starts packing my clothes as well.

While she does that, I dial Jake to deliver the news. He takes it well; we all knew this was coming. And he's quick to get off the phone so he can rearrange his schedule and book a flight to Tennessee. Next, I call Ari. Violet has finished packing and gotten dressed, so she heads downstairs to update Andre and Paul while I talk to my wife. One-handed, I tug on the clothing Violet laid out for me while the phone rings.

"Greg?" Ari answers.

"Hey, I um… Listen, Granny Millie died."

"Oh God, I'm so sorry."

I give her a moment to process. "The funeral is going to be on Monday. I don't know the exact details and times yet."

"Is it okay if I go?"

"Of course it's okay. That's why I'm calling." Despite everything, Ari is still family. Sure, legally, that will soon change. But between our Island-of-Misfit-Toys "family" in Austin and over a decade of shared history, we're family, and we always will be.

"Okay. Is it okay if I bring Alex?"

It's surreal that my wife is asking for permission to bring her boyfriend to my grandma's funeral. "Yes, it's fine. He can meet the family."

Surprisingly, it really is fine. Alex is a part of our family now too. Plus, apparently this is the perfect opportunity for everyone to bring their new loves home to meet the family. Jake is bringing Nicole too. Losing Millie is a sad occasion, but in a way, I think it's exactly what Granny Millie would have wanted, to bring everyone together.

Ari and I sit in the silence that stretches between us for a moment before she says again, "I'm sorry, Greg."

I know she means about Grandma Millie dying, but she's also probably saying that about, well, everything. And for the first time, I mean it when I say, "It's okay."

I check the time on my phone and say to Ari, "Well, I need to go. We're about to head out."

"*We?*" There's a sense of humor in Ari's question.

I let the smirk on my face color the tone of my voice when I say, "Yep. We'll see you soon."

Once I've hung up and finished dressing, I step into the kitchen, where Violet and the guys are packing up food for the road and filling a pair of travel mugs with coffee.

"Sweet Vee, are you sure you're ready for this?" Andre asks.

Violet frowns at her cousin. "Yes."

"To meet his family."

She nods.

"His *white* family."

That catches my attention. I respond defensively, saying, "They aren't like that."

Andre cants his head at me. "Everyone *thinks* their family isn't like that until it's *Guess Who's Coming to Dinner*."

"Dre, stop. I'm going," Violet says, and the tone of her voice brooks no argument.

A silent pall hangs heavy in the air between us as Violet continues to pack snacks for the road. There's a wariness in her eyes, the kind of exhaustion that comes from a lifetime of living in America as a Black woman.

I can only imagine what she's feeling. During my travels, there were parts of Asia and Africa where I was the only white person in a room. It's a strange experience, no doubt. But I never felt unsafe or unwelcome. The same cannot be said for the experience of Black people in white America. I hope she knows she can trust that I wouldn't take her into an unsafe situation. Though, maybe my definition of what's "safe" is different from hers.

I open my mouth to offer her a way out of this situation. But the look on her face tells me that rescinding my invitation would be an insult. She's the one to speak next, tossing some protein bars into a plastic sack as she asks, "You ready to hit the road?"

"I am."

"Goodbye, darlings! Tell Dolly I said hi," Paul says as he leans in and brushes us with hugs and air-kisses.

Andre embraces his cousin and whispers, "Be careful, baby girl," in her ear, then squeezes my shoulder, hard, silently warning me to keep her safe. Then, in a kind voice he says, "I'm sorry about your granny, Greg."

I follow Violet, who clasps my hand in hers and leads me down to the courtyard and out to the truck.

We don't have enough gas to run the air conditioner, so we roll the windows down and let the hot breeze whirl through the truck cab as I get us onto I-10. The sun blazes overhead, baking the roads and evaporating most of the Rita rainfall as we move through the city toward the bayou out east.

The sights out here are devastating. Terrible thoughts echo through my head like the obnoxious voice of an overly cheery tragedy tour guide. *If we look to our right, we can see the skeletal remains of amusement park roller coasters left for dead. And on our left, these rotting homes steeped in toxic floodwater for weeks represent the death of the American Dream. Don't forget to buy a commemorative Katrina shot glass in the gift shop on your way out. All proceeds go to somewhere else.*

At Lake Pontchartrain, we're detoured onto a little, old two-lane bridge, and to our right we see toppled remains of the interstate bridge. In some cases, the roadway appears to have shifted sideways. In others, it's collapsed into a series of chipped concrete slabs leaning like boat ramps out of the water to the low abutments they once sat atop.

"I wonder why that bridge collapsed and this one's fine?" Violet asks as she crosses her ankles on the dashboard and twirls a curl of her hair around her fingers.

"Hard to guess," I say, though I posit a few theories. "Could have been wave activity from the storm surge, wind shear between the surface of the water and the bottom of the bridge, faulty construction material or design—"

Violet laughs, and the sound whips around me with the whistle of the wind. "Oh yeah, I almost forgot you're an engineer."

"Sorry."

"Don't apologize. It's cute."

Cute. I smile.

For the next several miles, Violet peppers me with questions about the flood, the levees and pumps, and the engineering faults that failed New Orleans. I answer gladly, happy to entertain her with science as we roll across the long expanse of bridge into Slidell and meet up with I-59 to head into Mississippi.

Only then do we see gas stations with fuel at the pumps. I fill up the tank for the first time in weeks while Violet runs inside to the restroom. When she returns, she has a road atlas and a highlighter. She traces a line over our route as she kicks her sandals off again and stretches her feet across the dashboard, seeming to enjoy the drive. Now that we have AC again, I enjoy it too.

I've always loved traveling. Going to somewhere strange and new is exhilarating. And the farther we travel from the coast, the more the world functions as normal, which feels strange and new to us. Violet talks for a while, asking me questions about my family and friends and the places I've been. When we cross from Mississippi into Alabama, she beams at me. "I've never been to Alabama before."

"The first of many *firsts*." I want to take her everywhere; I want to share the world with her.

Strip malls and kudzu-covered trees smear past the windows, and the shadows grow long as we make our way through the state. The sun sets on us in Birmingham, and we stop for the night.

Violet insists any old roadside motel will do, but I want Violet's first night in a new state to be something special, so I head downtown to a historic hotel and rent us a room near the top.

I hug Violet from behind as she stands at the window, staring out at the view. The city's twinkling lights are beautiful from this vantage point, and Violet sighs contentedly.

"I'm sorry," she says.

"For what?"

"For enjoying this trip to your grandmother's funeral."

I chuckle as I nuzzle her neck, trailing soft kisses to her ear. "I'm enjoying myself too. I like traveling with you."

"Why's that?" she asks and tilts her head to give me better access to her neck.

"I like everything I do with you."

Violet turns in my arms, finding my mouth and planting a soft kiss. But the soft kiss turns hard after only a moment, and we blindly stumble toward the bed as we make out. This time, when I get her naked, I'm not slow or gentle about much of anything. I'm desperate to be inside her again and spare only the time it takes to get the condom on and make sure she's wet and ready before I shove inside. We both groan at the surge of sensation, and she arches off the bed like she's levitating.

Violet is not gentle either. She claws me with her nails as she takes every stroke, demanding more. We fuck faster, harder, and I like getting rough with her, knowing that I can trust her to express herself clearly and honestly if I ever veer too close to a boundary. So far, she's made it clear we're well within her comfort zone. She fucks me as hard as I fuck her, and when she comes, she clutches and claws and screams in ecstasy. I can hardly hold on to my control, and stars spark through my vision when I finally let myself go. Gasping, I collapse and flop onto my back beside Violet, spent.

She giggles and says, "I definitely like doing *that* with you."

I chuckle. "Me too. I've never had sex in Alabama before."

Violet smacks my chest. "New rule: we fuck in every state we go to."

"Sounds like a fun itinerary. We'll have to hit Mississippi on the way back through."

She laughs, and the sound fills my heart with joy.

"You hungry?" I ask.

"Starving."

"What do you want?"

"I'll take me a big juicy steak and a piece of pie, please."

I roll over to the phone and call room service to put in our order. They don't have pie, so I get us two slices of cheesecake.

"Ask and you shall receive." Violet grins at me when I hang up. "How does an unemployed drifter afford steaks and a fancy room like this?"

"I had a six-figure salary for almost a decade and rarely spent any money. I can afford to be unemployed for a while longer."

"Yeah, but your wife will take half of that in the divorce."

I climb out of bed and throw the condom away. "Ari is practically allergic to money. I'll have to force her to take the money, and she'll probably donate it to charity."

"Must be nice." Violet smirks, her experience with money decidedly different from Ari's or mine.

"Even factoring in her half"—I shrug as I tug on my boxer briefs—"I can afford this." And I want to spend it. I want to spoil Violet. I want to give her the luxury of not having to care about money either. Then, I ask, "How's the theater going… Or rather, how *was* it going before the storm?"

Violet guffaws, "Before the storm—that's a hell of a caveat—things were going well. Not six-figures well, but I was showing a profit. I had a good staff, but they've scattered to the four winds, and we were gearing up to host an indie film festival in the fall—fifteen films by up-and-coming Black filmmakers. All my plans have scattered to the four winds too."

"Do you know if they'll return? I mean, the people…not your plans? Of course your plans will come together again."

She laughs at me. I love when she does that. It makes my awkwardness less awkward when she finds it amusing.

But in answer to my question, she shrugs. Then she turns the question around on me. "What about you, Daddy Warbucks? Will you keep on drifting on the wind until you figure out what you want to do with your life?"

It takes me a moment to realize what she's really asking. This is a huge question, and to ask it while we're both still mostly naked, bared to each other, makes it feel important.

"I'm not drifting anymore, Violet. I know what I want to do."

"Oh yeah. What's that?"

I open my mouth to speak, but there's a knock at the door. Violet grabs the sheets and tugs them around her to cover her nakedness while I answer the door and take the food tray from the waiter.

The smell of the food overwhelms our senses, and the conversation is tabled as I set the tray on the bed between us and lift the stainless steel cloches off our steaks. We moan at the aroma, and it sounds like we're having sex again. After we've devoured the meat and dessert, I set the tray outside our door and lie with Violet in my arms, falling with her into a contented sleep.

21

SUNDAY, SEPTEMBER 25, 2005

"Greg!" Mom's voice rings brightly through the house as I walk inside. I didn't bother to knock; they still don't lock the doors during the day. She sets a tray of food on the dining table and comes at me, ready for a hug. I knew to leave the luggage in the truck until after introductions, so it's easy to fold my petite mom into my arms. I bury my face in her hair and breathe in the familiar scent of her perfume as she clings to my waist.

My dad comes out of the kitchen as Mom and I come apart, and I take the moment to step back and put my arm around Violet. "Mom, Dad, this is Violet Devollier. She's the woman I went to New Orleans to find. She has a theater there, where I met her, and I've been staying with her and her cousin and his partner and—"

"I'm his girlfriend," Violet says with a smile, winking at my surprised expression.

"Yeah." Okay. I guess we're officially dating now. I turn to face my parents. "Violet is my girlfriend."

"Oh my goodness." Mom glances between us, then she pounces on Violet with a hug. "It's wonderful to meet you."

Violet reacts a bit wide-eyed as she's swallowed up in Mom's affection. I turn to Dad, who's beaming. He might not be a crier, but he's definitely a hugger. He holds me tight and pats a solid hand on my back as we connect. Then he steps past me to hug Violet.

With introductions made, Mom starts the ritual feeding process. It begins with her offering hearty helpings of everything she's already cooked, followed by heartfelt offers to cook anything else, should the current selection not meet our needs. She quizzes Violet about food allergies and preferences, then suggests Dad can run to the store for alternative options. Finally, when Violet and I begin to stuff our faces with the amazing food Mom has made, she relaxes enough to eat her own meal.

Mom and Dad ask Violet questions about her theater, life in New Orleans, and the hurricanes. Violet answers graciously, and I have to remind my parents to give her time to chew and swallow her food between questions. So they turn the interrogation toward me.

"Greg, are you still working at Crawford?" Mom wants to know.

Oh, right, I forgot to tell them. "No. I was"—marched out the door by security—"let go." Their outrage on my behalf is heartwarming. "I'm glad to be gone from there. It frees me to find something new, work I care about."

"What do you have in mind?" Dad asks.

Well, a few levees need to be rebuilt, and an entire city down in the bayou needs our attention. As if she can read my thoughts, Violet's gaze connects with mine, and she says, "I'm sure there are a lot of job opportunities for a structural engineer in New Orleans right about now."

And just like that, we're back to the conversation from last night. I look at her, trying to read the meaning beneath her words. Is she inviting me to stay in New Orleans, or is she inviting me to stay *with her* in New Orleans? I mean, she did announce she's my girlfriend, but we haven't talked about anything long-term, and the uncertainty makes me nervous.

"Are you moving to New Orleans then?" Mom asks. Her tone is cautious, like she's afraid she's putting me on the spot to come up with an answer. But it's a fair question. After all, I did show up with a girlfriend they didn't know about from a city they thought I was visiting temporarily.

"I…don't know. I'd like to. I think I want to stay." Then with more confidence, I state, "But right now we're focused on getting everyone back on their feet. I can sort out my situation later."

Violet rests her hand on my thigh under the table. I don't know what the gesture means. I glance at her nervously, but before I can read anything in her expression, the front door bangs open and in walks my brother, Matt, and his family. His wife, Robin, is carrying my newest nephew, and the other three kids make a racket as they run to greet their grandparents.

Mom and Dad go into hug mode while I stay back and tell Violet everyone's names and a little about them. I don't expect her to remember any of the details, but I hope having the information will make her feel more comfortable, less like she's surrounded by strangers—which she is.

When my brother and sister-in-law come around, I shake Matt's hand—we were never close—and hug his wife. They give Violet friendly hellos then wrangle their kids as they settle at the table. My mom has the baby on her lap so Robin can eat, and finally, Violet and I are not the subject of conversation.

At least not until my brother makes it so. "New Orleans, eh?" he asks, his tone suspiciously casual.

I nod. "Yep."

"So Violet, are you one of the Katrina refugees?"

Violet stares at my brother, and my Mom speaks up, explaining, "No, Matt, I told you, your brother is staying in New Orleans, trying to help rebuild."

"Ah." Matt chews and swallows, then asks, "So I've been hearing a lot of debate about this, and I would love your opinion: What do y'all think about this idea to *not* rebuild New Orleans? I know it's a controversial opinion, but you have to admit, it makes sense. The city is below sea level, and with all this 'global warming' and 'the sea levels are rising' mumbo jumbo the environmentalists are always spewing… I mean, strictly looking at a cost-benefit analysis, it would be smarter to move the city somewhere it won't flood."

Ice runs through my veins as Matt speaks, a little glint of excitement in his eyes as he expects Violet to answer him. My brother was always a bit of an ass. He bullied Jake and me whenever Mom and Dad weren't looking. I took his abuse back then because he was bigger than me. He's not bigger than me anymore, and I'll be damned if I let him bully Violet with bullshit politics dressed up as pseudo-science.

I try to keep my tone even. "Do you suggest we move Miami inland as well? What about Washington, D.C.? Both of those coastal cities are protected by levees. A recent study indicates almost twenty-five million people live in flood-prone areas along our coasts. Should we move them all to Kansas, Matt? But what about tornadoes? What about the tens of millions who live in the Los Angeles area—should we move them away from the San Andreas fault? What does that cost-benefit analysis look like, Matt?"

"Hey, man, I'm just asking questions, but you gotta admit it's a lot to ask of the taxpayers to keep rebuilding in a place that's going to keep flooding, then expect us to come to your rescue every time."

I grit my teeth, holding back the words I want to say to my brother, instead going with science and engineering for my response. "If you're legitimately concerned about the rising tides and cost of flooding, then look to the Netherlands. Their flood mitigation system far surpasses the patchwork of levees we've built in this country. Amsterdam is six and a half feet below sea level, but instead of abandoning that city, engineers utilized technology to protect it. New Orleans is one of the oldest and most vibrant cities in the United States, and we're not going to abandon it."

"Okay, sure, but the best parts of New Orleans didn't even flood. Like, the French Quarter. It didn't flood, and that's where the culture and history are anyway, right? So let's protect those parts of the city and let the swamp reclaim the slums that flooded."

"*Slums*?" Violet says, her voice sharp as a knife.

"Hey, no offense, but facts are facts, and the fact is New Orleans has been the murder capital of the country for a decade. Maybe this storm was a message from God to save the good people of that city by moving them out instead of rebuilding the same old cesspool of crime and corruption."

I'm seeing red at the edges of my vision, and I want to slam my brother's face into his dinner plate. I promised Violet she'd be safe here, and he pulls this shit?

"First of all, only a jackass who never explored New Orleans beyond a drunk weekend on Bourbon Street would think the French Quarter is the cultural center of that city." I try to temper my tone, but it's impossible. "And you've got a lot of fucking nerve to condescend to my girlfriend with your 'no offense' remark right before suggesting her city was smote by God."

Matt's wife blanches at my use of foul language in front of her kids. *Tough shit, Robin, you're the one who married an asshole.*

I turn to Violet as I reach for the keys to the truck. "Would you like to go? I can give you a tour of—"

"I'm okay here," Violet says to me, then turns on my brother. "I grew up in one of the parts of New Orleans you call a 'slum.' My childhood home was destroyed by Katrina. A lot of good people lived and *died* in the neighborhoods that were destroyed. But they were largely Black neighborhoods, which makes me wonder if that's what you really mean when you talk about *good* and bad people."

"Now you're calling me a racist? I didn't say one word about race, you did. And I'll have you know—"

"Matthew Allan Hendricks, that is enough!" My mother's tone brooks no insolence from Matt. I straighten my posture too. It's been over a decade since I heard that voice out of Mom, and it's still terrifying. "You are being extremely disrespectful to our guest. You will not say one more word on this subject. Do you understand me?"

Matt fumes, his face turning bright red, but he says, "Yes, ma'am."

Mom holds my father's gaze in some silent conversation for a moment, then softens her expression as she turns to Violet and says, "Violet, I apologize for my eldest son's behavior. I thought we raised him better than that."

Violet smiles at my mom. "They can't all be winners like your Greg, Mrs. Hendricks."

I choke on my mashed potatoes and wash them down with a gulp of water. If we weren't in front of my family right now, I'd have her across my lap, kissing the ever-loving shit out of her for that compliment/backhanded cutdown of my brother. *That was a thing of beauty.*

Matt scowls at the two of us for a moment, then turns his attention to Dad and asks about tomorrow's funeral arrangements.

Below the table, I squeeze Violet's hand and lean in to whisper, "You okay? Do you want to go—"

"No. Really. I'm good. Thanks for checking in," she whispers back.

"Well, you've officially met my least favorite family member."

"Aren't you always talking on the phone to your brother and telling him how much you love him?"

"That's Jake. My parents sort of adopted him. So he's my brother from another mother."

Typical Jake always hits his cues, and he comes through the front door as if we've summoned him.

"Is that my truck I spy in the driveway?" Jake says and drapes an arm around Nicole.

I bolt from my seat, keeping Violet's hand in mine as I go to greet my true brother and introduce him and Nicole to the reason I ran to New Orleans in the middle of a disaster.

Jake smothers me in a hug, like he hasn't seen me in a decade. When I pull away, I wrap an arm around Violet to make introductions. "Violet, this is my best friend, Jake."

She makes a strange sound as she stares at Jake. "Your brother from another mother is Jake Sixkiller from Mammoth?"

Oh. Yeah. I forgot he's a celebrity now.

She looks positively starstruck as she beams at Jake. "I saw you guys play back in July, right after they added you to the lineup. It was an amazing show."

"You listen to Mammoth?" I'm stunned.

She frowns at me. "There are layers of me you haven't peeled yet."

Jake cackles and grabs Violet to give her a hug. "Oh, I like you." To me he says, "I like her."

When I can finally get Violet back from Jake, I turn to Nicole, who looks amused by the whole thing. "And this is Nicole. She's Jake's... What are you guys exactly?"

"Engaged." Nicole holds up her hand, and there on her finger sparkles a black diamond ring.

I catch the look of intense pride on Jake's face and hug him again. "Congrats, man. I'm happy for you."

Next, I hug Nicole, who looks me up and down, saying, "It's good to see you healthy and alive again. I suspect you're at least partially responsible," Nicole says to Violet, then shakes her hand. "Jake was worried he'd relapse."

"Sober as a church lady on Sunday morning," I interject.

Jake introduces Nicole around to everyone else in the family, and we settle at the table, having to send Matt's children over to the card table Mom set up so the adults can all fit. I clutch Violet's hand tight as everyone talks and eats. It's like old times; I've eaten a million different meals at this table with family, extended family, friends, and neighbors. And it feels even better now with Violet at my side. She contributes to the conversation occasionally, but I don't, content to listen. I'm like my dad in that way. I glance over at him, concerned with how he's taking the passing of his mom—we've barely even talked about the loss—but he's smiling as he stares at his boys and the women and children we've brought into his home. He doesn't seem so sad right now.

"I like your family," Violet says as I wrap her in my arms and nuzzle her neck, standing with her at our hotel room window. Jake and I gladly let Matt and Robin and the kids sleep at Mom and Dad's while we got ourselves hotel rooms. I opted for a high room with a mountain view so Violet can wake up to the sight of the sun rising over the peaks in the morning.

"Even Matt?"

"Eh...not so much him. He's an ass, and not an original one. He didn't say anything I haven't heard before. Now, your mom, on the other hand, with her 'mom voice'—that was amazing."

I chuckle. "To this day, that voice fills me with terror."

"She seems like a good mom."

"She is."

Violet turns in my arms, grinning up at me. "And I felt like a very bad girl, sitting at her table, imagining all the dirty things I wanted to do to her son."

Okay. This is a new game. "Is that so?"

She bites her bottom lip.

I'm instantly hard and straining the zipper of my jeans, which comes as a surprise considering how exhausted I feel. As much as I love (most of) my family, being around so many people zaps my energy. Violet appears to be the opposite in that way. While my batteries are drained, she seems recharged and ready to go.

"What sort of dirty things are we talking about?" I stroke my hands up her arms to rest against her neck.

"For starters, I want to suck your cock so hard you can't see straight or stand up, but I won't let you come, not until you're inside me."

Fuck.

"Then, I'm going to turn around, bend over, and press my hands to this window so your hometown can watch you take me from behind."

Batteries recharged. Violet's words electrify me. I take her mouth in a sloppy kiss as I strip her out of the cute dress she wore to meet my family. Getting it caught on her shoulders, she has to wiggle the rest of the way out while I get busy kicking my shoes across the room and stripping off my socks.

I want to assist as she slips out of her bra and underwear, but Violet avoids my touch, forcing me to wait as she performs a tease for me. Then she lays her hands on my chest and starts to tug at the buttons on my shirt. When it's open, I shimmy it off my shoulders, hissing at the sensation of her hot mouth as she melts kisses down my chest. I want to kiss her, to take her, but every time I move to touch her, she barks an order to stand still, not to touch. The denial makes me want her more. I'm desperate, starved for her.

She unfastens my jeans and shoves them, along with my boxer briefs, down my thighs. I grab for her again, but she slips through my fingers as she drops to her knees and swallows me whole.

"Oh fuck." I groan and nearly collapse, my knees trembling under my unsteady weight. Violet grabs my ass to hold me strong, even as she makes me weak. I tilt toward the window, pressing a palm against the glass, staring down at my girlfriend as she sucks my dick.

I don't care anymore that the curtains are open and there might be people with a view of this window. It doesn't matter to me if anyone is watching. All I can focus on is Violet's mouth and the way she twirls her tongue around the head of my cock. Then she hollows out her cheeks and sucks me so hard I might not make it to act two of this sex scene we're performing.

But Violet isn't going to let me come too soon; she intends to make this last. Her lashes flutter as she looks up at me, seeming to delight in my torment as she takes her time, dragging her mouth up and down my length at a maddeningly slow pace. She gives me everything I need, almost, holding me right at the edge of ecstasy, and it drives me mad.

I think my madness was her goal all along. When I grab her shoulders and yank her to her feet, she squeals with excitement. Gruff with desperation, I'm not gentle as I grab her hips and spin her to face the window. She presses her hands to the glass, bends over, and spreads her legs for me.

Outside, any voyeurs have an exquisite view of her breasts hanging heavy between her arms, but I'm the lucky guy who gets to see this spectacular ass and the glisten of her wet pussy.

Fuck. Me.

Now I'm the one on my knees, worshipping her. I smooth my hands up her thighs and over the round globes of her ass, then tease my fingers down the center line, tickling the bud of her ass before I stroke her slit. She moans and shivers, so I do it again.

Then I clasp my hands on her ass cheeks and push my face against her pussy, licking long strokes over the slick folds. She moans again and presses back against my face, demanding more. I give it, going to town as I eat her out from behind, occasionally tracing my tongue all the way up to tease her ass too. It's probably too soon for ass play, but someday I'd like to explore that territory with her too.

Someday. What a thought—that this splendor before me isn't temporary or a fleeting thrill. Maybe, just maybe, there's a *someday* for us.

For now, though, thoughts of the future are a distraction. I pull Violet's thighs apart and push my tongue deep inside her pussy as I use my fingers to tease her clit. She bucks against my face, and she comes on my tongue, shaking and holding herself up against the window.

I'm so hard it hurts. I need to be inside her. *Now.*

Condoms. Condoms. Where are the condoms?

"Have you been tested?" Violet asks as I stumble over shoes to go rummage through our luggage.

"Huh?"

"For STDs."

"Oh. Yeah." After New York, I got paranoid. I had my doctor check me for everything even remotely transmissible by sex. I'm fortunate. Despite my stupidity that week, I tested negative for it all.

"Me too," she says. "And I'm on birth control."

"Oh." I stand up, staring at her perfect ass bent over and begging for my attention.

"So get over here and fuck me raw, Hendricks."

"Oh."

"*Now.*"

I don't linger any longer. My cock crying for her, it leads me like a dowsing rod to water, and I press inside her wetness with one glorious stroke. *Oh God, the feel of her.* I smooth my palms over her ass and clutch her hips, pulling out and slamming home again.

"Yes." She pants and lets her head hang between her shoulders. But I want more from her than this one connection. I reach forward and grab her neck, wrapping my fingers around her throat, then pull her up so her head comes back to rest on my shoulder. I kiss her, taking her mouth as I pound into her pussy, so desperate for her now I'm grunting like an animal as I rut inside her.

Violet's palms squeak against the glass, and I take a couple of steps forward until her tits smash against the glass too. She's pinned to the window, and I'm pressed entirely against her. I piston my hips to fuck her harder and harder until she's coming out of her skin, screaming my name. She scrapes my neck with her nails and my ass, too, spurring me forward, demanding more.

I give her what she wants while I take and take and take from her. Reaching down, I press the heel of my palm against her clit, and the pressure sends her over the edge. She screams when she comes, and her pussy clenches my cock, milking me. I come, too, bellowing and stumbling forward until we're both mashed into the glass, coated in sweat and catching our breaths, neither of us seeming too eager to untangle.

Eventually, though, she shivers, and I worry she's getting cold, so I pull away. Coming out of her feels all wrong, but linking our fingers as I lead her to the shower feels all right.

Under the spray of the water, I rest soft kisses where my fingers had clutched her throat, and she scratches gently up and down my back. Out in the room, everything we did to each other was hard. But in here, our tastes and caresses are soft. We're back to being sweet to each other again, and I love the way our affection swings from rough to gentle. I love both. I love it all.

"Thank you for coming," I whisper as I trail wet kisses up the column of her throat.

"I should be thanking you for making me come."

I chuckle. "I meant on the trip."

She looks up, her eyes twinkling in the dim light of the steamy bathroom. "I'm glad I came, too, Honey Eyes."

"Honey Eyes again?"

She strokes her palm down my cheek and presses a lingering kiss against my lips before she whispers, "I can see the light in them again."

22

MONDAY, SEPTEMBER 26, 2005

I'm in the front row. Violet sits to one side of me, holding my hand, with Jake and Nicole by her side. Dad is on my other side, sitting stoic with Mom's hand in his. Matt and his family flank Mom.

Ari is here, too, sitting with Alex and her parents a few pews behind us. We waved as we all filed into the chapel, but we haven't spoken yet. It's strange. Less than a year ago, she was the one by my side when Grandpa Chuck was buried.

At the altar, Pastor Rick tells a funny story about Granny Millie and her famous buttermilk pie at one of the church socials. Everyone laughs. This funeral is different from Grandpa Chuck's. There is less sadness this time. Not because the loss of Millie is any less painful but because Grandpa's death left Grandma behind. With Grandma Millie's death, she's left us all, but she's back together with Chuck, and I can't help but feel the rightness of that.

The air feels lighter today. Sun shines through the stained-glass windows, filling the chapel with bursts of color. And when people eulogize Grandma Millie, they speak through smiles instead of tears.

At the graveside, Violet and I stand at the back, letting our elders and Jake's pregnant fiancée take the limited seating. Violet hasn't let go of my hand since the day began, occasionally stroking her thumb across my knuckles to remind me she has me in her grasp.

I think she knows how much this sort of thing exhausts me because when she links her hand with mine, it's like she's pumping energy back into me, helping me get through the long day. It's possibly the most romantic thing anyone has ever done for me, and I can't stop grinning at her every time I catch her glance.

Back at Mom and Dad's house, the air smells like warm cheese, perfumed by the myriad of casseroles cluttering the dining table and dotting the kitchen counter. Everyone within a fifteen-mile radius has brought food.

Everyone is eating, and they're all drinking too. Each time I'm stopped so someone can share condolences and small talk, they offer to get me a drink. This is exhausting, too, but Violet's soft hand in mine gives me strength. And after a few nosy cousins ask why I'm not drinking, she starts to run interference, distracting people with friendly questions about their accessories or aftershave so they forget all about me.

Violet once told me she didn't want to be my crutch, and now I see why. She's a caretaker. Her natural tendency is to support others, and it's so easy to lean on her. So as the day wears on, I make a concerted effort to stand on my own two feet.

It's easier when we get some plates of food and a couple of sparkling waters dressed up to look like vodka tonics. Coming off the feast Mom fed us yesterday, I'm not hungry today, but after weeks of food insecurity, we eat our fill. Violet is eyeing the pie selection, looking for pecan, when Ari makes her way toward us, having left Alex across the room to chat with Jake and Nicole.

I warn Violet. "You're about to meet my ex-wife."

"Oh!" She perks up, looking excited, which makes me laugh.

Ari's focus shifts between the two of us, probably unsure of what's funny.

"Hi, Ari," I say and put an arm around Violet's waist. "This is Violet."

"Oh my gosh, hello. It's wonderful to meet you, Violet." Ari gushes, her overly friendly tone coming out a little awkwardly. She's trying so hard to make everything okay between us, and for the first time since she left me, I appreciate the effort.

Violet seems as surprised as I am by Ari's weird friendliness. "You as well. Uh…" Her gaze moves from Ari to me as she says, "I'm going to see if your mom needs help in the kitchen."

Ari and I watch her leave, her silky black dress covered in tiny purple violets swaying enticingly with each step she takes.

"I hope I didn't chase her away," Ari says when it's just the two of us.

"Of course not. I think she thinks we need a minute alone to talk."

"Oh." Ari bites her lip. "Do we?"

I consider the question, searching my brain for anything meaningful I want to say to Ari, but nothing comes to mind. Standing here, looking at Ari—the woman I once loved with all my heart, the woman I thought I would grow old and die with—I'm surprised by all the emotions I *don't* feel.

The thrill is gone, but the pain is gone too. The emptiness in my chest, the weight on my shoulders, the ache that stretched through every part of me: they're all gone now. The anger and helplessness went away too.

"No. We're good."

She nods. "How's New Orleans?"

"Good. It's good." *Jesus, what am I saying? I suck at small talk.* "I mean, as good as can be expected…all things considered."

Ari ignores my awkwardness, saying, "You found Violet."

"I did."

"And you brought her here."

"I did."

"Is it serious?"

It's not her business anymore. Still, I proudly proclaim it is, indeed, getting serious, grinning when I say, "Yeah."

"I'm happy for you, Greg. Truly."

"Thank you, Ari."

I yelp when Violet elbows me in the side. She hands me a little plate with a fat slice of pecan pie in the center, and says, "Look what I found in the kitchen." She holds up two forks. "I was going to take a sliver for myself, but your mom says you look thin. I tried to explain that we inhaled half the buffet table, but she wasn't hearing it. She dished up this hunk and sent me out here with an extra fork. So what do you say, Honey Eyes? You want some of my pie?"

I laugh. "Was that a euphemism?"

She winks and mumbles, "Yes," around a mouthful of pie. God, she's cute. I kiss the tip of her nose, then take a big bite of her pie.

Jake comes up behind Ari and loops his arms around her neck, resting his chin on the top of her head. "Anyone seen that pip-squeak Two Shoes around here? Could have sworn she was just here a minute ago."

Ari giggles and tickles Jake's side. It's nice, like old times, the Musketeer trio together again. Only now we're six deep as Nicole steps up beside Jake, and Alex settles against Ari's side.

"Oh, speaking of pip-squeaks." Jake transfers his chin from the top of Ari's head to the top of Nicole's and rests his palms against her belly. "Guess who's kicking?"

"Jake, that wasn't a kick. That was indigestion," Nicole grumbles. "The baby is about the size of a strawberry, but he's convinced everything is a kick."

Despite her complaint, Nicole looks blissfully happy, practically glowing as she settles her own hands atop Jake's, like they're embracing their baby together.

"Y'all are real cute," Violet says as she feeds me another piece of her pie.

"So are y'all," Jake says.

Someone puts a record on the stereo and cranks up the volume. Jazzy piano competes to be heard over the chatter of all those conversations, and it doesn't take long before the conversations cease.

Louis Armstrong sings about being in heaven in his classic duet with Ella Fitzgerald, "Cheek to Cheek," and everyone smiles sadly. This was Chuck and Millie's favorite tune, but the lyrics hit harder today than they ever did while they were alive.

Happy memories of my grandparents dancing to this song fill my head, and I'm nearly brought to tears. Instead, I take the dessert plate from Violet and set it aside—it's just crumbs now anyway—before asking, "May I have this dance?"

She hesitates a moment, looking around the room, perhaps wondering if it's appropriate to dance at a funeral. But I can't imagine a better way to honor the memory of my grandparents. After a moment, she sets her hand in mine, and I pull her toward the center of the room to sweep her into my arms as we start a slow foxtrot.

My dad steps into the kitchen and grabs my mom, bringing her out to dance. Jake and Nicole, too, start to sway, as other couples pair up and dance in the center of the room.

I clutch Violet a little closer to me, feeling such a sense of well-being when I have her in my arms, like my cares vanish when we dance together. She centers me, giving me a reason to smile and laugh. When Ella takes over the lyrics, I spice up the dance a little, pulling Violet in for a kiss. She giggles against my lips, and the sound is more musical than the song.

I press my forehead to hers and say it all; everything that's in my heart comes rolling right off my tongue. "Violet, I… God, I feel so good with you. I always feel so good with you. And I wish I didn't need you so much. I wish all I did was want you, but I want you, *and* I need you, and it feels like it's too soon to need you this much. I mean, it's only been, what…four weeks…five? How can I need you this much? But I do… I'm overwhelmed with need and…I'm overwhelmed with the *rightness* I feel with you. It's like we fit. Like you hold a piece of me I didn't know was missing."

I gesture around the room. "It's like, life is a puzzle, and all these people—plus those who aren't here anymore—they're pieces of that puzzle. Except, they're pieces of my jigsaw history. And I was still trying to add pieces to that old puzzle. Then you come into my life, and it turns out the piece of me you hold—it's for a different puzzle, and now I'm ready to build the picture of my jigsaw future. Jesus, why am I talking about puzzles?"

Violet raises her brows, seeming amused. I should stop talking, but I'm on a roll now, a runaway train of thought.

"Forget about puzzles… It's like…a story, okay? And I used to think that my life with Ari and my career at Crawford, that was the whole story. But I'm starting to realize it was only a chapter in my story. Or, not even a chapter, it was the prologue… Shit, I've gone from puzzles to prologues. I'm saying this all wrong. What I'm trying to say is—"

"Greg." Violet silences my rambling with that one syllable, and the golden glow of the setting sun glitters through the window to halo her beautiful face. "I love you too."

I stop dancing. I stop moving and thinking and doing. I just *stop* and stare at her as everyone and everything spins and twirls around us. *Those* are the words I've been reaching for. So simple, short and sweet, yet packed full of meaning, full of everything I feel. "I love you too…too."

Violet smiles, and I kiss her. Still standing in the center of everything, like we're the axis the world spins on. And there, at the center of everything, I kiss the woman I love. When we come apart, she glances around like she feels self-conscious. I resume our dancing, feeling over the moon with my love in my arms. If heaven is a place on earth, I've found it.

23

TUESDAY, SEPTEMBER 27, 2005

It's early the next morning when Violet and I climb into Jake's truck and head southeast toward the mountains. After the exhaustion of socializing and mourning yesterday, I'm looking forward to some peace and quiet with Violet in the Smokies.

You can see the edge of the forest from Knoxville, so Violet has been staring at the hazy green peaks for two days now, but nothing beats the experience of going through the national park. And I can't wait to show Violet the view from 6,643 feet.

On our way through Pigeon Forge and Gatlinburg, Violet insists we stop at some of the weird little souvenir shops and load up on all the best Dolly swag. She also buys a pair of matching bedazzled sunglasses for us to wear. I look ridiculous, but I don't care. The smile on her face is worth any fashion indignity she wants to subject me to.

Her excitement is contagious. I'm floating on cloud nine as she pops a cassette—an Appalachian country-and-western compilation she found in one of the shops—into the truck's tape deck, and we harmonize with Ronnie Milsap about the Smoky Mountain rain.

It's not raining today. Sunlight beams brightly in shafts of shimmering light that burst through the canopy of green. Between the blue sky and the yellow sun, everything here is green. Towering conifers and deciduous trees meet over the middle of the winding two-lane road, and on both sides, the forest floor is painted green as well, thick with hobblebush and berry brambles.

We weave and meander higher and higher on switchbacks and curves, slowing at every bend to see the view. I stop at each overlook, giving Violet the opportunity to get out, stretch, and smell the mountain air. We listen to the wind as it blows through the boughs and needles of the trees. Violet takes pictures of it all with a camera I found in my bedroom in Knoxville. It will be fun to get the photos developed later and remember all this, but the photos will never do this forest justice.

Nature isn't something you can ever truly translate to film. The photos can guide our memories back to this place, but the splendor will live best in our memories. So we take our time, noting every little detail. When we're back in New Orleans, sweating through next summer, this place can exist in our minds too.

The higher we go, the colder it gets. Most of the other tourists have thrown on extra layers as we travel with them from one lookout to the next. But we revel in the cold. We roll down the windows and let the crisp mountain air whistle through the truck cab, smiling as we shiver.

Violet has her road atlas out. She's navigating, but I don't need the help. I know these roads intimately. I spent my entire youth hiking and camping these hills and dales, and I know every road and trail, in every season and condition. Still, exploring them with Violet feels new again.

About halfway through the national park, we cross the Appalachian Trail, and I turn off onto a smaller road. Almost immediately, we cross the state line into North Carolina. Violet winks at me, and my mind goes to some wicked places as we weave higher and higher, meandering between Tennessee and North Carolina a few times before we reach the crowded parking lot at the end of Clingmans Dome Road.

"Where are you taking me?" she asks as I pull into a spot.

"You said you wanted to see the mountains, so we're going to the top of the tallest peak in Tennessee."

"I thought we were in North Carolina."

"Right now, we are. We're going to walk up that mountain into Tennessee. You ready?"

"Hell yeah!"

Violet leaps out of the car, beaming at me as she shivers in her short sleeves. It's downright cold up here, probably around fifty degrees, and we're not properly dressed for the half-mile hike to the top of the trail, but neither of us seems to care. She clasps my hand, and we move with the other sightseers up the wide path to the overlook tower on top of Clingmans Dome. It's not a terribly difficult walk, fully paved and handicap accessible, but the twelve-percent grade and the thinner air at this elevation have us both winded.

"Don't you dare tell Dre I'm struggling up this hill, Honey Eyes." Violet huffs. "He'll revert back to Corporal Andre Johnson and have us doing jumping jacks in the courtyard at dawn every morning."

"Andre was in the army?" I ask as we nod to an elderly couple who's taken a break on one of the stone benches dotting the trail.

"Yes," she says between puffs. "Let's stop and look at the view."

We step to the edge of the path and turn to see the miles and miles of mountains, undulating green waves of trees as far as the eye can see. It's beautiful, and a perfect excuse to pause and catch our breath. I'm in no hurry.

Not wanting to be outpaced by our elders, we cut our break short when the older couple gets up to resume their walk and make our way up the rest of the mountain. At the summit, I revel in the sound of Violet's laughter as she stares up at the observation tower looming overhead.

"It looks like a spaceship."

It does. It's a big, circular concrete disk set atop a towering pillar, with a spiral ramp leading through the trees up to its deck. Getting her second wind, Violet races me to the top, though we only speed walk—running would be rude considering all the other tourists sharing the path with us.

"Wow," Violet says, sounding winded as we make it to the deck and circle around to look in every direction.

It's mostly clear today, just a few tufts of fluffy white clouds below us to the north. Otherwise, I reckon we can see for a hundred miles in every direction, waves of hills in shades of green, blue, and pink that fade into the horizon.

Violet finishes shooting the roll of film, then settles beside me against the railing, staring into the distance toward the southwest. We both squint, like we can see New Orleans from here.

Wrapping my arms around her, I rest my chin on her shoulder and ask, "From a brackish bayou at sea level to the tallest peak in Tennessee, how does it feel to be six thousand, six hundred feet up in the air?"

"Pretty freakin' cool." Violet shivers. "Pretty freakin' cold, actually."

I squeeze her tighter, rubbing my hands over her bare skin to warm her up. Violet turns in my arms, and I forget all about the view as I stare down into the obsidian depths of her eyes.

"Did you mean what you said yesterday?" she asks.

I said a lot of things yesterday. It was one of my more vocal days.

"That you love me?"

Oh! That! Of course. "Yes. I meant it. Do you doubt it?"

Violet considers, then says, "Sometimes, I can be a bit pushy. And you can be easy to push around. Did I push you into—"

"What? No." I rest my palms on Violet's cheeks, feeling the chill of her skin as I say with total resolve, "Violet I've been falling in love with you since the moment I met you. Maybe it didn't seem like it at the time because it was slow. It's been happening gradually. Bit by bit, day by day, I trip and fall a little more in love with you."

She smiles. "I tripped and fell in love with you too. I didn't mean to. Didn't even want to. I'd given up on men and the trouble they bring. Then you came along. And certainly, you bring your fair share of trouble, but..." Violet pauses, takes a deep breath, and her voice is quieter when she continues. "When you first arrived in New Orleans, I was convinced you wanted to use me to rebound from Ari. As time went by and you literally never talked about her, I started to think I'd been wrong about you. But I still harbored some insecurities until yesterday.

"With Ari there, I figured I'd have to watch you moon over her all day. Instead, you paid all your attention to me and danced with me and told me Ari's a piece of your past puzzle and I'm part of your future puzzle, which was adorably awkward and somewhere in the middle of all that, I tripped and fell in love with you."

I hug Violet against me, breathing in the scent of her hair mixed with the chilly mountain air, then pepper kisses up her neck to her ear and whisper, "I love you too."

Violet sags in my arms like she trusts me to hold her steady. "I love you too, too."

She pulls away and plants a soft kiss on my lips before she turns back to the view, sighing heavily as she asks, "Do you feel homesick for the mountains when you're in New Orleans?"

Odd question. I haven't felt homesick for Tennessee in a long time. "No."

"Are you homesick for Austin?"

"No."

"Do you want to know what this view makes me feel right now?" she asks.

"Yep."

"Homesick for New Orleans."

"Well, then, let's go home."

Home. It's the first time I've called New Orleans home. It catches us both by surprise, I guess, because we grin at each other, and she winks when she clasps my hand in hers, and we walk back down the mountain.

"We're in North Carolina right now, right? This parking lot is literally *in* North Carolina," Violet says.

"Yes."

"Well then, we're in a new state, and we need to have new-state sex. Them's the rules, Honey Eyes."

"Where?" I glance around the parking lot, where retirees in RVs and on motorcycles mingle with families from other parts of the world as they queue for the bathrooms and photograph the landscape. There's not an inch of privacy around here.

"I'll give you road head on the way down the mountain."

I nearly swallow my tongue as I look around to make sure no one overheard her.

Violet laughs. "It is so easy to fluster you."

Oh, she's joking. I unlock the truck so we can get in out of the cold. But as soon as we turn out of the parking lot, she stretches her seat belt out, twists on the bench seat to come toward me, and unzips my jeans.

"Oh fuck, Violet. What are you doing?"

"Giving you road head."

"I thought you were joking."

"I never joke about road head." She reaches into my pants, teasing her fingers down the length of my painfully hard dick.

"But…wait…what if…"

She pulls her hand out of my pants and says, "If you don't want me to, Greg, I won't. Tell me the truth—do you want road head?"

I tighten my fists on the steering wheel until my knuckles are bloodless and my sweaty palms squeak around the synthetic leather. Of course I want road head; that goes without saying. "Yes."

Violet smirks. "I'm gonna need more enthusiasm outta you."

As nervous as I am at the prospect of getting caught or getting us both hurt while driving distracted on a dangerous road, I want this. The idea has my cock weeping with desperation. I stretch my legs to get comfortable, hovering my foot over the brake while we coast downhill. And this time, when I answer, there's no hesitation in my tone. "Come here and suck my cock. Next turnoff we come to, I'm pulling over so I can taste myself on your tongue."

"Now that's the sort of enthusiasm I want to hear," Violet says as she dips under my arm to bring her head to my lap. I huff out the breath I'm holding when she reaches into my pants and pulls me out, stroking my length then swallowing my cock down to the root.

My legs twitch, and I'm afraid I'll hit the gas too hard. I've never received road head before. It's intense, trying to focus on the road and make sure I don't jerk the wheel and send us plunging off the edge of a mountain. This is dangerous and stupid and fucking exhilarating.

I'm so keyed up, every nerve in my body responding to Violet's mouth, that it only takes a few minutes of her sucking my cock and tickling my balls with her fingernails before I come in hot jets that stream down my amazing girlfriend's throat. I sink with such relief and tap the brakes as we curve around another bend. Violet zips me up nice and proper, giving my shoulder a friendly pat as she straightens back up and licks her lips.

There's a turnoff twenty feet ahead, and I yank the wheel over, screeching to a stop in one of the parking spots. Throwing the truck into park, I unstrap and slide across the bench seat until I'm crowding Violet against the window. With one hand wrapped around the back of her head and the other pulling her hips against mine, I kiss the ever-loving shit out of her, tasting the salt of my come in her mouth.

"My turn now." I move like I'm going to strip off her jeans and eat her pussy right here in the parking lot, but a van pulls up beside us, thwarting my plans. "Damnit."

Violet giggles, and I straighten up, pulling her against me for another kiss. I press my forehead to hers and say with all seriousness, "Woman, I am crazy in love with you."

"I'm sure that's what all the boys say after a blow job."

"Yeah, but I mean it."

"I love you too, too." Violet kisses the tip of my nose. "And you can take your turn tonight."

I wink at her. "It's a date," I say as I reverse and hit the road again.

We travel the rest of the way in relative quiet, enjoying the view one last time before we head back home to where it's flat and wet and hot. In Gatlinburg, our phones chirp and chime with text and voicemail notifications. I ignore mine, but Violet reaches for her own and listens to a voicemail as I navigate the crowded roadway through the weird little town.

"Holy shit!" Violet screams.

I jump in my seat, startled. "What? What!"

"Paradise got the power back. We've got to get home, like, now. Can you drive any faster?"

The road is jammed with traffic, and tourists clog every pedestrian crossing. At my side, Violet calls Andre. When he answers, his voice booms so loud I can hear him too. "Baby girl, get your ass back here. It's lights, camera, *action* time!"

"We're on our way. His mom is cooking us dinner tonight, then we'll drive through the night." She looks at me as she says it, perhaps wondering if I'm okay to drive all night. I nod with exaggeration; it's not even a question. My new mission is to get Violet back home as soon as possible.

Suddenly, my builder brain kicks in, and I talk to Andre with Violet as a conduit. "Tell him to run the air conditioner today and tonight at seventy-two degrees so we can cool and dehumidify the space. Also, I'll need to know what the model number and sizes are for the filters you use on the air conditioner so we can stock up on replacements and switch them out regularly. Ask him to take my measuring tape from my tool belt when he returns so he can measure the missing drywall we cut out of the bathrooms and employee lounge walls too."

"Why?" she asks, and I can see she's pointing the phone at me so Andre can hear too.

"So we can patch the walls back together. We'll stop at a hardware store in Mississippi and get everything we need to start reconstruction tomorrow."

Violet turns the phone back to her ear. "Did you get all that, Dre? Cool. Call me with the information."

When she hangs up, she stares at me. I shift my glance from the road to her and back. "What?"

"I like your take-charge voice, Mr. Hendricks. I'm looking forward to hearing you bark more orders."

"I wasn't barking—"

"Honey Eyes, that was a compliment. Just accept it."

I chuckle to myself and change the subject. "You excited to get back to Paradise?"

She sighs long and heavy and says, "More than I thought I would be. I miss that place like it's my baby."

"Well, let's get home and take care of her."

24

"Let me get this straight," Jake frowns at me, "you want to trade your BMW, which is probably worth thirty thousand dollars, for my piece-of-shit truck that's held together with baling wire and prayer?"

"Yes," I reply patiently. "And it's in decent condition. I drove it up to Clingmans Dome today with no trouble."

Jake clearly doesn't grasp the concept. "Still. Why?"

"Two reasons," I explain. "First, I'm not sure when I'll be back in Austin to return it to you, so unless you have a sentimental attachment to the truck, it makes sense to trade cars. Also, I need a vehicle that can haul building materials. My only concern is Ari."

"Me? Why am I a concern?" Ari chirps from the other side of my parent's dining table, where she and Alex are enjoying this version of our Family Dinner Night. My bio brother flew home with his wife and kids this morning, so Mom and Dad gathered their other two sons as well as our little family—including Ari and Alex—for this last supper together before we all head back to our homes.

I turn to her. "Technically, the car is half yours."

"Oh." She waves my concerns away. "It's all yours, Jake. I never liked that car anyway."

"You didn't?"

She shakes her head. "It always felt too rich for my blood."

Interesting. It's another thing Ari never told me while we were together. Though, to be fair, I never bothered to ask. Still, I like that nothing seems to go unsaid between Violet and me. If she ever hates my choice of car, I trust she'll tell me, loud and clear.

"Y'all are so weird. Have you no concept of value?" Jake jokes.

"Yes, I do. And right now, a truck that can haul drywall is more *valuable* to me than a fancy car."

Jake presses his palm against his chest and says, "It's just... I feel like, emotionally, I'm not ready to own a beamer. It's a very grown-up step."

"For the love of God, Sixkiller, say thank you and accept the car." Nicole elbows him in the side. "It's either this or a minivan."

Jake shivers and relents. "*Fine*. We'll take the BMW."

"And..." Nicole raises a brow at him.

"Thank you," Jake says to me amid a round of laughter, and asks, "So you're moving to New Orleans, then?"

It's the question of the hour. Mom grilled me on the subject until her dinner guests started arriving. I chew and swallow my food, then say, "Yes. Obviously, I need to come back to Austin at some point so we"—I gesture to Ari—"can finalize the divorce—"

"And be there for my wedding and Tommy's birth." Jake adds to my to-do list.

"Yes, brother, of course," I say, but stumble over the name he's said. "Tommy? Do you already know the sex of the baby?"

Jake shrugs and answers enigmatically, "Sixkillers are always boys."

"Will they even let you back into New Orleans? I heard they weren't letting residents return to their homes," Ari says.

"I'd like to see them try to stop me." Violet's answer rings with finality, and she takes another bite of her food.

I add, "We stewed in that city without power or running water for weeks. We stood in line for our Red Cross administered tetanus boosters. We adhered to every curfew and managed to stay safe and healthy the whole time. Now that the power is on in her neighborhood—"

"Our neighborhood." Violet corrects me, and my heart leaps in my chest.

"Our neighborhood." I smile. "I don't see why they would stop us from returning."

"Gotta say, Violet, you're pretty much my new favorite person... right after Nicole, of course," Jake says.

"Oh?"

"I haven't seen this guy smile this much in ages."

Everyone nods, even Ari.

"So, Violet, what sort of theater do you have? Movie or performances?" my mom asks.

"It's an old movie theater."

"A midcentury classic," I add. "With a big blade sign and marquee out front. It's a real beauty, something you don't see too much these days."

Violet agrees. "It's very pretty if I do say so myself. Well, it was..."

"It will be again," I say.

Violet nods, adding, "When we get it cleaned up, you're all invited for a show."

"How badly was it impacted by Katrina?" Nicole asks.

Violet details the damage, and everyone listens with keen interest. They question her more about her theater, her family, her life in New Orleans. Everyone is curious to know this woman who has inadvertently changed the course of my life.

By Violet's side, surrounded by my family, I feel centered. Before, I thought I had my shit together because I had all these plans for what my life was supposed to be. Then that vision of life went to hell, and I lost my way for a while. Now, though, I see my path, and it isn't some vague notion of what my life *should* be. It's finally, for the first time, what I *want* it to be. And that feels so good.

The space behind the truck seat is stuffed with coolers containing casseroles. Mom sent us away with most of the funeral food and instructions to share it with the "Beaux Ballroom boys," as she's taken to calling Andre, Paul, Clifton, and the others. We're stuffed with food, too, as we roll out of town.

It's late in the day when we leave, and the plan is to drive to Meridian, Mississippi, about six hours away. We called around to the hotels in the area and booked one of the few rooms available—most of the lodging in central and southern Mississippi still serves as temporary refuge for people displaced by the storm. The hotel clerk assured me that a nearby hardware store has been resupplied several times and should have everything we need, even though Katrina spawned several tornadoes in the area, and people here are rebuilding too.

Shopping in Meridian means driving about three hours with drywall hanging out of the back of the truck. But none of the stores closer to the coast answered our calls.

We head southwest on I-75 to Chattanooga, where we connect with I-24 at the bend around Lookout Mountain and join I-59 in Georgia. Violet winks at me as she announces the new state we've entered—we have a lot of new-state sex to make up for in Meridian—and says a quiet farewell to the mountains as we head home to the swamp.

She's been on the phone most of the trip, getting a shopping list from Andre, chatting with an agent at her insurance company, working with her mortgage company to arrange payment forbearance, and sitting on hold with FEMA. When we drift out of cellular range, the call to FEMA drops, and Violet groans, exhausted by bureaucracy.

The sun sets in our eyes, and we don our bedazzled sunglasses from this morning. It feels odd, like eons have passed since we last wore the goofy specs on our trip up the mountain, even though it was only hours ago. We're heading back to regular life again, irregular though it may be. The carefree jaunt to mountaintop splendor is in our rearview mirror. The road ahead paved with hard work and paperwork as far as the eye can see.

Once darkness falls, Violet dozes against the passenger door while I listen to the Appalachian classics cassette again, and John Denver sings about the country roads that will take me to where I belong. When we reach Meridian, I navigate to the hotel and check in. The room key in hand, I wake Violet so she can resume her rest on the lumpy queen mattress.

But when I come out of the shower and settle onto the bed beside her, Violet is wide awake and giving me that naughty grin I've come to love so much. She curls closer and kisses me, soft and sweet, as her hand roams across my chest and down beneath the sheets. Suddenly, I'm wide awake too.

Who can sleep when we have so much sex to make up for? There was our first time in Mississippi, when we drove right through, same for Georgia, and I still owe her a big thank you for that North Carolina blow job.

I wrap an arm around her waist and move like I'm going to roll on top. But Violet pushes me onto my back, her voice a purr when she says, "You've been driving all day. Why don't you let me do the steering for a while?"

That's thoughtful of her. But if she thinks I'm the type of man who'll lie there while she does all the work, she has a lot to learn about me.

She slides on top, her firm thighs straddling my waist. I won't complain about this view, though. With my eyes adjusted to the dark room, I revel in the sight of her magnificent tits, swaying as she curls her hips forward and back, her wet heat sliding over the shaft of my cock.

I reach up, grabbing her breasts, so warm and soft and heavy in my hands, then rise off the bed so I can take one into my mouth, sucking and nibbling and teasing her nipple into a tight peak. Caressing my hands down to the curve of her perfect ass, I squeeze. She moans and moves a little faster, a little harder over me. I trace my fingers up her spine, clutching her neck to pull her down so I can kiss her. More than kiss, though—I consume her. I breathe her in and taste her essence; I claim her with my mouth. And when I'm hungry for more, I urge her to crawl up my body and sit on my face.

It doesn't take much convincing before she plants her knees by my ears. I grab the firm globes of her ass and pull her down, penetrating her with my tongue. She gasps and clutches the headboard as she rides my face. She's dripping wet, drenching my chin and cheeks as I drink my fill. I use my fingers to fuck her, curling them forward to reach her

G-spot, and flick my tongue on her clit until she comes to pieces all over me.

That's for North Carolina.

Violet collapses to the sheets beside me and giggles when I rub my wet face across her breasts then lick them clean. She hugs me against her, running her fingernails through my hair, and my eyes roll back in my head at the sensation. She seems to delight at discovering one of my erogenous zones and does it again.

I kiss her as I stroke my hand down her body to settle between her thighs. She has the prettiest little pussy. I want to pet it for hours. But we have an early day tomorrow, so I don't dawdle as I tease the most sensitive parts of her and demand she come for me again. She drenches my fingers as I drive them inside her, pressing my palm to her clit.

That's for Georgia.

Violet giggles again as I bring my hand up and lick my fingers. "Goddamn, Greg. I said I was going to do the work."

"I don't like to lie down on the job." I trace her bottom lip, leaving it glossy with her wetness, enticing her to open. When she does, I lay my fingers on her tongue, and she sucks the rest of her come off me, groaning like she loves the flavor. She pushes me onto my back, pinning my shoulders to the mattress, and pulls my hand away so she can lick and kiss my chest, sucking one of my nipples into her mouth and teasing it taut with her teeth.

This time I stay put, content to lie here and watch as she slides her tongue down my abdomen and circles my navel before she tickles the tip of my cock and sucks it deep. Every muscle in my body spasms in response. This woman's mouth is sinfully sweet and deliciously naughty. It's so sexy the way her lips stretch around my cock as she fucks me with her mouth, but I'm too close to the edge. I could come at any moment, and we're not finished yet.

I pull Violet away, and her mouth releases my dick with a juicy pop. She gives no quarter, not even a moment for me to calm my libido, before she climbs up my body, angles my cock at her entrance, and drops down, impaling herself on my length.

It's perfect; *she's* perfect. I revel in her warmth and wetness, the drowning heat, the tight grip she holds on me as I sink deeper. This right here—*this* is paradise. Violet rides me in long, slow strokes. She folds her arms over her head, sending her tits on a glorious ride of their own. I reach for them, catching one with my mouth and the other with my palm as they undulate above me. I taste and touch, teasing her taut nipples with my tongue and fingers. She makes the most perfect sounds, and I take such satisfaction in her moans.

I need her to come again. So I slide my hands up her legs and reach the apex of her thighs, using a thumb to stroke her clit in sync with her rolling movements. Violet gasps and cries out, and her pussy clenches around me as she climaxes. *Yes.* She takes her pleasure from me, riding me harder, and I am eager to give her whatever she needs. Even when she freezes, her orgasm cresting, I continue to touch her and fuck her. I don't stop until she collapses onto me, trembling in my arms and gasping for air.

That's for Mississippi.

This next part, though, this is for me.

I wrap her in my arms and roll us until I'm on top. With her pinned beneath my weight, I lace our fingers and stretch her arms over her head so I'm in complete control. Her orgasm still ebbing and flowing through her veins, I take her hard and fast.

"Oh my…fuck… Yes!" Violet screams. She arches her back off the mattress and tangles her legs around mine, trying to top from the bottom.

"You like it rough, don't you? You're my dirty girl, aren't you?" The questions come through gritted teeth as I pound into her.

"Yes." She gasps and squeezes her palms against mine, her nails clawing into my hands. It hurts so good. "Oh God… More. Harder. Faster."

Violet's hips slam up to meet mine, taking me deeper, harder, bruising us both. We're coated in a sheen of sweat that makes it easier to slide together and apart. My heart races, pounding like it's hitting my ribs in the same frenzied rhythm that the bed bangs against the wall.

This could kill me. I might die tonight. Still, I don't slow, never stop. I give her what she wants: more, harder, faster. With every ounce of energy in me, I fuck her fucking brains out.

I let go of her hands and clutch her ass, pulling her tightly against me, angling her hips to take me deeper. She claws my back, pulling me down so our chests are flush, not an inch of space between any part of us now.

I'm barely hanging on, and my orgasm is coiled tight and threatening to spring loose each time my balls slap against her ass. I put my mouth to her ear. "Come for me, Violet."

"Oh God, yes," Violet says and scratches her nails up into my hair, scraping my sensitive scalp.

That's it for me. I'm done for. My cock jerks, and I huff out all the air in my lungs as I come. Violet spasms in my arms and cries out, her orgasm taking her breath away like mine did to me.

We lie there together for a good twenty minutes, I'd guess, catching our breath. I feel like I have vertigo and can't move without getting dizzy as I float down from this high. Eventually, I shift so I'm not crushing her with my weight, and she pulls the blanket up to keep out the chill as the AC cools our damp skin. We curl together, keeping our arms wrapped around each other and our legs tangled. We're lying in the wet spot on the sheets, but neither of us seems to care.

"I love you too," she says with a soft kiss to my jaw.

"I love you too, too," I reply with a feathery kiss to her temple, and then every bit of energy drains from me, and I fall into the blissful abyss, safe in the arms of my love.

25

"What's that?" I ask as we come into New Orleans, and Violet pushes a cassette into the truck's tape deck.

"I found this in your old bedroom. Your mom said I could have it."

"Oh?"

Violet winks and starts to shimmy as the bebop guitar and piano intro to Meatloaf's classic "Paradise By the Dashboard Light" starts.

"My *Bat Out of Hell* tape? Where did you even find that?"

"I'm an expert snooper. If you were harboring some big secrets, FYI, I know them all now."

I laugh. No big secrets, just some awkward fashion choices in middle school. I shrug—if she's going to love me, she deserves to know the truth about my *Miami Vice* blazer and the tight-rolled jeans.

Violet isn't paying attention to me anymore as she sings along with the song. She's a Meatloaf fan? "Woman, I cannot wait to peel your layers."

"Oh, dirty boy, save it for tonight, lover," Violet says with a wink, and her words send my heart racing. Then, in sync with the song, Violet sings the part of the woman demanding to know if Meatloaf loves her before she'll let him sleep with her.

I crank the volume on the scratchy old stereo playing a scratchy old tape and sing along with Meatloaf's role in the duet as we make our way toward, well, Paradise…guided by the dashboard light. I chuckle at Violet's sense of humor.

There's more traffic and activity in New Orleans than when we left, so clearly we're not the only people ready to start restoration. Some of the streets that had been blocked by debris are cleared; rusty cars, bits of homes, fridges taped shut—a few with "smells like Bush" spray-painted on them—and other refuse are piled on the sidewalks like plowed snow banks full of sharp edges and *staphylococcus*.

We pull up in front of Paradise to the smiles and waves of Andre and Paul and the cadre of volunteers who've come to help. Violet bursts from the truck—Meatloaf still crooning through the open door—and leaps into her cousin's arms, hugging him like they haven't seen each other in years. I shut the truck off as she makes the rounds, hugging everyone else. I'm caught by surprise when I come around the fender and walk through the same gauntlet of affection. Everyone who hugged Violet comes to do the same to me. Even Clifton—looking so different now that he's shaved and showered—hugs me. I can't help the stupid grin that plasters my face; I hadn't truly realized I was part of this family until right now.

After a few quick words, we store the perishable food in the one working cooler at Clifton's shop, then it's time to explore the theater. We let Violet lead the way inside. The lights are out, and only the glow from the doorway we came through illuminates the space.

Overhead, the air conditioner hums its glorious white noise while it works its magic. The air doesn't stick to my skin anymore or smell like dampness and rot. To think, when this theater was first built, cooled air was one of the attractions, and finally we're able to enjoy that simple comfort of modern life again.

Violet crosses to the panel of switches behind the concession stand and lets out a shaky breath as she triggers the overhead spotlights, one by one. The bleached glass and brass of the candy shelves gleam, but where the floor had once been an ocean of red with gold stars, it's nothing but dingy concrete now. Where the walls were neatly painted and adorned with movie posters and the homage to her father, the plaster is chipped and muddy, and the drywall is cut away at the water line.

We take a moment to stare at the space and process this new reality. It's ugly, sure, but overall, in good condition. Our mold remediation has worked. The bleach killed most of what grew here. Now, with the air-conditioning to dehumidify the air, we can spot treat any areas of concern and proceed with reconstruction.

However, this is just one room. Like we're sharing the same thought, Violet steps around the concession counter and crosses to the back wall, going into each bathroom and employee lounge to trigger those lights too. I follow, scoping out the damage. The bathrooms are in good shape, only need a quality scrub. The employee lounge, however, is a mess.

Before the storm, this room had been a combination office and kitchenette. The fridge is gone now, still waiting for removal from the curb by the dumpster. The remaining appliances and office electronics are probably fried and destined for the dumpster as well. The kitchen cabinets were cleaned during our last work weekend here, but they need to be disinfected before we put food back in them. Some of the doors are damaged, too, beaten by a file cabinet that caught a wave during the flood and buffeted the room like a battering ram.

Most of the paperwork in that file cabinet had been soaked, turned into a pulpy mush that we shoveled into garbage bags and tossed. But anything that's somewhat legible, we laid out to dry. Now, brittle pages of contracts and invoices are scattered everywhere.

Three tall file cabinets remain standing against the wall behind the desk. The files in the lower drawers were lost. But the files in the upper drawers were spared. Violet crosses to the first cabinet and opens the top drawer, then gags from the stench and shoves it closed.

Okay. Clearly we need to salvage what we can of the paperwork before it all rots.

Violet straightens her shoulders and marches back out to the lobby. She takes the stairs two at a time to the balcony above. I follow close behind, not wanting her to have to do this alone. Andre and Paul come too. Everyone else remain silent in the lobby.

Violet swings the auditorium doors open, and we all step into the pitch blackness. She flips the lights on, and the room goes from total darkness to blinding brightness in an instant. We hiss and cover our eyes like vampires on a sunny day but eventually adjust to the light and take in the sight of this damaged space.

The ugliness takes my breath away. Around the screen, the beautiful red velvet curtains are too short, the bottom four feet hacked off unevenly, like a kid cutting their own bangs. A stretch of stair-runner carpet is torn up in lopsided angles, too, and the first several rows of seats are stripped bare to their metal skeletal remains. The lower portion of the walls I helped Violet paint are stained up to the high-water mark, and the electronic lights that once traced the edges of the steps are dead.

The worst part, though, is the screen. It was high enough that it didn't get wet in the flood, but the damp air in this cave-like room has been a perfect breeding ground for an aggressive colony of aspergillus. The once white display is now speckled with dark plumes of black-and-green mold spores.

Again, though, despite the ugliness of the destruction and the creepy colony of microbes, the damage is surface deep. The structure is sound. The problems here will be relatively easy to fix, but that doesn't make the wreckage of this storm any easier to stomach.

Violet's breathing turns ragged, and a few tears trickle down her cheeks as she stares at her auditorium. I open my arms to offer a hug, and she comes in for it, softening against me, letting me hold her up as she falls apart.

Feeling Violet tremble and silently cry breaks my heart. I take her pain personally. Desperate to avenge the woman I love, massacring this colony of mold just rocketed to the top of my to-do list. It's the one thing I know I can do to make this better. I will fix this for her.

I read recently that women don't like when men do that—they want us to listen rather than always try to fix their problems—but I'm betting these are extenuating circumstances. This problem is imminently fixable.

"You go through the paperwork, okay? I'll get a crew together, and we'll take care of this room," I say to Violet and kiss the top of her head.

"And Paul and I will work on the lobby," Andre says.

See, I'm not the only one trying to comfort her by fixing what's broken.

Violet nods but stays put, wrapped in my arms, her tears dampening the front of my shirt. Andre and Paul come closer and rest their hands on her shoulders. We stay like this for a moment, letting her feel what she needs to feel. Then she straightens, wipes away the tears, and we get to work.

As soon as we join the crew of helpers in the lobby, the mood lifts. Everyone here is ready for a hard day of labor, but they approach it with laughter and comradery. They are, after all, the people who've survived this entire ordeal. They're sick of being sad and angry, and they're ready to get their lives and community back to normal and operational.

Someone brings in music: an iPod full of dance hits and a speaker that boosts the tunes through the whole space. I can even hear it down at the bottom of the auditorium. I went out to the truck earlier to collect some supplies, including N95 masks that I distributed to everyone. Now we can protect our lungs from the mold and chemicals while we sing and dance and work.

Federico joins me in the auditorium. He knows more about fabrics than anyone here, so I get his advice on how to clean the screen. We use natural fiber brushes and dish soap, rather than bleach, to scrub it clean.

He attacks from the bottom, and I climb the rickety old ladder I remember from my first visit here, scrubbing the higher blooms on the screen until my arms ache and my back screams for me to stop. We keep going until every piece of that mess is mutilated, then Galen and James use a couple of those high-powered water guns to rinse the soap off.

It comes down in sudsy waterfalls to the muddy floor, and a guy named Steve squeegees the excess water out the fire exit door as best he can. Galen, James, and Steve have scrubbed and rinsed the plaster walls, and now we mop the floor.

When we're finished, the screen is slightly discolored where it's wet, but the mold is gone. The walls could use another coat of paint, but the caked-on mud has been washed away. The stair-step carpet needs to be patched, but the floor is clean.

We point a couple of box fans at the screen and bump the thermostat down a few degrees to dry this space as quickly as possible, then we head out to the balcony to see how the other teams are doing.

Andre and Paul have a crew of seven, and they've made amazing progress in the lobby. A carpenter is among them, and he's managed to rehang both doors so they can open, close, and lock. Paul leads a few others in cleaning the walls and the floor. And Andre has several helpers measuring and cutting drywall to fit the ruined portions of the walls we cut away once the water receded.

Someone hands me a bottle of cold water as I descend the stairs, and I accept it graciously, stepping outside to remove my mask and drink it down. I glance up the block to where another group of people is helping Clifton with his shop. And on the far end of the street, a few other residents and business owners have arrived to assess their own situation.

I finish my water, wipe the sweat off my brow, and don my mask to go into Clifton's shop. They've scrubbed and mopped it clean, and two electronics guys now work on fixing more of the cooler units. I grab a sanitary wipe from the front counter and clean my hands before I go to the one working cooler and find the pecan pie.

When Clifton notices, I quickly say, "It's for Violet."

Clifton smiles at me. "Smart man. A well-fed woman is a happy woman."

"Did you read that nugget of wisdom in *Cosmo*?" I ask.

"*Men's Health*," he counters with a cackle and hands me a paper plate and plastic fork. I cut off a slice of pie and wrap up the rest to return to the cooler. Before I take the food out the door, Clifton adds, "Tell her to stay hungry. I'm hosting dinner at my place in an hour."

"You cooking?" I ask with surprise, not used to this hospitable side of Clifton. He's always seemed a bit crotchety and well armed.

"I'm reheating all that food your mom and them sent. We've got a funeral's worth of people to feed tonight, don't we?"

"That we do. See ya in an hour."

Back in the theater, I hold the pie high over my head as I dodge busy workers and aim for the back office and my girlfriend. *Girlfriend.* Violet is my girlfriend. Jeez, that will never get old.

She's on the floor—which is clean, to my great relief—surrounded by papers. All the lights are on, but still she uses a flashlight to scrutinize each document before deciding if it's keeper or trash.

She's oblivious to the group of people scrubbing the kitchen cabinets clean. And she doesn't notice me until I sit on the floor behind her, straddle my legs around her, and lower the plate in front of her face.

"Pie!" She turns and gives me a grin. At least I think she's grinning. It's hard to tell with the mask on, but the corners of her eyes crinkle a little, suggesting a smile.

"I love you too," she says as she pulls down her mask and accepts a bite of the food.

"I love you too, too," I reply.

"Whoa!" Andre hollers from where he's been attaching wall board to divide this room from the lobby. I realize this is the first time Violet and I have used the L-word in front of him. "Whoa, whoa whoa, whoa, *whoa*! Pump the brakes, Cowboy. Did I just hear you say, 'I love you, tutu'?"

"That's what I heard," Paul says as he joins his partner to stand in the doorway, and they smirk at each other.

"How, with all the nouns on God's green Earth, did you land on 'tutu' as your chosen term of endearment for my cousin? It's not her initials or some cute little animal you want to cuddle or a delicious treat you want to eat. It's a ballerina's skirt. It's the great Archbishop Desmond's last name. It's a Miles Davis album…"

Paul posits, "In French it's slang for 'ass.' Maybe he loves her ass."

Violet and I ignore them. They can have their fun; I'm busy feeding my girlfriend.

I've been on Clifton's roof dozens of times but never inside his apartment. It is roughly the same layout as the shop below, with one big room up front for his living and dining needs and a few smaller rooms off the back for cooking, sleeping, and showering.

The walls are bare, like any other bachelor pad, but on a shelf beside the television are a dozen framed photos, images of Clifton at a younger age, graduating the police academy, receiving accommodations, and there's one of him with a beautiful young woman wrapped tightly in his arms. I want to ask about her, but the fact that nothing indicates the presence of a woman in Clifton's life suggests the story won't have a happy ending.

I'll keep my probing questions to myself, for now. This isn't the night for tales of heartbreak. Tonight, we celebrate. We achieved a lot today. And we did it together, as a community that's become a family. Tonight, we come together for this Big Easy version of Family Dinner Night. It's ironic, and oddly appropriate, that the meal we share is left-over funeral food.

The room is hot as Clifton's oven works overtime to reheat all those casseroles. We help ourselves with a mismatch of ladles and serving spoons to bits and pieces of the different delights. I take my fill of lasagna, chicken and rice, macaroni and cheese, and something involving green beans.

There are more people than seats, so Violet and I sit on the floor, sharing nibbles of our favorite things. She feeds me a bite of ambrosia salad I'm sure one of my grandma's church friends made and laughs at the face I pull when I try to choke down the gritty shredded coconut. Not my favorite.

"A little birdy told me you two finally realized you're in love," Federico says as he settles on the floor beside us.

I chuckle as I swallow the last shreds of ambrosia, washing them down with a soda, and glance around the room. Every conversation has stopped, and everyone watches, waiting to see what Violet and I will say. All this attention is overwhelming. I don't know what to say. But Violet answers decisively, "Yes, he's all mine."

My heart soars, and Violet's words ring in my ears like bells. She's claimed me, loudly and proudly, in front of her family and friends, right in the middle of our Family Dinner Night. *I'm all hers.*

When the attention has drifted away from us, Violet sets her plate aside and turns a little in my lap, draping her legs over one of mine so we can look at each other when she says more privately, "At least I assume you're all mine."

"I'm all yours—mind, body, and soul."

Violet clasps her hands on my cheeks and delivers a kiss that feels less sexual than any we've shared before. This kiss isn't about sex; it's about everything else that's between us. This kiss is a pact, a promise. Like a vow, only better than the vow I once made to Ari because this vow feels indelible.

We kiss for whole minutes, maybe hours, only coming apart to breathe. Violet presses her forehead against mine as she whispers, "I love you too."

I whisper back, "I love you, *tutu*."

EPILOGUE
THURSDAY, OCTOBER 13, 2005

It takes a few weeks before we're ready for showtime. When businesses began returning to the city, our crew of helpers dwindled as they returned to work at old jobs and new. But that's okay. Most of the remaining work has been a two-person job anyway.

We enlisted the help of a carpet layer to get the lobby floor and stair-runner carpeting replaced, and Federico helped with the drapery around the screen and the chair upholstery in the auditorium. Otherwise, Violet and I have worked tirelessly to get everything ready for opening night, which is tomorrow. Tonight, we paint. Like that first night we met, music rings through the cavernous room, and the smell of fresh paint fills the auditorium as Violet pops the lid on a can of Tibetan red, and we coat the bottom part of the walls.

When we're finished and stand back to admire our work, it's even more awe-inspiring than the first time Violet showed me this room. This time, it's beautiful and scarred, those scars telling the story of what this beauty had to overcome.

The most notable scar is the seam in the drapery around the screen. Instead of replacing those curtains entirely, we evened out the cut along the hacked-up bottom, and Federico sewed a four-foot velvet extension to the hem, the seam forever commemorating Katrina's high-water mark in this room. The theater's lived history is also apparent in the seating. We couldn't find an exact match for the original chair upholstery, so we got as close as we could and have taken to calling those first few rows the VIP section.

The true homage to the recent history of this place, however, is in the lobby. Right beside the framed portrait of Violet's father is a new collection of photos showing the damage and the cleanup effort, along with a framed section of the wall we left unpainted, a shadowboxed display of the high-water mark labeled Katrina 8/29/2005.

But it's not Katrina we honor with the tribute, it's all the people impacted by her. Tens of thousands of New Orleanians have returned in the last few weeks to find their own horrible project waiting for them. They stand amid the rubble and try to decide how they will start rebuilding their lives, their businesses, their community. Friends and neighbors are gone, and some won't be coming back. There has been death. There has been heartbreak and loss. There has been a diaspora, a drain of talented and creative people who evacuated the storm and may never return. With the reopening of Paradise, we honor them all.

Tomorrow, we will show a print of *It's a Wonderful Life*, which we had to drive to Houston to find, and sell concessions with restaurant equipment we picked up in Baton Rouge on the way back.

Admission is free. Donations to the Angel Wings Fund encouraged. After all, were it not for the fund, none of this would be possible yet. It was the fund that allowed us to purchase the décor and equipment the theater needed to reopen without waiting for the wheels of bureaucracy to turn. Once Violet's insurance and FEMA claims process, we'll reimburse the charity and let that money go to help others on their rebuilding journey.

With the auditorium painted, we prop the doors open and set out a couple of fans to speed up drying. We're finished working for the night. The theater is ready, and so am I.

Tomorrow, I will finally get to see *It's a Wonderful Life* in Paradise. I still have the ticket Violet gave me all those months ago and intend to redeem it for a free hug and a show. In the meantime, I steal a hug, wrapping my arms around Violet as we stare down at the empty lobby from the balcony railing.

That old Prince song "Let's Go Crazy" comes up on her playlist, and I remember this was playing the first moment I laid eyes on Violet. It was on another opening-night eve when I'd barged into Paradise looking for something. I hadn't known what I was looking for that night, so how could I know I'd found what I sought in her. Now, though—now I know.

I hug her a little tighter as we listen to the song's introduction: Prince preaching about the challenge of getting through life. When the rhythm starts, I clasp Violet's hand and spin her out, then bring her back in to tuck against me. She gasps and giggles but dances right along, a wide smile on her face as I twirl her again and dip her before we start really dancing to the music.

It's like déjà vu all over again, except everything is different now. I'm different. She's different. Paradise is different.

And this *different* state we're in, it's good. It was a struggle to get here, hard battles we fought together and alone, but we fought them, and we won, and we came out trusting our strengths. Now we know we can weather the storms that come our way, and we will, together, here in Paradise.

Prince rocks his way through an epic guitar solo at the end, and I pull Violet against me, swaying with her in my arms as we catch our breath.

"Paradise," I say, the first words we've spoken in a while. "It's not just a place, is it? It's a state of mind."

Violet pulls away enough to meet my gaze. "Indeed."

"I don't think I've ever been to this state of mind before. Have you?"

Her grin turns wicked. "You know, this is a new state of mind for me too."

I stroke my fingers down the length of her spine and clutch her ass in my palms as I press my mouth to her ear and ask, "Wanna have new-state sex?"

"Quit talking and fuck me already, Honey Eyes."

EXTENDED EPILOGUE

The trill of my phone startles me awake. Blinking my eyes open to the darkness, I panic. A phone call at this time of night is rarely good news. I see Jake's name on the display, and my heart pounds in my chest. Could it be…?

I answer in a hurry, and before I can say a word, Jake announces, "It's happening."

My smile stretches wide, and I glance over at Violet. She looks so cute in her hot-pink hair bonnet, up on an elbow watching me as she rubs the sleep out of her eyes. I confirm her suspicions: "It's go time."

She leaps out of bed and starts to dress, tossing clothes at me to change into. Rushing around the room, she packs phone chargers and other necessities into the bag we've had waiting by the door for the last two weeks.

I turn my attention back to Jake and pinch the phone between shoulder and ear as I hop into a pair of jeans. "How's Nicole doing?"

"Good. Cranky, but good. We just got back from the hospital."

"Wait. What? Why'd they send you home?"

"Apparently we have to labor at home for a while—" He laughs. "Listen to me saying 'we' like I'm doing anything other than standing around wincing. Nicole's doing all the labor, and she's pretty pissed about it. Anyway, we're supposed to stay here until her contractions are closer together or her water breaks…or something like that. I don't know. Tynisha is on top of the details. Thank the fucking Lord for her because I'm useless right now. My brain is just screaming 'Holy fuck!' over and over again."

"Take a breath."

Jake pauses his rambling panic to inhale deep and exhale long. He sounds like he's winding up to start talking again, so I order another breath. We both inhale deep and let the air seep out of our lungs like steam.

"Thanks, brother," he says. "I needed that. You're always the level-headed one."

Not always. Flashes of memories from my trip to rock bottom run through my mind. It's been—how long? —sixteen months since Ari and I redefined our marriage before eventually ending it. Everything is so different now. I glance over at Violet as she brings me a steaming cup of coffee, then grin when she plants a quick kiss on my lips.

Turning my attention back to Jake, I tell him, "You got this, brother."

"I do?"

"Fuck yeah, you do. You're Jake Motherfucking Sixkiller."

"I'm totally going to be a motherfucker soon, aren't I?" Jake chuckles.

"That's right, so be the best motherfucker you can be. Hold Nicole's hand for every step of this journey, no matter how many bones she breaks. You're a badass dude, and you're going to be a badass dad."

"Fuck yeah, I am."

"That's the spirit. We're leaving right now. Be there as soon as possible."

"Okay. Yeah. Thanks. See you soon."

When I'm off the phone, I turn to Violet, who's waiting with a giant smile on her face. Violet loves babies. She's been dying to meet Tommy since the moment she met Nicole. Her baby craziness is contagious, and lately we've wondered aloud if we might let her birth control prescription lapse and just see what happens. The conversation hasn't turned serious yet, but I know I'd be fucking ecstatic to have a happy accident with Violet.

With a huge smile of my own to match Violet's, I slip on a shirt and grab the bag from her. Out in the living room, Violet leaves a note for the guys that just says, "Baby Time!" and we rush out the door, hop in the truck, and head to Austin.

"How far along is she?" Violet asks.

"They sent her home from the hospital because she wasn't far enough along, apparently."

"Then we have plenty of time to get there."

I frown. "It's a nine-hour drive."

"Yeah, and labor usually takes a lot longer than that."

"*Jesus.*" I groan, feeling a little sick at the thought. Of course, I've known all along that labor takes time, but the reality of how much time is sinking in tonight. Nicole will suffer through countless waves of contractions while we drive across the bulk of two states.

Violet chuckles. "We keep telling y'all that women are tough. When ya gonna listen?"

"Women are amazing. You don't have to convince me." I lace my fingers with hers as we merge onto the highway and aim toward Texas.

Violet finds some music on an old blues station, and it seems fitting to listen to the jangly guitar of Delta blues as we watch the sun slowly rise over the swamp. On the other side of Houston, we gas up, grab some food, and swap seats.

"Wake up, Uncle Greg."

Wait. What? Where are we? What's happening? When did I fall asleep? Uncle?

I rocket awake, jackknifing in my seat and blinking the sleep away. I look around, recognizing the parking lot of the downtown hospital in Austin. Shit. Violet must have driven the rest of the way.

"Did I miss it?"

"Haven't missed anything yet. Let's go, Honey Eyes."

"I thought Nicole was at home."

"You sleep like the dead, my love. Jake called and told me where to find them. It's here."

Holy shit! It's happening. Suddenly wide awake, I grab Violet's hand as we hustle through the lot toward the doors of the ER. Inside, a nurse I vaguely remember from when Ari got hit by a car checks our IDs to make sure we're not rabid Mammoth fans or gossip magazine reporters looking for photos of the rockstar's baby—Jake's status has blown up in the last few months—and directs us to the maternity ward.

It feels like it takes years for us to clear the security precautions and make our way to the private waiting area, where we find a crowd of friends and family. Ari and Alex are there, looking like they fell asleep leaning against each other. Sheryl—sporting a T-shirt that says, "I'm the Cool Aunt"—is bouncing off the walls as usual. Tynisha and Rachel have a jigsaw puzzle spread out on a coffee table. In the corner sits a big Indian man, who I instantly recognize as Jake's Uncle Eli, even though I haven't seen him since I was a teenager.

I rush over to him first, offering my hand to shake. Eli stands, looks me up and down, and instead of shaking my hand, he wraps me in a giant bear hug.

"Greg. It's good to see you again." He holds me at arm's length, and tears shine in his eyes as he says, "I owe you a debt. You were always there for Jake, and I thank you so much for that."

My own eyes shine with tears now, and I'm almost embarrassed to speak these words in front of everyone, but I whisper, "There is no debt. Caring about Jake has never been a burden. If anything, I've been the burden."

Eli smiles, chuckles. "Welcome to the club."

Now we shake hands, sharing a kinship in our love of the man who's ready to become a father in the next room. I wipe at my eyes with my arm when we separate, and I turn to the rest of the room, ready to say hello. Ari is already hugging Violet, and then she comes to me, wrapping me in her gentle arms, such a difference from my bear hug with Eli.

When she lets me go, she gives a status update. "Nicole's been in labor for fourteen hours. Jake's a mess. I've never seen him so scared."

"Can we see him?" I ask.

Ari shakes her head. "He's in there with her, doing the Lamaze thing. He pops out from time to time to update us. They're worried that they might need to do a c-section, but otherwise things are progressing as expected."

Not waiting for Ari to finish talking, Sheryl leaps at me and gives me a bone-crushing hug as she peppers me with questions. "How's NOLA? Did Miss Jewell get the purple beehive wig I sent her? When are you and Violet going to have babies? I need more babies in my life. Ari and Alex are not on board with the plan, but I need babies to spoil. Don't disappoint me, Greg."

I blink at her, then look over at Violet, who bursts into laughter. The whole room seems to let out some steam, everyone laughing now, as if they've all been tied in knots for hours, and this is the excuse they needed to let some of the anxiety go.

"God, I need coffee." Jake comes into the room, looking paler than I've ever seen him.

He spots Violet first, standing with Ari near the door, and a smile takes over his face. "You're here!"

He hugs Violet as Sheryl hops off me to fetch Jake some caffeine.

I go to my friend, and his smile widens when he says, "I'm glad you're here."

"I wouldn't have missed this for the world, brother." I fold the guy into a hug.

He feels smaller, somehow, like his fear has shrunk him into the little boy I used to know, the boy with a morbid fear of hospitals. I remember hugging him the night his family died. Two boys clinging to each other in a hospital waiting room much like this one. Twenty years has hardly changed the terror of this sort of crossroads.

"Jake." I hold his gaze. "Nicole is the strongest person I've ever met. She'll be okay. They both will."

The look on Jake's face tells me how much he needed to hear that. A few months ago, when we gathered in Tennessee for Christmas, Jake told me the details of their surprise baby. Nicole's history with an ectopic pregnancy, as well as other complications Jake didn't detail, had led everyone to presume a successful pregnancy would be something akin to a miracle. Now, here we are, one miracle baby coming right up.

But the miracle nature of this baby has kept Jake on pins and needles for the entirety of the pregnancy. He's too accustomed to losing people in hospitals, not gaining them, and his emotions are bouncing between the wavy crests and troughs of excitement and fear.

Jake hugs me again just as Sheryl brings him a steaming cup of coffee. He takes a drink, let's it settle his nerves a little, then he smiles wide at Violet and kisses her on the cheek.

"Thanks for getting this guy here. It's good to have the band back together. Now, I gotta go help Nicole debut the newest addition."

Violet slips her arm around my waist, and we watch Jake make his way back to Nicole's room. As confident as I sounded for Jake's benefit, I worry too. We all do. Once he's left the room, we all simmer silently with nervous excitement.

Eli watches his nephew return to Nicole, then settles back into his seat and begins to whisper in Cherokee; it sounds like a prayer, and it soothes my nerves. I settle into the plastic seat beside him and take his hand. Violet comes, too, taking my other hand, and before long, we're all seated around the perimeter of the room, joining in Eli's prayers for Jake, Nicole, and little Tommy.

It's difficult to know how much time elapses while we all sit there, praying together and apart, sending good energy and vibrations and whatever else we think might help Nicole as she does all the work to bring Tommy safely into the world. Outside, the light changes as the day moves forward, but otherwise it's all the same. Just helpless waiting. At one point, there is a flurry of activity, a couple of nurses moving quickly toward the door where I last saw Jake.

My stomach tumbles to my feet. Is something wrong? Is something right? What's happening? This waiting is killing me. This helplessness is too hard. Seeming to sense my unease, Violet squeezes my hand. I glance over at her; she's smiling at me.

"What's so funny?"

Violet giggles. "You're so cute when you're worried. I'm just imagining what a mess you'll be when it's our turn."

"Our turn? We're going to have a turn?"

"We've talked about this, Honey Eyes. I want babies. You know this."

Okay, so I guess we're having that conversation now. "Absolutely. I'm ready. One hundred and ten percent ready. When can we start?"

Now it's not just Violet who laughs, so does everyone else in the room.

"Love that enthusiasm, Greg," Tynisha chimes in.

Violet answers, "Let's find a house first, then we can dive into parenthood."

I nod. "Good plan. Just say the word anytime you're ready. My sperm is all yours."

"Aww," Sheryl clasps her hands over her heart, "that is so romantic!"

Everyone howls with laughter, but the sound of footsteps in the hall captures our attention, and we all turn as Jake steps into the room. He's holding a swaddled bundle of baby boy in his arms. Daddy Sixkiller looks ten feet tall, so full of pride, and he's beaming the biggest smile I've ever seen on the guy as he looks down at his son and back up to announce, "Everyone, meet Thomas Jacob Rollins-Sixkiller."

We all rush over to meet this precious tiny little human who is half Jake and half Nicole, and wholly incredible. I'm honored when I'm the first person Jake lets hold his son. I could cry with joy and terror and everything in between. Staring down at this child, I can't fathom how so much goodness and joy can fit into such a small little person. Instantly, I'm in love with Tommy.

I look to my best friend while I hold his son in my arms and try to think of what to say. But words don't do this emotion justice, and I think Jake understands that. We both just smile at each other.

I hand Tommy to his great uncle next. Eli and Jake whisper softly in Cherokee as Eli cradles and rocks the baby. It's a beautiful sight to behold, three generations of Sixkiller men, together.

I feel Violet's arms snake around my waist, and I turn to wrap her in a hug and kiss her forehead. In a whisper, she says, "Not to be crass, but watching you hold that baby did powerful things to my lady bits. What do you say? Are you ready to ditch the birth control and see what happens next?"

"I've never been more ready for anything in my life."

Keep reading for Sheryl's story in the final book of the Lost in Austin series, *All the Rest*.

ALL THE REST

CHAPTER 1 - THURSDAY, NOVEMBER 25, 2010

The house looks like the *Addams Family* mansion, all creepy and kooky with its sweeping gables and gothic corbels. I half expect a cloud to pop up out of the clear blue sky and flicker lightning all around, like this is a dinner party at a haunted mansion rather than Thanksgiving with the family at Jake and Nicole's new place.

My street skates clatter over the road, and I grimace at the other houses that dot the wide expanses of manicured lawn. This neighborhood, with its beige bougie opulence, seems very much *not* a good fit for Jake and Nicole—Jakole for short. But now, as my eyes take in their weirdly wonderful gothic gem, I love it.

And I'll bet the president of their home owners association is shitting actual bricks. Seriously, I'd pay cash money to see these neighbors challenge Nicole over her design choices. That would be a fight worthy of pay-per-view prices.

My skates squeal as I come to a halt in front of an eight-foot-tall wrought iron gate, an ornate design featuring bats and spiders and a bull's skull adorning the top. I try to push it open, but it won't budge.

Glancing around, I spot two cameras trained on my position and a security keypad beside the driveway. With all this security and walls as tall as Jericho, I have to wonder if any of Jake's obsessed fans have tried to get a little too close to Mr. Big Shot Rockstar.

"Hello! Let me in!" I shout at the keypad as I push all the buttons at once. Then I blow a kiss at the cameras and do The Macarena until someone buzzes the gate open, and I slip through.

The driveway winds up toward a bluff overlooking the lake, and I put some muscle into my ascension. I aim for the chimney stacks of Jakole's gothic mansion, which peak above the bows of the mesquite trees.

When I've reached the apex of the driveway, clotted with cars, I see the wee ones playing in the yard. Blowing kisses at my adoring fans— all two of them—I execute a pretty impressive arabesque before spinning to a stop. Tommy and Mia erupt in delighted squeals. Cute little fuckers, those two.

Tommy—Jakole's son—is five and adorable. He looks like his

daddy—complete with long black hair parted in the middle and braided to his waist—but he has his mom's gorgeous green eyes.

Wiggling beside him is Mia, Greg and Violet's feisty three-year-old daughter, in the cotton-candy cloud of a powder-pink princess dress. Don't let the dainty outfit fool you, though—Mia is a tornado of energy with a black belt in badassery just like her mama.

"Shaywall." Mia butchers my name adorably as I skate right into her and lift her up in a spin, like she's a Disney princess on ice. She squeals with glee, at a frequency so high only dogs can hear it. When I set her down, I tickle Tommy until he dissolves into a puddle of giggles. Once I'm sure the kids have adequately trumpeted my arrival to the adults in the house, I let each of them take a hand and tug me inside.

"Take your skates off in my house. What, were you raised in a barn?" Nicole hollers at the precise instant I cross the threshold. I stick out my tongue at Momzilla. She might be retired from roller derby these days, but it was awfully naive of her to install floors you can't skate on.

"I was raised in Florida, so...kind of." I shrug as I bend over and unlace my skates. I'm sporting my Ryan Gosling socks. Each foot is a different half of his face, and I can make him waggle his chin with my toes. Big hit with the TSA agents whenever I fly.

Tommy runs to his momma and tangles his arms around her leg while she watches me take off my skates like a good girl. When I straighten up, I ogle Nicole's belly. "Dang, woman, you're as big as a house."

Nicole smirks and settles her hands on her big ole preggers belly. Jake knocked her up again, this time with twins. She's fixin' to pop and complains all the time about it, but she's over the moon. I never would have pegged Nicole for the mom type, but damn does she love making babies with her rockstar.

I can't help it—I touch her belly. Even though it's considered rude, and with Nicole I could lose a finger, I do it anyway because I love baby-on-board bellies, and I think Nicole and I have achieved the I-can-touch-her-without-permission stage of friendship.

She smacks my hands away. "No touching the merchandise."

Or not.

Feeling some weird need to carry a baby myself, I pick up Mia and hold her on my hip. She plays with my hot-pink hair, delighted with how it matches her dress.

Tommy points at his mom's belly and informs me for about the eighty bajillionth time, "That's my bwothers in there."

"What? No way!" I gasp. "Your brothers? How do they fit in there?"

"They're little."

"Not that little," I say to ruffle Nicole's feathers.

She mouths the word "bitch" so her precious first born can't hear, and I wink.

Then Nicole gasps and grabs my hand, holding it to her belly so I can feel one of the little nippers bend it like Beckham. Gotta hand it to Nicole, she breeds fighters. Tommy, as sweet as he can be, came out screeching like a banshee and yanking on his daddy's hair within half an hour of touchdown. He hasn't stopped moving or talking since.

I turn to Tommy, who has also set his hand on his mom's belly. "So, T-Man, when do you get to meet your brothers?"

"In five days." He holds up his little fingers with their cute little fingernails that his dad helps him paint black. "Daddy says if they don't get here soon, Mommy is going to reach in and pull them out herself."

"Well that's…graphic." I grimace at Nicole.

I lace my fingers with Tommy's, swinging our arms together, and change the subject. "What are you going to call them?" It's a prompt more than a question. Everyone within earshot for the last eight-and-a-half months knows the answer, but I never deny the proud big brother his fifteen minutes. Soon, those twins will steal the show, so I make it a point to shower Tommy with attention, like he's his daddy on stage at Madison Square Garden.

"One is named Gregory, like my uncle, and the other one is Hezekiah, like my grandpa," Tommy declares with glee.

"Daddy," Mia squeals as her papa—aka Tommy's Uncle Greg—turns a corner and joins us in the entry, apparently summoned by the call of his name.

"Mia Monster, tell your daddy you want to join the roller derby rec league in the Big Easy," I say as Greg kisses my cheek and unwraps his daughter from my neck.

"Daddy, I wanna join the whoa er derby weckley in da bickeezy."

"Close enough." I shrug.

"We'll look into it." Greg kisses his daughter's cheek, then smirks at me. I only smile. His daughter is a future derby diva whether he likes it or not. Violet tells me she can't get the girl into normal shoes since I mailed her a pair of tiny toddler skates for her birthday.

When Violet comes out of the kitchen, I see she has a baby bump now too.

"Damn, what's in the water around here, and where do I get a glass? Y'all are popping out babies like it's the new fashion or something."

"Good to see you too, Sher." Violet hugs me.

I swallow the lump in my throat and try to ignore my jealousy. I've been baby crazy pretty much my entire life, but these sharp pricks of bitterness and resentment are new. I love seeing my breeder friends happy. Really, I do. But why can't I be a happy breeder too?

"Sher Bear!" Ari comes out of the kitchen to hug me, saving me from my downward spiral.

"You're not preggers too, are you?" I ask, just to be sure.

"Oh, God no." Ari laughs as Alex, that gorgeous man she calls a husband, comes out and hugs her around the waist. I've never understood why these two don't want kids. I mean, I get it: everyone has their reasons and can make their own choices in life. But, damn, they'd make beautiful babies, like, seriously, top-shelf, premium-quality babies.

Jake comes out of some room down the hall. I think it's a recording studio or practice space or something. He told me once, but I wasn't listening, too focused on staring out their picture window overlooking the pool and displaying a ridiculously expensive view of Town Lake. Tommy goes running into his dad's arms, and the big ole warrior man comes padding across the black marble floors barefoot, carrying his son.

"Did you work out the details on that last song?" Nicole asks when

Jake slides his free arm around her, resting his hand on her big belly and kissing her neck.

Jake answers, "Yep. It's brilliant, going to be our next big hit."

Since joining Mammoth, Jake and the singer, Aidan, have become a transatlantic songwriting duo, penning more than a few chart-topping songs over web-cam. One even earned a Grammy last year. All while their wives pop out adorable little spawn. Must be nice to have it all.

Dang, there's that green jelly monster again. Today is Thanksgiving. A time for feeling thankful for what I *do* have. Not envy and covet what I *don't*.

Sheryl Ann Novak, do better, girl!

"Now that our late little lassy is here, we can start Family Dinner Night. Everyone grab a drink and a seat." Nicole directs, and the whole house springs into action.

Taking one of Alex's beers from the fridge, I grab my usual spot at the table. Everyone settles into their little family pods around me. I have no pod. I'm the seventh wheel—ninth and soon to be eleventh wheel when you count the kids. I'm the last orphan of this weird family of ours, and it's been this way for over five years.

Perpetually single—that's my curse. Not because there's anything wrong with me; I'm awesome. It's all the lame dudes. I may be small in size, but I've got a personality as big as Texas. Some might say it's *too* big. I've yet to meet the man who can handle this much woman. So I remain single...and childless...and I'll be thirty-five next month! Growing up, I always assumed I'd be a mom by now. But here I am with no baby and no prospects, my biological clock banging like a gong.

"It's that Sixkiller sperm. It's unstoppable," Jake says. He's been bragging about his sperm since they found out they were having twins.

"Please don't talk about your sperm at the dinner table," Nicole grumbles as she pats her belly.

I could use some of that Sixkiller sperm right about now.

"Uh...what?" Jake frowns at me. "I suddenly feel very uncomfortable."

Whoops. "Did I say that out loud? Ignore me."

"Gladly."

But, seriously, why didn't I think of this before? I don't need a man to have a baby. I only need his sperm. How hard could it be to find some sperm? Not from Jake, obviously, since he's eyeing me like I'm an evil witch trying to steal his seed. But surely there is some guy out there willing to give me the baby batter I need to bake a bun in my oven.

My body is ready. Let's do this.

I make the decision at the same time I make the announcement. Standing, I clink my knife against my glass so loudly everyone turns to me, looking worried, like maybe I've broken something. I clear my throat, raise my arms, and proclaim, "I'm having a baby!"

They look stunned and a bit confused with their mouths hanging open, food frozen on forks in midair. Their shock lasts only a brief moment before everyone speaks at once.

"What?" they say in such harmony you'd think it was choir practice.

"You're pregnant?" Ari asks.

"Not yet, but I will be."

"Huh?" Jake frowns.

"I'm going on a sperm hunt."

"A hunt?" Greg asks. "Like, with a gun?"

What? "No! Duh. With my feminine wiles. Or I might pay them. I haven't decided."

"Wait. Wait. Wait. You're going to hire a guy to"—Jake stops himself, takes a deep breath, then spells his question—"f-u-c-k you?"

"Um! Mommy, Daddy spelled a bad word," Tommy says.

"How do you know it's a bad word?" I ask Tommy.

"Because you only spell words when they're bad."

"Oh yeah? Well, what does I-L-O-V-E-Y-O-U mean?"

Tommy blinks at me, so I help. Using the sign language I've been teaching him, I say and sign, "I love you."

Tommy giggles, and it's the sweetest sound in the world. My smile reaches all the way down to the tips of my toes.

Meanwhile, the adults are still fixated on the details of my plan, as if I somehow magically know the details. We're in the infancy phase here, people. Well, the pre-infancy phase, really.

"I mean, maybe, if the guy's super smart and good looking and worth the money, then I'd pay for some seed." I shrug. "I'm also open to the idea of a one-night stand."

"What's a one-night stand?" Tommy asks.

Jake leans back in his chair to dole out some fatherly wisdom to his son. "You know how you have two nightstands in your bedroom, one on each side of your bed?"

Tommy nods.

"Well, some people only have one nightstand."

Nicole laughs at Jake's explanation and chokes on a sip of water.

"No! No. No. No. No. No!" Ari looks legitimately upset as she sets down her fork and scowls at me. "I one hundred percent veto this idea, Sherrie."

"It's called Operation Insemination, and you're not the president of me. You don't get a veto."

"I will be damned if I let you f-u-c-k a bunch of dudes *raw* so you can get pregnant."

"Oh, that's rich coming from you, Little Miss Hedonistic Self-Discovery Girl."

"Excuse me? Are you s-l-u-t shaming me right now, because—"

"Ari, you know I love you and I love s-l-u-t-s, but you've literally slept with every man at this table—"

"Not me!" Jake declares.

Greg and Alex remain silent, smirking at each other. I laugh out loud at their comfort with one another these days. It wasn't always so easy going. When I first met Ari, she was married to Greg, but they'd agreed to open their marriage. Ari was footloose and fancy-free, fucking her way through the men of Austin. That's how she met Alex. I'd called it from the start—she was so in love with him—but it took her a minute to come to the same conclusion.

"Fine," I amend, "you've slept with two-thirds of the men at this table. Plus, like, half of Austin. Now you want to turn around and tell me I can't?"

"Sher, it's not the same thing at all."

"How is it different?"

"Well, for starters, every one of my, uh, nightstands wore a condom."

"Daddy, what's a condom?"

Jake chuckles. "A piece of latex."

"What's latex?"

"Rubber."

"What's rubber?"

"You're the one who wanted to teach him English," Jake says to Nicole.

Ari continues, "You can't just *do* a bunch of random dudes without protection unless you want to get knocked up with a whole lot of STDs along the way."

"Mommy, what does S-T-D spell?"

"Nothing, honey. Aunt Ari doesn't know how to spell. Ignore her."

"Okay, fine," I huff. "I'll ask them to get tested first or something. I don't know. I'll figure it out. Stop raining on my parade."

Ari softens. "Sorry. You're right—I'm being a needless pain. You're a smart woman. I have faith in you. So… Congrats, babe, you're going to have a baby!"

"Oh God!" Nicole shouts, and the tone of her voice is pained. Every other conversation in the room stops. We stare at her, concerned and confused. Her posture changes, curls forward a little as she looks down at her big baby belly then over at Jake, her eyes wide as her complexion pales. "It's happening."

Grab a copy of ***All the Rest*** to keep reading
Sheryl & Manic's story.

It's been five years since I found my family. Not my bio-family—my found family of friends. I love them to pieces, but lately they aren't enough.

I want a baby.

All my friends have family units with cuddly babies, and I want that too. But I turn thirty-five in less than a month. Clock's ticking, so I've got to hustle. I need some baby batter to bake a bun in my oven as soon as possible.

One problem: baby batter comes from men, and I'm really tired of men and their heartbreaker BS.

Manic, though, is different from the other men. A retired sideshow circus performer with piercings all over the place, he's different from everyone. I really like him, and I think he really likes me, too, but he flat out refuses to get me pregnant.

Is Manic worth giving up my dream of being a kickass mom? Maybe.

THANK YOU

Thank you for reading *After the Storm*. If you enjoyed Greg's story, please spread the word!

xoxo,
Christina

And don't forget to subscribe to my newsletter
subscribepage.io/Td7TPB
or join my reader's group
facebook.com/groups/christinaswildberries
for the latest news and new releases.

ACKNOWLEDGMENTS

To the readers: Thank you so much! There's still more to come. Next up is the final book in the series: Sheryl & Manic!

I hope you enjoyed Greg's story and this tribute to the people of New Orleans. *After the Storm* is the most difficult book I've ever written. After doing tons of research about Hurricane Katrina, it was a challenging line to walk in telling an entertaining love story without exploiting a real tragedy. It took me years to get it right. Then, halfway through the final edit, I suffered a stroke. The last few weeks have been scary and strange, but having this story to focus on helped me work my injured brain and come back fighting. I guess this book about two phoenix stories (Greg and NOLA) has become one itself.

But enough about me. This is about everyone who helped make this book happen. Rock stars, all of you!

Nikki DaVaughn: Your friendship, patience, and love mean so much to me. I looked up the date when we went on the book research trip to NOLA. It was January 2018. Dang, it took me a while to write this thing. It's been a strange journey, and I couldn't have done it without you. I love you, lady!

Christina Consolino: You are my rock. Without your friendship and editorial expertise, I don't think I'd have the energy or confidence to indie publish.

Meghan Scott: Thank you as always for your real world and book world medical info.

A big heartfelt thank you to my wonderful beta and sensitivity readers: Paula Dombrowiak, Marcella Bell, Emily Williams, and Alex Molnar.

Finally, to my family and my family of friends: Thank you! I'm very lucky to have a life filled with so much love and support. This book, like all my books, could not have happened without my amazing husband, Errek. I sure do love you, baby. Mom and Dad and Karen: These last few weeks have especially reminded me how lucky I am to have such a wonderful and supportive family. I love you all so much. And to my extended family of friends: I want hugs. Gimme. xoxo

ABOUT THE AUTHOR

Christina Berry is an award-winning author of sex-positive contemporary romance. Her debut novel, *Up for Air*, won "Sexiest Consent" in the 2021 Good Sex Awards, and her first two Lost in Austin series books won the Readers' Favorite Gold Medal in Romance - Sizzle in 2021 and 2022.

A citizen of the Cherokee Nation, Christina is originally from Oklahoma, and currently resides in Austin, Texas. When not writing, she's usually helping her husband with their never-ending home remodeling adventure or marathon watching true crime television.

www.christinaberry.com

facebook.com/christinaberryauthor
instagram.com/authorchristinaberry

www.ingramcontent.com/pod-product-compliance
Lightning Source LLC
Chambersburg PA
CBHW021153310726
48971CB00002B/609